Saving Laura

Also by Jim Satterfield

The River's Song

SAVING LAURA

A Novel

Jim Satterfield

Oceanview Publishing

Longboat Key, Florida

ISBN: 978-1-60809-078-5

Published in the United States of America by Oceanview Publishing,
Longboat Key, Florida
www.oceanviewpub.com

10 9 8 7 6 5 4 3 2 1

PRINTED IN THE UNITED STATES OF AMERICA

For Papa

Acknowledgments

I am deeply grateful for the help of many generous and talented people. My wife, Gloria, read every page warm from the printer, providing supportive but critical editing and a woman's point of view. I had a blast writing the first draft for my critique group, GPASC (Grammatical Parallelism Anonymous Social Club), a fun and enormously helpful audience. I thank my first readers, Mike Korn, Ron Aasheim, Tom Peck, Ingrid Antony, and my sister, Lee Hamre, for their thoughtful reviews and suggestions. Debbie Burke read several drafts, generously sharing her remarkable editing talent. My agent, Elizabeth Kracht of Kimberley Cameron & Associates, gave fine editorial suggestions and wonderful advice and encouragement. I am exceedingly fortunate to work with Drs. Pat and Bob Gussin of Oceanview Publishing, who have provided the kind of support and belief in my work writers crave. Furthermore, it has been a joy to work with Frank Troncale, David Ivester, and the entire Oceanview staff. Artist George Foster created an awesome cover. Finally, I thank Dennis Foley and the Authors of the Flathead for years of support and instruction.

Prologue

Tom Tucker sold the best cocaine in Aspen. Strong, uncut, and customers always got a full, honest gram for their $100. He was also well supplied and accessible, even in the 1970s before the days of cell phones and e-mail. Lots of folks relied on him for their blow. He was almost an institution. Good ol' Tom Tucker.

Tom had only one problem—his mouth. He loved to brag on famous pals, like Willie Nelson and Jerry Jeff Walker. Tom was a Texan, and he adopted his native state's unofficial motto, *Everything's Bigger in Texas*, as his personal credo. He played the big man and made no secret of having a ready stash and a cool place on Highway 82 outside of town to party. Tom loved to sell his clients toot, then help them use it all up in the comfort of his living room.

Along the way, Tom managed to piss off a lot of people. Like friends and relatives of women he turned into coke whores. Like parents who saw their children tumble into hopeless addiction. Like spouses who watched husbands and wives piss away all their savings on the white marching powder.

Through the late seventies, Tom enjoyed a charmed life, never busted by the cops or even ripped off by his clientele. Although his lifestyle had aged him well beyond his thirty-something years, he figured that was a small price to pay for the glorious ride. Hell, he knew he was a rotten turd, but he'd never made anyone buy one speck of dope. He just enabled their dark side. If he didn't, they'd find someone else who would.

One fine evening in mid-September, when the slopes above

Aspen were in their full golden glory, Tom received his comeuppance. For days he had boasted of a big deal he was about to make with his Vegas connection. He usually traveled to Sin City to re-supply, but this time, on the promise of a wild Aspen weekend, his man was delivering the dope to Tom. The day of his guest's arrival, Tom paraded through all the watering holes in town like a peacock, singing the praises of this batch of cocaine and taking orders on spec.

In those days, Aspen Airport wasn't much more than a warehouse and a lengthy run of tarmac, with virtually no security or staff present, particularly between flights. After Tom greeted his supplier at the edge of the runway, they retired to Tom's vintage Mercedes-Benz 220SE and sipped whiskey from a silver flask until the rest of the passengers and airport personnel departed. When they were alone in the parking lot, Tom asked to examine the five kilos of Peruvian flake. Seventy-five thousand dollars waited in a blue North Face travel bag stowed behind the driver's seat. They consummated the deal, then Tom shared some of the stuff with his pal.

Unbeknownst to either of them, they were not alone in the airport. A young man, tall and thin like a runner, hid in the enveloping darkness behind a private hangar. Through his binoculars, he watched and waited until the right moment. Then he adjusted a respirator over his face and crept to the parked vehicle. In one graceful instant, he opened the unlocked door on the driver's side of the Mercedes and sprayed both men with an entire can of mace. The robber took the money and cocaine from the car, while Tom and his supplier choked and cried, helpless to resist. There were no witnesses to the theft.

How do I know what happened? I was the robber.

Saving Laura

Chapter One

I'll start my story in the town of Baggs, Wyoming, not much more than a wide spot along State Highway 789, just a few miles north of the Colorado border. Even though this all happened nearly thirty years ago, I vividly remember the early fall evening in 1979 when I climbed out of the eighteen-wheeler and thanked the trucker for the ride from Laramie. I don't recall the man's name anymore, but I still laugh at him warning me not to forget my rucksack as I scrambled to get out before he headed up to Rawlins. He was needling me for keeping the pack at my feet the entire trip rather than letting him stow it in the rear of the cab. No way I'd let that pack out of my sight.

I hopped off the last step and waved as he headed north. In the dying light, I made my way across the road to the only restaurant and hotel in town, the Drifter's Inn. Dog-tired and hungry, I'd been on the run for days and couldn't remember when I'd last slept well or eaten a real meal. I pulled open the heavy double doors and let two drunken highway workers stagger outside before I entered the old wooden building. Inside, I walked down a dark corridor lined with ratty old deer heads and glanced into the open doorway of the bar to my right.

The place was packed and you could have cut the smoke with a chainsaw and sold it. Most of the revelers were highway workers staying at the inn, a few cowboys scattered about, and some hunters, too, judging from their camouflage. A big mahogany bar was stocked with every kind of booze you could imagine as well as the obligatory gallon mason jars of pickled pigs feet, sausages, and hardboiled eggs. I softly cursed when I spotted two sheriff's deputies hulking over a man seated at the end of the bar. Edging back from the doorway, I turned toward the restaurant across the hallway.

I took a seat at a table for two with my back against the wall and my pack at my feet. Gazing out the west window, I was just in time to watch the last bit of sun slip behind the sagebrush hills. The joint wasn't too smoky, not nearly as bad as the bar, nor was it as crowded. Drinking was evidently a higher priority than eating for most of the Drifter's guests. Fine with me. I planned to enjoy a quiet meal before I found another ride that night south into Colorado.

A waitress brought me a glass of water and a menu. She was around fifty and wore her gray hair in a tight ponytail. Judging from her ruddy complexion, lined and creased from wind and sun, I guessed she lived on a nearby ranch. Her name tag read "Donna."

"Beef ribs are the Friday night special, hon," she said, as she wiped my table clean.

"I won't need that, then," I said, nodding at the laminated menu. "I'll have the ribs."

"They ain't that good, though," she said in a whiskey-and-to-bacco-seared voice. "They're pretty tough."

"What's good?"

"Nothin', really."

I chuckled and shrugged my shoulders. "Well, I'm hungry. I gotta eat something."

"You probably can't go wrong with a hamburger."

"I'll have two, and fries."

Donna jotted down my order and moved on to freshen an old rancher's coffee.

I sipped my water and kept an eye on the doorway leading to

the entrance hallway. I tried to relax a while before I had to hit the road again. All I needed was about half an hour of peace, and I'd be fed and on my way to Colorado. I left my seat for a moment, keeping an eye on my pack, and fetched the *Rocky Mountain News* from the end of the counter. I just wanted to catch up on the news and enjoy my meal.

I was in the middle of the sports page when my food came. I put down the paper and eyed the burgers hungrily, smelling the wonderful aroma of greasy cooking.

"Anything else, hon?" She asked in that raspy voice of hers.

"Just a check, ma'am."

"Check? You ain't even et yet."

"I might have to leave quick," I said. "Wouldn't want to stiff you—"

As if on cue, the two deputies entered the restaurant and took a seat on the other side of the room, next to the doorway. Donna looked over her shoulder and saw the two lawmen. Then she looked at me and spoke low, "You're in trouble with them, ain't you?"

I said nothing.

"I know 'em both," she said. "Worthless as tits on a boar hog."

As scared as I was, I still laughed.

"See the fat one? I went to high school with him. He couldn't track an elephant with a nosebleed in six feet of snow. T'other one ain't as tall as this tabletop, but he's a mean little bastard." She looked me in the eyes with kind of a sideways stare. "You ain't done nothing too bad, now, have ya?"

"I haven't hurt anyone, but—"

"How old are you?"

"I'm twenty-one, ma'am."

She rubbed my freshly shaven face. "You look all of about sixteen," she snorted and walked away.

Out of the corner of my eye, I watched her serve the lawmen

coffee. They didn't speak much to her, and I could swear they were both looking my way. I wolfed down one hamburger in about four bites, knowing I wasn't going to be able to stick around much longer. I pulled a ten spot from my wallet and placed it partly under my plate. Donna headed my way, stopping to top off the old rancher's coffee again.

"How are those burgers?" she asked in an overly loud voice. Before I could answer, she whispered, "They're talking about you. Better git."

Using the waitress to shield me from their view, I asked, "Any way out of here, besides through that doorway where they're sittin'?"

"Only other way out is through the kitchen."

I wondered how I was going to heft my pack and get out without drawing their attention. She read my mind. "You'll have to make a run for it."

Just about then, one of the deputies, the short one, rose from his seat and left the room.

"He's either headed to the can or the pay phone at the end of the hallway. I'll try to distract fat boy, then you git."

"Why are you helping me, ma'am?"

"You remind me of my own boy."

I thought I saw her eyes water, but before I could thank her she turned on her heels and headed toward the rotund lawman. I wrapped my second hamburger in a paper napkin and put it in my jacket pocket. Eating my fries as nonchalantly as possible, I tried to appear disinterested in what was happening on the other side of the room. When she stood squarely in front of the deputy, blocking his view, I grabbed my pack and slipped into the kitchen.

My head swiveled, looking for the exit to the outside and temporary freedom. To my right, the cook recoiled from the grill, apparently not used to strangers barging into his kitchen. He was dark skinned and a mane of black hair flowed from under his white cook cap to well past his shoulders. He yelled, *"Salga de aqui!"* and waved a spatula at me.

"¿Donde esta la puerta?" I hollered, hoping he could understand my piss-poor accent.

He nodded toward the far corner of the room by the two walk-in freezers. I nearly slipped on the greasy vinyl floor and bolted for the white metal door. Leaving the kitchen, I heard him yelling and recognized a few familiar cuss words. I didn't stop, though, just dashed into the darkness of the rear parking lot. Hiding among the cars and trucks, I shouldered my backpack and tried to decide on my next move.

Across the road and a hundred yards south stood an old Sinclair station, with a green dinosaur emblem on the window. A white truck pointed south next to the nearest pump. I ran for the rig, praying the driver would give me a lift. At the edge of the parking lot, I heard two men yelling behind me, but I didn't stop, just sprinted across Highway 789. Nearing the station, I saw a young fellow, probably a high school student, filling a battered Ford pickup that had Colorado plates. He was tall and skinny and wore a black cowboy hat. I took a pretty girl with big blonde hair in the passenger seat to be his girlfriend.

I slowed to a brisk walk to keep from alarming the lad and asked, "Headin' towards Craig?" Before he could answer I followed with, "I'll buy that tank of gas for a ride!"

He stuck his head in the cab and spoke to the blonde, then he looked my way. "Mind ridin' in the bed?"

"Not at all." I glanced at the pump and dug a twenty out of my wallet, which more than covered the gas. I glanced back toward the Drifter's Inn and watched the two deputies sweep the parking lot with their flashlights. I threw my pack in the bed of the truck and climbed in, looking for a hole amongst the fence posts and rolls of barbed wire. I sat low and held my breath, waiting for the young cowboy to pay the station attendant. He used the change to buy a six-pack of Budweiser, which was fine with me. I just wanted to get the hell out of there.

Before he got in the cab, the fellow asked me, "Goin' all the way to Craig?"

"Nope, just a ways past the border," I said. "I'll tap on the rear window when I'm ready to get out."

He nodded, and I got my first good look at him from under that big hat. He was a redhead and looked like he'd fallen in the freckle barrel. "Have a beer? You paid for 'em." He laughed and waved the six-pack at me.

I was tempted, but figured I better stay clearheaded, because I doubted my running was done for the evening. "I'll pass, but thanks anyway."

"Suit yourself." He jumped in the truck, and we sped away south into the night. The truck ran rough, and I hoped it would get us where we were going. We motored up a long uphill grade, and I looked back toward Baggs. When we neared the top of the hill, around half a mile south of town, I saw the red lights of a police car leaving the Drifter's Inn and coming our way. Then we reached the summit, and I lost my view of the little town. With the help of good old gravity, the Ford picked up speed. Through the cab I heard Merle Haggard singing "Mama Tried."

Chapter Two

I had graduated a few months earlier with an English degree from Mesa College in Grand Junction. Only taking one course in math, *College Algebra and Trigonometry for Non-Majors*, I didn't claim to be a whiz with numbers, but as we hurtled down the two-lane highway toward the border, I ran sketchy calculations through my head. I figured we had about a thousand-yard lead on the vehicle chasing us. Peering through the cab window—not easy with two rifles and a lariat resting in the gun rack—I discerned my unwitting accomplice was driving his truck around eighty miles an hour. Even if those lawmen drove over a hundred, they'd have a hell of a time catching up with us before we drove another mile and a half to the state line.

I sat with my back to the cab and ate my second hamburger, watching for the emergency lights to clear the northern horizon. The country was hilly, the road like a big roller coaster ride, steep hills followed by long downhill runs. As we reached the bottom of a swale and labored up the next summit, red flashing lights appeared behind us. The border loomed beyond the next hill. We were going to make it, I thought.

We reached the next hilltop and again sped downhill. I knelt and looked over the top of the cab to the south. On our left, a wooden sign with a picture of a cowboy riding a bronc read, "Leaving Wyoming, Come Again!" and then out of the darkness on the right shoulder of the highway a shiny metal sign emerged. "Welcome to Colorful Colorado!"

I laughed in the cool night air. Only eight more miles to the county road where I'd be bailing out. I dropped my guard and enjoyed the evening. The moon rose, full and nearly red from the dust of the windy range, and stars twinkled overhead, a good evening for a hike. To the east, beyond rolling hills, loomed my destination, Baker's Peak, a dark silhouette towering above the prairie.

At the bottom of the next swale, I nearly choked on the last of my hamburger when I looked behind us and saw red flashing lights. Well past the Colorado line, those Wyoming boys weren't giving up the chase. They had cut our lead in half, and were gaining, within a quarter of a mile now. Over the din of Charlie Daniels's "Devil Went Down to Georgia," a siren keened. How long before my young driver pulled off the road? Was there enough cover on the dark prairie to make a run for it?

The music died and the truck accelerated. The blonde stuck her head out the passenger window and hollered, "Hold on, dude! We ain't stoppin' for no pigs!"

At first, their temerity elated me. Then I wondered how I was going to exit the truck in the midst of a high-speed chase with rogue Wyoming lawmen. I glanced at a mileage marker along the shoulder of the highway and calculated my destination lay only five miles to the south. Behind us, the pursuers had lost ground, but they were still coming, no more than a half mile away. We flew by another mileage marker, and I shouldered my pack. One way or another, I needed out of that truck bed in short order.

Heading up the last hill before we reached my turnoff, the old Ford pickup solved my problem for me. First, I heard a loud blast, like a rifle, and figured the cops were shooting at us. Then I realized the explosion had come from the exhaust pipe. I smelled burning oil and a dark cloud of oily exhaust spewed from the rig. We lurched to the top of the ridge as the engine ground itself in death throes with sickening screeches and rattles. After one final shudder, it stopped dead in the middle of the highway. A few hundred yards away, the patrol car bore down on us.

I bailed out of the bed and ran east up a hill overlooking the highway. By the time I pitched my pack over a barbed wire fence and climbed through, the siren's wail was earsplitting. Aircraft-grade headlights lit up the dead Ford. Away from the pool of blinding tungsten, I ducked behind a chest-high sagebrush and peered through it. The Wyoming cruiser pulled within fifty feet of my recent rescuers. A scratchy voice blared from the metal speaker mounted on the roof rack. "Come out with your hands up!" Both doors opened on the cruiser, and each deputy knelt behind one, revolvers drawn and pointed toward the truck.

I expected the young couple to emerge from the Ford with arms raised. There'd be reprimands for the short chase and open containers, along with a stern admonition to get the hell back to Craig or wherever the two belonged. But once the Wyoming boys learned they had lost their quarry, me, they'd slink back across the border. At least, that's what I figured would happen.

In one fluid motion, the young cowboy slipped out the door, scope-sighted rifle in his hands. He fired at the driver's door of the cruiser, and the fat deputy collapsed on the pavement. Gunfire burst from the other side of the sedan, shattering the rear window of the truck.

The young woman, still inside the cab, shrieked, "They shot me! I'm hit!"

The skinny cowboy slipped around the front of the truck and poured several shots into the open passenger door of the cruiser. The second deputy stumbled from the vehicle's cover onto the gravel shoulder of the road.

The cowboy dropped him with one well-placed shot to the chest. The young man pitched the rifle and lifted his girl out of the truck. Blood blossomed from a wound to her shoulder as he helped her into the passenger seat of the cruiser. He ran around the sedan, losing his cowboy hat in the process, and jumped in the driver's seat. Tires screeched as they sped away, heading south. Just before they cleared the horizon, the emergency lights died.

I was alone in the darkness.

"Son of a bitch!" I muttered. I closed my eyes and shook my head in disbelief. Now what? I stood and went to fetch my pack. From the road below, I heard moaning and crying.

I hesitated, backpack slung on one shoulder. Plaintive calls for help drifted through the night air.

As if I weren't already in enough of a fix, now a wounded cop had only one hope for survival: me.

I could walk away in the darkness. No one would ever know I'd been there.

"Will, help me!" the strangled voice pleaded.

Guilt got the best of me. I slipped out of my backpack and leaned it against a fence pole. Rummaging through the pack, I found my flashlight and hopped over four strands of barbed wire. I sidestepped down the slippery slope and ran to the highway. The driver, the fat deputy, was sprawled in the middle of the north-bound lane, writhing in pain. I quickly shuffled past him, looking for the other lawman. I found him, facedown on the far shoulder of the road. As soon as I rolled him over, I knew he was dead. Blood from two wounds to his chest covered his torso, and his eyes were open and glassy, like a dead deer.

Returning to the wounded man, I knew I'd better get him off the highway. If another car came along, he'd likely be run over. We were at the crest of the hill, out of sight of traffic until it was nearly on top of us. I knelt next to the man and pointed my light at his face. He clutched a wound in his stomach and opened his eyes. "Will?" he asked.

"No, sir," I answered, "I'm just a passerby, but we need to get you off the road before any cars come along." I switched on the emergency flashers on the young cowboy's dead truck, then went back to the deputy. "Can you walk?"

"No," he groaned, still clutching his stomach.

"I'm gonna have to drag you a ways." I went behind him and knelt to slip my arms under his armpits. His blood felt warm and sticky on my hands. Unable to lift him to his feet, I dragged him a few inches. I figured he must weigh well over two hundred and fifty pounds, way heavier than any deer I'd ever killed, and I'd killed some big ones. I sucked in a deep breath and yanked, moving him another few inches. With every lurch, he cried and swore. Finally, I got him off the pavement and safely beyond the shoulder to the edge of the hill overlooking the highway.

I ran to the Ford and looked in the cab for a blanket or clothing to cover the deputy. Broken glass glittered on the seat in the dome light. The girl's blood stained the upholstery. Behind the seat, I found a ratty old army surplus blanket. I returned to the wounded man and covered him.

"What about Will, how is he?" he muttered through clenched teeth.

"He's dead," I answered.

Walking toward the center of the highway, I heard him whimper, "Don't leave me."

I walked on to the crest of the hill, looking in either direction for headlights, but saw nothing but empty darkness in both directions. It could be a good long while before anyone came along this road. In the meantime, the deputy would likely bleed to death. With the patrol car long gone, I had no idea how to get help.

Returning to the wounded man, I asked, without much hope, "Either one of you have a radio?"

"Will should have one . . ."

I trotted across the highway and scanned the dead man with my flashlight. Sure enough, a radio sheathed in black leather was hooked on his belt. I grabbed it. Except for a short-lived career as a CB operator, I knew nothing about using a radio. After *Smokey and the Bandit* came out when I was in college, CBs were all the rage for my buddies and me.

With the help of my flashlight, I figured out how to turn the thing on and thumbed up the volume. Squeezing the bar on the side of the unit, I said, "Can anybody hear this? Come back if you can, over."

Replying so fast it startled me, a woman's terse voice responded, "Carbon County dispatch, identify yourself, over."

I ignored her demand. "There's been a gunfight about ten miles south of Baggs on Colorado Highway 13. One of your deputies is severely wounded and the other's dead, over."

"Who is this?" A deep male voice came over the airwaves. "Identify yourself."

"Just a passerby. We need an ambulance. This is no joke, over."

"What's your twenty? Over."

"Right on Highway 13 near mile marker 38. There's an abandoned Ford truck in the south lane. Hurry up."

I turned off the radio and returned to the wounded deputy. He moaned and squirmed even worse now, but he hadn't died. I held his hand and said, "Hang tough, help's on the way."

"Don't leave me," he pleaded again.

"I'll stay as long as I can."

Chapter Three

I planned to keep my word to the deputy, but the instant I heard sirens or spotted emergency lights, I'd be hightailing it out of there. The county road to Baker's Peak was less than a mile to the south, and I needed to be on my way soon if I were going to reach the peak before dawn, a walk of around eight miles.

I remembered what little first aid I'd learned as a referee and umpire for Pop Warner and Little League. Keeping the patient from going into shock was important, so I did my best to keep him warm and awake. I could only imagine the pain he must be in with a bullet in his gut. But if he didn't lose too much blood, such a wound could take a long time to kill a man.

I knelt next to him and tried to carry on a conversation to keep him from slipping away. "What's your name?" I asked, not expecting an answer.

He grunted and I saw him wince in the rising moonlight. "Chance, Chance Stewart. What's yours?"

I raised my eyebrows, surprised by his curiosity, but answered, "John, John Doe."

He chuckled, then groaned.

I studied the man. "Just testing you, see how alert you were." He was big and balding, with blue eyes and a clean-shaven face. He reminded me of Hoss on *Bonanza*. "You ever hear you look like Dan Blocker?"

"Yeah." He squirmed under the blanket and rolled over on his side to look at me. "Who the hell are you?" he asked between grunts.

"That's for me to know . . ."

"You're the guy from the Drifter's."

Afraid to hear the answer, I asked, "What'd you fellows want with me?"

He shuddered from what I took to be a shot of pain, but answered, "There's an APB out for a guy—no name—fits your description." He rolled on his back and breathed deeply. "When they gettin' here?"

"Any minute, Chance," I said, without much conviction. Blood seeped through the army blanket, and I decided to take a more aggressive approach. "Wait a minute, I'm gonna go get my first-aid kit."

"Don't go . . ."

I hustled up the hill and dug into my pack. For years I had carried an army surplus dressing for bullet wounds in case someone I was with got shot on a hunt. With the flashlight I found my water bottle and the green cardboard box, about the size of a candy bar, and ran back to Chance. The package read, "Dressing, First Aid, Field, Individual Troop, Camouflaged, 4 x 7 inches." I tore it open and found some sketchy directions. "This might hurt, but I want to dress that wound, try to slow the bleeding, okay?"

I took his grunt for approval and removed the blood-soaked blanket. Carefully unbuttoning his shirt, I cleaned off his stomach with a little water and found the bullet hole a few inches above his navel. He had no exit wound, and I realized the door of the police cruiser must have taken a lot of steam out of the bullet. Otherwise it would have plowed clear through him, causing a lot more damage. Blood seeped out in a slow, but steady flow.

"Chance, this is gonna hurt." I unwrapped the dressing and applied the white gauze to the wound. Fortunately, the bandage came with extra-long tying tails, because I needed them to get the wrapping tied around his belly. After rolling him over to tie the dressing, I covered him again with the blanket. "The wound's not as bad as I expected. Don't give up, you're gonna make it."

"Hurts like hell," he answered. "I'm cold, now—so cold."

I ripped off my jean jacket and covered his chest. Clutching his hand, I said, "Now all we can do is wait."

Getting folks hurt wasn't part of my plan. I blamed myself for what happened. If the Wyoming deputies hadn't been after me, they'd have never run into the ersatz Bonnie and Clyde from Colorado. I sat next to Chance, held his hand, and glanced at my watch in the bright moonlight. I talked to the wounded man, let him tell me about his wife and kids. He liked to hunt and fish. He didn't sound like a bad guy.

I settled in for a long wait, helping the suffering deputy tough it out until help arrived. The nearest towns in Wyoming were Dixon and Savery, around five and ten miles to the east, respectively. But they were even smaller than Baggs, and I doubted enforcement staff was stationed in either tiny hamlet. That left Riverside, another forty miles east, as the most likely source of help. There might also be highway patrol in the area. A rescue by the Moffat County sheriff from Craig to the south was also possible. When a brother officer was wounded, I knew cops were likely to converge from all directions.

To the east, a pack of coyotes broke the stillness of the calm evening, yodeling and barking. Then, another bunch of the little prairie wolves called from the other side of the highway. I realized they might hear something I couldn't. I knew of hunters using sirens to locate coyotes. I rose and stepped away from the fallen lawman. Closing my eyes, I cupped my ears and strained to hear what might have stirred them up.

"Chance, I think someone's coming. I hear a siren!"

I scooted to the crest of the highway and saw a distant red light on the southern horizon. Returning to Chance, I gently patted his shoulder. "Help's coming up from Colorado, be here in a few minutes. I got to get—"

"Wait, wait—"

"Listen to me, Chance," I said. "I didn't have any idea them folks meant you harm. I was just tryin' to hitch a ride to Denver." I lied to throw off any more pursuit. Now I heard more than one siren nearing and stood. "Hang tough!" I bolted up the hill and cleared the fence as lights from an emergency vehicle flooded the highway. Shouldering my pack, I headed due east across the prairie, making a beeline for Baker's Peak.

Chapter Four

The blare of those damned sirens followed me. Long after I topped a low-lying ridge that blocked the flashing lights behind me, the discordant music of the emergency vehicles still rang over the prairie. With one deputy dead and another seriously wounded, I expected a lot of heat, likely every cop within a hundred miles. I was in big trouble. Treeless prairie rolled away to the base of Baker's Peak. I needed to cross those sagebrush-sprinkled hills by dawn. Reading my watch by moonlight, I figured five, maybe six more hours before sunup.

Named after the famous Indian fighter, Jim Baker, the isolated mountain on the edge of the Bears Ears range was part of the Baker family ranch for most of the 1900s. In the early 1970s the family subdivided the five-thousand-acre ranch into bite-sized parcels of forty to eighty acres. My maternal grandfather bought a choice lot on the north side of the mountain. We built a small cabin together the first summer after I lost my parents. The Old Man called it therapeutic. I called it lonely, backbreaking work, but I came to love the place.

I'd always liked hiking at night. A few weeks earlier, rattlesnakes might have worried me, but a cool fall had chased them into their dens early. Now all I had to watch for was stepping in a badger hole and breaking my leg. Still, I moved at a ground-eating trot across the rolling prairie. After an hour, I stopped for water and a breather. I pulled my binoculars from my pack and glassed south, where the county road ran parallel to my route. A rig moved slowly east with a spotlight scouring the surrounding countryside. Could be kids shooting jackrabbits. More likely the law, looking for the mystery man from the Drifter's Inn.

The Old Man had gotten himself into trouble once, might have even spent some time in the big house. He never said. Still, I figured he'd have rolled over in his grave, seeing me in this fix. I hoped, thought he'd understand, if he knew it was for a good cause, not greed or selfishness. He'd broken the rules a time or two himself when they got in the way of true justice.

I had run track in high school, ran for Mesa College, too. I never met anyone who could stay with me in the hills. I'd be damned if some flat-footed, donut-eating lawman was going to catch me on ground of my own choosing. I moved on, resigning myself to traveling cross-country rather than taking the easier route of the county road.

With my senses in tune with the prairie night, I fell into a simple rhythm, jogging an hour, followed by five minutes of restful walking. By my third cycle, I was nearing the base of the peak. Stunted junipers cast long shadows across the moonlit ground. Mountain mahogany and serviceberry portended aspen and pine, another thousand feet up the mountain. I skipped the next walking interval and loped for the waiting timber above.

I felt safe when I entered a big stand of aspen, running like a belt around the 7,500-foot elevation line of Baker's Peak. When I was still hours to the east of my cabin, the first violet hues of dawn crept upon the eastern horizon. In the timber, though, darkness reigned. I drifted like a ghost, always bearing east and a little up-hill. To my right, I gazed across miles of open ground to the west and that ribbon of a road from a bad dream, Colorado Highway 13. South, towards Craig, the lights of a few remote ranches twinkled in the predawn quiet. I turned east and picked up the pace of my run through the white-trunked trees with shimmering leaves.

I was looking for a barbed-wire fence running north, right up the side of the mountain, all the way to the top. I hiked on, and when golden light poured across the aspen slope from the east, I hit the boundary fence of Baker's Peak. I pitched my pack over the top strand and climbed over, using a handy tree stump. I hefted my pack and slowly walked to the edge of the grove.

A wide grassy meadow stretched beyond the trees. Kneeling behind the last large tree, I studied the rolling grassland through my binoculars. Near the edge of the far timber, a herd of two dozen or more mule deer, does and fawns, quietly browsed along the edge of a patch of mountain oak. At the bottom of the valley, the glassy surface of a small pond shimmered in the growing light. A beaver motored toward the willow-choked dam of its recently constructed home. In the growing warmth of the blue-sky morning, I found a sunlit patch of short grass in the security of the trees. I lay down to rest and spied the vapor trail of a jet cutting the morning sky in half.

So far, so good. It didn't look like anybody knew who the hell I was. Traveled across half of Colorado and into Wyoming over the last week, and all they had was a description here, a sighting there. A story, but no name. Even ol' Hoss, Chance the Wyoming deputy, said there was an APB, but no name.

All I had to do was stay out of sight for a while. Maybe two or three months at the peak. That'd get me to the holidays and the New Year. I was hoping things would be cooled down back home by then.

The smart play, the right play, was to hide in the timber until last light, then hightail it across the ranch on one of the many four-wheel-drive roads. I didn't want to run into a snoopy landowner, a bow hunter, or the conservation officer. My salvation depended on no one discovering I was there.

On the other hand, I didn't want to lay up for an entire day, so close to the cabin. I was tired, hungry, and impatient. So, late in

the morning, when the last of the mule deer drifted into the timber, I shouldered my pack and headed cross-country for my little
retreat.

I followed a game trail on the high side of the grove until the
path cut the main road through the ranch. My home lay only a
couple of miles away. I was sorely tempted to fly down that narrow
jeep road. At least I exercised a little restraint here, as I kept well
off the road, traveling on the uphill side of the trail. If I had to
leave the road, I could always go cross-country to the cabin.

My eyelids were growing heavy, my head foggy. I wanted to
sleep.

I would have heard him coming but for want of rest.

"Howdy, fella. Looks like you've had luck." A short, thick man,
clad in camo, stepped out of a trail entering the meadow I was
crossing. He pointed at my arms and chest.

With a start, I realized he was referring to Chance's blood on
my shirt and hands.

Chapter Five

I faked a cough to give me a second to come up with a story. "Yeah, got a fat doe this morning, right at legal shooting time." I pointed vaguely to the west, in the direction from which I'd been running all night. "Left my bow with my kill."

"Need any help?" He raised his eyes hopefully, like maybe he was bored or looking for something to do out of the ordinary. "That's kind of a strange outfit you got for archery huntin'."

"Nah, thanks the same." I grinned and pointed back toward the top of the peak. "I'm with some friends." I nodded uphill.

"Well, all right, then." He extended his hand and looked me deeply in the eyes, like he was taking a picture. "What tract you got, anyhow?"

I shifted in my pack and started to move on. The curious little pain in the ass might try to follow. "We just call our property the Old Man's shack, out of respect." I nodded curtly and headed up a steep hillside. Glancing backward, I saw the man watching my every step.

Within a few minutes, I cleared the ridgeline and dared to travel the main ranch road for the last mile to the cabin. Despite the surprise encounter with the hunter, I felt safer, way up on the north-facing slope of the peak. I'd hear any vehicle approaching a mile or more away, grinding up the rocky, twisting, four-wheel-drive road in gas-guzzling granny gear. Most of the other owners forsook this portion of the property, with its steep terrain and poor road access.

Entering a large aspen forest, I remembered the Old Man calling the place "Eagle's Grove." Deer browsed around every new bend in the road and a herd of elk worked the area, judging from their fresh scat and cattlelike trails. Walking through the grove, I left the road and veered to the right. I followed a trickle of a creek for a few hundred yards, then headed toward a small stand of spruce, seemingly misplaced on a bench of willows and wild roses.

The Old Man and I had carried all the building materials in the wheelbarrow he had constructed with plywood and a couple of bicycle tires. Took us two days to get nails, lumber, tools, camping gear, and everything else we needed hauled to the site. I kept asking why we couldn't build along a road like everyone else did. "Someday, you'll thank me for doing this the hard way," was his only rebuttal.

It took us five days to build the Old Man's idea of a hunting shack. Most of the lumber came from standing dead pine he felled for some local boys to saw into rough-cut boards. Counting the windows, roofing, stove, and nails, he had about a thousand dollars into it. The one-room cabin measured eleven by fifteen feet inside, and we furnished it with bunk beds, a table, two chairs, and bookshelves, all made from our limited supply of lumber. We hung the walls with the tanned hides of mule deer, coyote, badger, and beaver.

I breathed easier when I took in my first view of the cabin and detected no damage from fallen trees, bears, fire, or vandalism that might have happened during the month I'd been gone. Local pine used for siding had aged over the last five years, blending in well with the surrounding forest. A green metal roof attracted little attention, closely matching the canopy of spruce.

I unlocked the stout Master Lock and opened the heavy door we had made from leftover siding. Light poured into the dark room, and I entered to the familiar smell of wool, wood, and kerosene. Spreading the canvas window curtains was like turning on lights. I hefted my pack on the top bunk bed and sat on the bottom one, pondering everything I needed to do. The kitchen shelves were well stocked with canned goods, and an old metal breadbox held dried beans, rice, pasta, and other food that might attract mice. One five-gallon water container was full, two others empty. On my last visit, I had split and stacked plenty of wood next to the stove and behind the cabin, but I could always cut more if I ran out of work to do.

Fetching water from a spring the next ridge over would only take an hour using the old wheelbarrow. I could go a while on five gallons, even it was a little stale. Same thing with the grub. Canned goods would do for a few days, but sooner or later, I'd be hunting for fresh meat. In the meantime, my most urgent project involved hiding the contents of my backpack.

After washing up and changing my shirt, I stepped outside and knelt to peer under the floor joists of the cabin. My posthole digger and pry bar rested where I had left them. A narrow-bladed fencing shovel lay next to the pry bar along with a storage container I had purchased earlier in the spring at a Denver gun show. At first glance, the white tube resembled a four-foot length of eight-inch PVC pipe. However, closer examination revealed a well-made container with fine threading on the end and a rubber gasket in the cap. The long-haired fellow who sold it to me wore camouflage and had cannabis-stained fingertips. He guaranteed it would keep any contents dry for years. He winked and repeated, "Anything, man."

I figured a half day to dig a four-foot hole and bury the tube. I'd chosen the plastic container because it didn't have any metal on it, so a metal detector couldn't find it. But I had to carefully document the location of my cache, or I might lose it myself.

I walked back inside and locked the cabin door behind me. I was too scared to sleep and too tired to work, but I mustered the will to dump the contents of my pack on the bed and take inven-

tory: A few canned goods and candy bars remained from my last
truck stop pit stop. Dirty socks and underwear, a clean chambray
shirt, and my raingear. But the cabin had plenty of work duds. A
compass, flashlight, hatchet, parachute cord, and small survival kit
tumbled onto the bunk.

I stared nervously at the last two items jammed into the bottom
of the cavernous pack. I removed a blue North Face travel bag
and a plastic-wrapped box the size of a loaf of bread.

Unzipping the bag, I stared at the most cash I'd ever seen outside of a bank. Seventy-five thousand dollars in used bills, mostly
tens and twenties. Someone had used rubber bands to organize
the money into thousand dollar bundles. Made it easy to count, I
guessed. I zipped the bag and stowed it in the sleeping bag on the
top bunk until I could bury my storage container.

Then I pondered the plastic-wrapped package.

The first time I saw anyone use cocaine was in high school. I
figured it must be pretty fun, everybody laughing and having a big
time. A few years later in college, I tried it myself at a bachelor
party. After one snort, I knew that shit wasn't for me. My head
spun, and I thought my heart would explode. All my pals started
grinding their teeth and talking a million miles an hour. Within
ten or fifteen minutes, they all wanted more. I drank my beer and
watched with fascination, as people I thought I knew revealed an
entirely different side of themselves.

The drug was euphoric, but it didn't look like the high was
worth the hangover. I saw friends fight and lie and scheme to get
their hands on coke. Once they figured I wouldn't touch the stuff,
they'd sometimes ask me to hold onto a little for them for special
occasions. They couldn't trust themselves to lay off it for even a
day or two.

Now I was staring at eleven pounds of blow. At a hundred dollars a gram, each pound had a street value of forty-five thousand
dollars. Eleven pounds was worth about half a million dollars.

Before I started my run, I'd come damned close to dumping the shit in the garbage. Or I could get a hell of a lot of fish high, dumping it in the creek. Or I could be a damned hypocrite and try to sell the coke. How much good could I do with the ill-gotten profits? How much harm? I already had a pretty good idea what to do with the money, but I still worried about the dope. If I had my way, this dope would never see the street, but I finally decided to keep it a while for insurance. For now, I stuffed the box in the top bunk sleeping bag along with the money and thought I'd try to nap for a couple of hours.

I closed the curtains on most of the midday light and sat on the bottom bunk. I unlaced my boots and lay on the narrow bed. On a wooden footlocker next to the head of the bunk rested a small framed picture of a lovely young woman. She sat on a boulder at the edge of Warren Lake, with the towering Williams Mountains of the Hunter-Fryingpan Wilderness in the background. Her brunette hair glistened in the summer sun and even in the photograph her dark eyes beckoned me. She looked happy. She was happy. I knew, because I was the photographer. She could have been mine, but "until death do you part" scared the hell out of me.

Now I was glad for the sleepless night of running. My mind started to race, but this time I was tired enough to choke it off. I closed my eyes and soon I was back with Laura in the high country. We followed a faint trail over the pass to No Name Creek. Before slipping into the next drainage, I paused to locate the sound of the vehicle that broke the stillness of the quiet fall evening . . .

Chapter Six

In the cabin's dim light, my eyes fluttered awake. Every muscle knotted. I heard the unmistakable roar of a four-wheel-drive rig climbing the road to the top of the peak. There were no other cabins beyond mine on the mountainside. Were they only hunters looking to gain elevation the easy way? Maybe, but I had my doubts.

Rubbing the sleep from my eyes, I jumped up and jammed my feet into boots. The vehicle stopped, somewhere close to the trail leading to the cabin. I grabbed an old canvas jacket and daypack hanging near the door and locked the cabin behind me. I was apprehensive about leaving the money and coke behind, but still entered the woods to investigate, figuring I'd only be gone a short while.

Slipping through the timber, I left the trail and made a straight line for the road. I peered through the trees with my binoculars. I wanted to see them before they spotted me. Reaching a little rise, I sat and studied the rocky, four-wheel-drive road a few hundred yards below. A red pickup truck stood out, shining in the slanting rays of the late afternoon sun. Two men exited the cab and lingered on the road.

I slipped off the knoll and flew through the timber toward the rig until I reached the last low ridge above the road. Slowing, I walked on the balls of my feet and dropped to my knees when I reached the little rise above the truck. I hid behind a fat tree trunk and spied two men, standing in front of the truck.

They were around twenty yards away. Loud voices rose in argument.

"I'm telling you, Larry, I think the guy I ran into this morning is the hitchhiker they're talking about on the radio."

I slowly raised my binoculars and studied the man speaking. Damned if he wasn't the same chubby, nosey fellow I'd stumbled into earlier that morning. He was still clad in camouflage, but now he wore a gun belt, complete with looped cartridges and a shiny revolver.

"You've seen too many movies, Stan." The tall, husky man with a three-day beard towered over the little pain in the ass.

"He said he was headin' for the top of the mountain," Stan said. "Said he was stayin' with friends up here."

"You know as well as I do there aren't any places this far up—"

"Larry, I just want to go to the end of the road. It's only another half a mile or so. Maybe they got a camp up there."

"Okay, but I'm not drivin' my new Ford any farther." The big man pointed up the road. "You want to go any farther, then we'll walk."

"Fine with me, let's get goin'."

I waited until they were out of sight, then dropped down to the truck. Using the Ford to screen myself in case the two men reappeared, I dug a small tool from my pack and scooted to one of the rear tires. I unscrewed the cap on the tire stem and removed the valve. Air whistled from the tire and within a couple of minutes it was flatter than hammered dog shit. I replaced the cap and valve, then crawled under the bed of the truck and partially deflated the spare as well. I scooted back into the woods and watched for Stan and Larry. They were about to learn these rocky roads could be damned hard on tires.

Waiting for their return, I sat against a tree trunk and remembered my first taste of vigilantism. The Old Man lived in a modest home along the municipal golf course of our hometown. He had always enjoyed access to the fairway behind his house until the city planned to place a chain-link fence, complete with concertina wire, along the perimeter of the course. For days, a surveying crew marked the boundary in preparation for fencing. "It sure would be a sad thing if something were to happen to all those god-damned stakes," he muttered one evening.

Late that night, after the FBI report and the "The Star Spangled Banner" ended the TV broadcast, I slipped from the house and pulled every one of those stakes. Took me most of the night, but the Old Man enjoyed another few months of unimpeded access to the course for his evening strolls. Funny thing, he never asked about those stakes, and I never told him what I'd done.

By the time I heard the two men returning from their hike up the mountain road, it was getting cold and dark. I shivered behind a tree, listening to them noisily kicking rocks and talking as they neared the truck.

"I told you there wasn't anybody up there, Stan."

"Just 'cause we didn't see anybody along the road doesn't mean he's not up here," argued the shorter man.

"Just what the hell you gonna do, even if you find him?" asked Larry.

"Arrest his ass—"

"Hell, you ain't got the authority to do that, Stan."

"I'm a deputy sheriff, ain't I?"

"Reserve deputy," scoffed Larry. "You're not supposed to do jackshit on your own."

"If I catch that son of a bitch, there's no way they can pass me over again," said Stan.

"Let's just get off this damned road before it's dark," said Larry. He pulled the keys from his pocket and unlocked the driver's door.

"Goddamnit!" he bellowed. "I got a fuckin' flat tire! I told you I didn't want to come up here."

I covered my mouth and laughed silently.

"That son of a bitch probably did that while we were gone," said Stan, as he walked around the truck and inspected the tire.

Larry said, "Now you sound like a nut!"

"I'll crawl under the bed, get the spare," said Stan. "You get the jack and the lug wrench. We'll be out of here in no time."

About the time the big man found the tools, Stan shared the rest of the bad news. "Larry, your goddamned spare is nearly flat!"

I strained to contain my laughter.

When they finally changed the tire and limped off the mountainside on that low spare, it was darker than the inside of a cow. I watched with satisfaction as the red glow of the taillights faded into the gloomy night and finally disappeared around a bend in the road. Archery season ended in a few days, and I hoped that'd mark the end of their stay at the peak. But I figured I hadn't seen the last of them, or at least of Stan.

With the aid of my penlight, I returned to the cabin. After lighting a single candle, I slumped on a wooden bench. The growl of my stomach reminded me I hadn't eaten all day.

I settled for a cold can of spaghetti, not wanting to risk chimney smoke. Eating in the quiet cabin, I stared at the AM/FM radio resting on the windowsill. Reluctantly, I switched it on and found the local Craig station, 550 Big Country.

The excitement of Stan and Larry's visit had just about worn off. I was played out and hardly found the energy to eat, listening to Barbara Mandrel belting out "Sleeping Single in a Double Bed." When the local news came on, the DJ recounted the day's top news story in a booming, urgent voice. "Last night, a shootout between two Wyoming deputies and an unidentified teenage couple along Colorado Highway Thirteen has left one deputy dead, the other in critical condition after being airlifted to Cheyenne."

Adrenaline jolted through me.

"The couple left behind their stolen vehicle and fled south, stealing the Wyoming deputies' cruiser," said the DJ. "The young man is between six foot two and six foot four, one hundred seventy pounds, with short red hair and freckles. His accomplice, a young woman, approximately five foot six and one hundred twenty pounds with long blonde hair was believed to be wounded in the shoot-out."

I nearly choked on my food when the DJ continued, "A second man is also wanted in connection with the crime. He is described as twenty- to twenty-five years old, six foot to six foot two and weighing one hundred sixty pounds, with medium brown hair, last seen leaving the scene of the gunfight, approximately ten miles south of the Wyoming-Colorado Border."

The DJ's report ended with the warning, "Anyone having knowledge of the identity or whereabouts of any of these individuals is urged to contact the Moffat County sheriff. All three should be considered armed and dangerous and should not be approached."

The law must have gotten the descriptions of the redhead and blonde from the Sinclair station attendant. They could have gotten mine from folks at the Drifter's Inn and, maybe, Chance, if he'd been able to talk.

I was devastated to be mentioned in the same breath as Red and the blonde. The only good news was Chance must have had made it through his operation.

I rose and stepped outside. The night air braced me. Breathing slow and deep, I tried to keep my wits. Despite being a part of the shoot-out, I was still a nameless stranger. Nothing had changed. I still needed to lay low until after the holidays. In a month, after rifle season ended, the peak would be deserted and I'd have the place to myself. I only had to stay out of sight, avoid folks. Most of all, I had to avoid that damned Stan.

But, I knew he'd be back.

A month was a long time when the law was looking for you. Even if the law was a pompous little pain in the ass whose only authority existed in his own mind. He was still a threat, maybe even more so than the regular law, because he sounded bound and determined to prove himself.

A sudden chill ran through me. Had I erred in flattening that tire? I wanted to dissuade Stan and his partner from snooping around my neck of the woods, but had I inadvertently revealed my presence? I'd have to be more careful.

I thought I'd planned this whole spree well enough. But I was learning there was a hell of a lot more to being a criminal than I'd ever considered.

Still, I didn't regret what I'd done. Someone needed my help. I'd made a vow. Tom Tucker would rot in hell, and Laura would be free.

I had to last out the month.

Chapter Seven

A week later, early snow covered the woods in a white mantle, as pristine as a bride, as innocent as her blush. The day after reaching my cabin, I had buried the storage tube containing the money and dope. Now, six inches of fresh snow hid any sign of my cache. I was relieved to be rid of that contraband, at least until I left the peak.

I had fetched water from the next drainage over and split enough wood to keep the cabin heated for weeks. I laundered my clothes and bathed every other day or so in a crude shower I'd built earlier that summer. Caught up with my chores, I turned to rereading my limited supply of magazines and books. Dog-eared copies of *Outdoor Life*, *Field & Stream*, and *Sports Afield* bore the Old Man's name and mailing address on the subscription label, reminding me of his silent presence.

I read A. B. Guthrie's *The Big Sky* for the umpteenth time. The Old Man had given me his worn copy, autographed by the author, when I graduated from high school. As I took it from him, he held on to it for a moment and looked me in the eye. "This is one you'll always come back to." Boone Caudill might have been the protagonist, but Dick Summers was my hero. He did everything right, no shortcuts, no lies, no excuses. He was the kind of man I wanted to be.

Reading about buffalo hunts and mountain men cooking fresh meat over coals whetted my appetite for something besides my dwindling supply of canned goods and dry staples. Archery season had ended days before, and I'd heard no vehicles since. I had a window of a few days before rifle hunters would be coming to the peak. As the snow lightened in the early morning light, I left the cabin to kill a deer.

Staying off the road, I slipped through the buckbrush and serviceberry, keeping the light breeze in my face. The fresh snow silenced my steps, and I paused every few minutes, peering into the forest through the binoculars around my neck. After a few hundred yards, I stopped at the edge of a small meadow and hid behind a patch of willows. To my right, I spotted a small herd of mule deer, less than fifty yards away.

The deer browsed in a patch of mountain mahogany, nibbling on the new year's growth. A forkhorn buck mingled among the does and fawns. Kneeling against a tall pine, I raised my little .22 rifle. Its movement caught an old doe's attention, and she snorted and stomped the ground with her front hoof. The deer all raised their heads and stared in my direction. I steadied the crosshairs of the scope on the young buck's neck and squeezed the trigger. The rifle cracked, spooking the other deer, which bolted for the timber. Left behind was the forkhorn, dead in the snow.

Walking into the meadow to fetch my kill, I grabbed an antler and dragged the yearling buck into the timber. The Old Man had been a stickler for following the game laws, but I needed fresh meat. Now, I was a poacher as well as a thief and fugitive. At least I'd honor this deer. I wouldn't waste a bit of it.

I skidded the animal downhill into a dark grove of spruce. Gutting the deer, I saved the liver and heart, which I placed in a small garbage bag. I tossed a wadded length of parachute cord over the stout limb of a standing, dead tree and tied the end to a stick I ran through the deer's hocks. I managed to pull the carcass off the ground, well beyond the reach of any predators, and tied the cord around the base of the tree. After placing the plastic bag with my evening's supper into my pack, I headed uphill for the jeep road.

The peak seemed deserted, but I still wasn't going to leave a trail right from the deer to my cabin. The snow fell again, but lighter than before. I hoped it would cover my tracks and any sign of my hunt in the meadow. Making a big loop, I finally reached the cabin from the opposite direction. I was satisfied to see my tracks from that morning were already covered by snow.

Inside the cabin, I cleaned my rifle and knife. I trimmed the liver and heart and placed them in a cooler, half full of fresh snow. My mouth watered, thinking of fried venison, but first I needed to fetch the deer. Field-dressed, the young buck probably weighed less than seventy pounds, an easy load I planned to carry back to the cabin on an old Kelty pack frame.

Before leaving the cabin, I took a lunch break. I'd come to listen to the noon news every day on 550 Big Country. Over the last few days, the coverage of the shoot-out had died down a little. Red and the blonde were still on the loose, but Chance was on the mend and out of intensive care. The DJ still blared out a description of the young couple. But I nearly choked on my Vienna sausages when he continued, "A man meeting the description of the unidentified hitchhiker has been recently sighted in the vicinity of Baker's Peak, according to the Moffat County Sheriff's Department." He repeated my description and asked locals to report any sightings to the sheriff's office.

"Shit!" I muttered. Must have been that chubby runt, Stan. I'd have to be more cautious than ever about avoiding folks. My head spun, getting a handle on my predicament.

With Chance looking to recover, I wasn't worried about being implicated in the assault of the deputies. But I damned sure didn't want to have to explain what I was doing, hitchhiking across Wyoming and Colorado. And I still wasn't sure why there had been an APB out for me before I reached Baggs. Did Tom Tucker have the balls to report my theft to the police? What the hell could he have told them? *Some son of a bitch stole my buy money and over ten pounds of coke.*

After lunch, I grabbed my pack frame and left the cabin. I carried my binoculars, but left behind my rifle to save weight. The sun had burned through the clouds and the same light breeze blew in my face. Snow covered my tracks back to the deer, but I wasn't worried about losing it. I could have found it in the dark.

The first hint of trouble was an angry pine squirrel barking near the small grove where the forkhorn hung. I paused and spied the small cluster of spruce, fifty yards distant, with my binoculars. Movement caught my eye, a tawny blur shifting through small gaps in the trees. I felt naked without my rifle.

Studying the spruce further, I realized whatever was in the grove had climbed above the deer in the overhanging limbs. Then I heard the parachute cord snap, like a broken guitar string, followed by a heavy thud in the snow.

A gentle breeze cooled the back of my neck. The wind had shifted. A few seconds later, a low baritone snarl rumbled from the grove. Cold sweat ran down my back. "Puma," I whispered.

An instant later, an enormous mountain lion with a head like a melon emerged from the trees with the neck of my deer in its mouth. The lion stood as high as a big buck, but with three feet of tail nervously twitching about. As big as it was, probably close to two hundred pounds, it had to be an old tom.

When I rose, the lion dropped the deer and stared at me. I looked up into the slender trees in front of me, then realized the futility of climbing to safety. The lion crouched low in the snow and laid his ears back. He bared his teeth, revealing four glimmering canines, and hissed at me.

I froze and tried not to look into his coal-black eyes. After what seemed to be an eternity, but was probably only a few seconds, the lion clamped its jaws on the deer's neck again and dragged his prize away into the timber. I was glad to trade my life for the deer. The tom was welcome to it.

Several minutes later, I summoned the will to leave the false protection of the trees I hid behind. While I resisted the urge to run, I forsook stealth for expedience, making a beeline for my place. I made an oath not to leave the cabin again without a gun, remembering the Old Man's warning never to venture into these woods unarmed. With all the deer on my side of the peak, this old tom had found himself a fine home. I planned to give him a wide berth. A cat like that could be damned dangerous to an unwitting man.

Chapter Eight

I stayed close to the cabin for a couple of days. But I was already caught up with my chores and getting restless. Scared—but restless. I wasn't the most sociable fellow, but I hadn't been around any folks in weeks. I craved company, someone to talk to, find out what the hell was going on, besides the little chatter and news provided by 550 Big Country. The cops were looking for me, judging from the radio reports and the constant din of small planes I heard from dawn until dusk.

On the third day after being cooped up, I left the cabin at first light, toting an old canvas rucksack from my scouting days stuffed with lunch, water, and my storm gear. I felt reasonably safe, with the Old Man's Smith & Wesson .22 revolver riding on my waist in an old moose-hide holster. It wasn't very powerful, but I could keep all my shots in a five-inch circle at twenty-five paces. Good enough for rabbits and grouse, good enough to plink a mountain lion in the head, too, if need be.

Most of the snow had melted, giving me the confidence to venture a ways from my place without fear of Stan or some other pain in the ass stumbling upon my trail. After reaching the end of the four-wheel-drive road south of the cabin, I hiked cross-country to the top of the peak. With big game season starting at the end of the week, traffic would soon pick up. I worked my way up the timbered slope, careful to avoid any hunters scouting before the Saturday opener.

I was toying with the idea of visiting Wilbur Butternut, the local hermit and anarchist. Wilbur lived on the other side of the mountain, under the west shoulder of the peak, on an eighty-acre homestead. He was the first man to live year-round on the ranch and had been a good friend of the Old Man. I trusted him.

Wilbur hated anything to do with the "guv'ment." He had bought his property in cash, years before, with his military pension and disability payments. He made his own wine from chokecherries, tended a big garden, poached deer and elk all year long, dynamited fish in the local ponds when no one was around, and generally did whatever the hell he pleased. He had been known to rustle the odd beef when he got sick of venison, and discouraged wardens and other interlopers from visiting by shooting a round or two over their heads with his army surplus Springfield .30-06.

More important than making a social visit, I had to reconsider how I would get back to Aspen in light of my status as a fugitive. I had originally planned to hike to the highway after Christmas and hitchhike back home. Now, the last thing I wanted to do was thumb a ride on Highway 13.

Wilbur had an old Ford Bronco he drove to Craig every month or so, to stock up on whatever he couldn't poach, grow, ferment, dynamite, or swap for at the peak. He made a few bucks butchering deer and elk during hunting season and spent most of his cash on a lady friend in town. I was hoping he'd give me a ride to Craig sometime around New Year's. From there, I could take a Greyhound to Aspen.

I reached the bare ridgeline overlooking Wilbur's place a little before noon. Glassing down into the little valley framed in bare aspen, I spotted smoke rising from the stovepipe of his cabin, around half a mile below. I chuckled to see a salt block he had placed in a little clearing, around fifty yards in front of the front porch. It looked like a pretty easy way to ambush unsuspecting deer. Wilbur was home, all right. The problem was how to hail the cabin without getting shot.

I slipped down the steep hillside, weaving through buckbrush and serviceberry, until I reached the valley floor, fifty yards from the back of the cabin. I hollered, "Hello, the cabin, I'm coming around the front!"

When I reached the porch, Wilbur was waiting, a rifle in his hands. "Goddamnit, your ass is on private property!" He raised the rifle to port arms. "You best have a good reason for tress-passin'."

I froze, hoping Wilbur would recognize me. He squinted and cocked his head. I didn't dare move.

Nearing fifty, Wilbur had given up on his thinning hair and shaved his head, making his crooked nose look even bigger. Like any good woods rat, he wore all wool for warmth and stealth. He was a little man, maybe five six and a buck thirty, sopping wet. But what he lacked in size, he made up for in grit.

He decided not to draw a bead on me, so I smiled and took off my baseball cap. "Don't you remember me, Wilbur? I'm—"

"That you, College Boy?" His scowl melted into a grin. He lowered the rifle, then leaned it against the cabin wall. "Get your ass up here and shake my hand!"

Climbing up the steps of the porch, I took his hand, marveling at the power of his grip. I pointed back toward the salt block in front of the cabin. "I see you're still a damned poacher."

"Shit, College, man's got to eat, don't he?" Wilbur had taken to calling me "College Boy," or some variation, instead of my Christian name years before, when I eschewed an opportunity to work for him the fall after graduating from high school. He thought I should take a year off before going to college. At the time, it sounded like a good idea to me, too, but not to the Old Man.

Wilbur opened the cabin door and motioned for me to enter. "Let's get out of the cold."

Inside, the frame-built structure was paneled in rough-cut siding, providing a flat surface to hang the racks of deer and elk and tanned hides of just about every critter that frequented the peak, including a bear, bobcat, beaver, and raccoon, to mention a few. Pictures of Wilbur in uniform at Chosin Reservoir with his old Marine comrades hung in the small spaces between antlers and hides. An old sofa sat against the back wall of the big one-room cabin, a Confederate flag hanging over it.

Wilbur checked a blackened pot on his wood-burning stove. "Water's boilin'. Build you a cup of tea, boy?"

"Sure, I'd appreciate it." I leaned my pack against the wall next to the door and took off my old Filson Cruiser.

"I see you're heeled." Wilbur pointed toward the holstered pistol hanging from my belt. "Your grandpa's old kit gun, eh?"

I unloaded the little revolver and handed it to him. I knew he loved guns. Aiming at the far end of the cabin, Wilbur dry-fired the piece. "Damn, this is a sweet little darlin'." He handed the pistol to me, cylinder opened, like a man with good gun manners should and motioned toward the couch. "Go ahead, take a load off, you must be tired, hiking 'cross the mountain."

Wilbur poured an enamel cup full of steaming water and dunked a Lipton tea bag into it. He stirred in a heaping teaspoon of his precious sugar and placed the mug on the coffee table in front of me. Sitting in a rocking chair of his own making from pine branches and rawhide lacing, he nodded toward the tea. "That'll cure what ails ya." As an afterthought, he nodded toward a shelf in the kitchen corner, where a few miscellaneous bottles of liquor stood. "Sweeten that up?"

"That Jack's tempting, but I better pass," I said. "I still have to walk back home and there's something I need to discuss with you."

Wilbur watched me sip my tea, studying me, like a teacher appraising a student.

When I was younger, I'd had the foolish notion that anyone without a college education, let alone without a high school degree, couldn't be all that sharp. Wilbur was the first man to show me how ignorant I'd been. He was as clever and witty as any "college boy." He was also intuitive as hell, and right now I felt like he was reading me like an open book.

"Why do I get the feelin' you got something to do with all the law that's been running around here the last few days?"

Reluctant to talk, I realized I'd come to get his help. No sense in clamming up now. Before I could answer, Wilbur thumbed toward a transistor radio on the windowsill and asked, "You ain't been hitchhikin' again, now, have ya?"

Chapter Nine

I spilled my guts to Wilbur. Told him everything, robbing Tom Tucker and his pal, hitchhiking across Colorado and Wyoming, and witnessing the shoot-out between the Wyoming deputies and the young couple from Colorado. Maybe I was taking a chance, but already I felt relief from talking to someone.

Wilbur whistled low. "Holy jumpin' Jesus!" He shook his head and chuckled. "Didn't know you had it in ya, College Boy."

"I'm just trying to help my old girlfriend. I'd do anything for her, but I didn't plan on every cop in the country looking for me." I leaned forward on the couch and rubbed my face with both hands.

Wilbur rose from his chair and patted my back. "You'll have a hell of a time gettin' yourself out of this mess, College. Lose your nerve now, and I'll be visiting you in Canyon City or plantin' daisies on your grave." He walked over to the window and gazed toward the south, where his driveway ran to the main ranch road.

"Thanks, Wilbur," I sighed. "You're making me feel lots better."

"Cops is thicker than fleas around here." He paused and added, "Bet you want me to haul ya to Craig, huh?"

"I hadn't figured to ask, Wilbur," I said, trying not to show how relieved I felt that he'd offered. "I was planning on hitchin' a ride, but now—"

"You done enough thumbin'. I'll get you there." Wilbur pointed toward one of his Marine photos. "My company got trapped above the 38th Parallel in Korea, back in June 1950. Spent three months getting back to our line." He grinned and thumbed toward the window. "This'll be a piece of cake, compared to dodgin' them North Koreans. When was you lookin' at heading south?" Wilbur returned to his homemade chair and rocked.

"Well after hunting season, late December."

"Think you can stay outta trouble 'til then?" Wilbur asked.

"Hope so, just one problem though—"

"That limp-dick Stan?" Wilbur raised his eyebrows and laughed. "I'd like to stick a pickle fork in his ass."

"You know that guy?"

"Hell, yes," said Wilbur. "We're practically neighbors, lives two properties over. Snoops around here, sometimes. Been braggin' about how he's gonna pinch the mysterious hitchhiker." Wilbur looked at me intently, eyes narrowed, and not a trace of a grin. "I may be a loner, but I still got my ways of keeping up with the doin's 'round here."

"He came up to my side of the mountain, with one of his pals," I said. "He's some kind of reserve deputy—"

"Yeah, I heard," interrupted Wilbur. "Makes his real livin' running his mother's Ben Franklin in Craig. Accordin' to his crew, he works fewer days a year than ol' Santie Claus."

I laughed.

"Yeah, he's a lazy bastard, but he's got a lot of time on his hands to cause trouble."

"He's already been a pain in my ass," I said.

"As long as we're gossipin' like a couple of ol' ladies," said Wilbur, "something else you ought to know 'bout Stan."

Now my curiosity was piqued.

"Stan married this gal, one of the salesladies at his mother's store, four or five years ago." Wilbur spoke low, like someone might overhear him. "Anyways, this woman had a son, maybe fifteen, or so. I think his name was Jimmy."

I already didn't like where this was heading.

"After Jimmy's second or third trip to the emergency room, folks started wonderin' what the hell was goin' on."

"Jesus, what'd he do to him?" I asked.

"Broken arm, busted lip, bruises," Wilbur snorted. "Lotta accidents in that home."

"Didn't anybody do anything about it?"

"Well, the boy moved away to live with his dad in Texas, but the mother, Stan's old lady, stayed with Stan."

"Good God."

"Ol' Stan didn't come out unscathed, though," said Wilbur. "Rumor is the sheriff got involved, knew all about it. Now Moffat County will never hire Stan's sorry ass as a real deputy."

"Well, at least that's some justice."

"I just thought you should know what sort of man you're foolin' with, College Boy."

The late afternoon sun shone through the western window. "Getting late, Wilbur." I finished my tea, savoring the last syrupy sip. "Ought to be heading back. I've got to go cross-country, stay off the road." I figured the law had been patrolling the ranch. I was grateful for my hideaway tucked away on the back side of the peak. But I remembered that big puma. I didn't want to be traveling through his territory after dark.

"I'd put ya up here, College Boy, but I think you'll be safer at your place," said Wilbur. "How you set for chow? Got plenty of meat?"

"I'm fine, but a big cat stole a nice young buck from me a few days ago."

Wilbur jerked his head toward me. "You see his tracks?"

"No, sir. As soon as he dragged my buck away, I hightailed it back to the cabin. By the time I cut his old trail this morning, all the snow was gone."

"Well, I'm guessin' he's the same tom I snared last week. Caught his front paw, but he managed to pull away right before I got off a shot." Wilbur grimaced. "He lost a toe, though. Won't be hard to pick out his sign from now on—"

"Couldn't it be a different cat?" I asked.

"Nah, ain't no way a big ol' tom like that would allow another male in his territory."

"Well, he is a big son of a bitch. Losing that toe won't help his mood," I added.

Wilbur sprung up from his rocker, like a man bent on action. "I haven't run my Bronco in a few weeks, the battery could use chargin'. I'll give you a ride over t'other side of the mountain."

We walked around his cabin to a little grove of spruce. In the center of the trees, Wilbur had built a small shed. He unlocked the double doors and motioned for me to enter. Sunlight poured in, revealing several carcasses hanging in the dark storage area. A deer, an elk hindquarter, and a side of beef. I grinned and patted the enormous carcass. "Hell of a moose, Wilbur," I quipped.

"Nope, slow elk," said Wilbur. "Made the mistake of wanderin' onta my place."

In Colorado, the legal burden fell on landowners to keep neighboring cattle off their property, but Wilbur didn't see that as justice. He took a knife from a little worktable along the wall and carved a hefty piece of sirloin tip, probably ten pounds, and a two-foot length of loin. He placed the beef, cool and fresh, in a burlap bag. "Here, stuff this in your pack. That'll keep you in meat 'til you can kill another deer." We left the shop and Wilbur locked the door behind us.

"Thanks for the beef, Wilbur, but you sure it's safe to drive across the ranch?" I wanted the ride, but not at the expense of another run-in with the law.

"They ain't lookin' for me, College Boy."

Chapter Ten

Wilbur kept his Bronco parked at the end of the driveway, in a little copse of aspen a hundred yards in front of the cabin. I unlatched the gate and waited for him to drive through the narrow opening. The yellow Bronco, a '68 with a 289-cubic-inch small-block V-8, sputtered and coughed when Wilbur turned it over. Within a few minutes, the engine purred and Wilbur drove through the gate, then stopped for me. When I started to climb in the front seat, he thumbed toward the back of the Bronco. "You're gonna have to be a little bit more careful than that," he said. "You ride in the back—and keep your head down."

Wilbur had long since removed the rear bench seat for more hauling capacity. I cleared a spot for myself and my pack amongst the tools, chain saw, and spare clothes. Sitting on a folded tarp to soften the ride, I leaned against the back of the passenger seat. "I'm good to go, Wilbur."

We lurched into motion, my view restricted to blue sky interspersed by the top half of aspen, spruce, and pine, bordering the four-wheel-drive road. I tracked our progress mostly from my recollection of the turns we made along the way and the hills we climbed up and crawled down. I was grateful for the ride, saving me several miles of walking with a heavy pack loaded down with my regular gear and at least twenty pounds of Wilbur's rustled beef.

We didn't try to talk much over the din of the noisy Bronco, grinding up the mountain pass in low range. So it startled me when Wilbur blurted out, "Shit!" and downshifted into first gear. "Speak of the devil," he shouted over the roar of the engine.

Without rising from my seat, I hollered, "What's wrong?"

"Got somebody headed our way—your pal, Stan."

"Can't we just drive around him?"

"Not here, College. Road's too narrow. We'll have to stop, let him pass." Wilbur slowed down and looked over his shoulder at me. "Cover yourself with that tarp you're sittin' on."

I scrambled to conceal myself as Wilbur pulled off the road. He softly cursed and spoke low, "Stay quiet, College Boy. The worthless prick is gettin' out. Looks like he's coming up to talk."

I crawled into a fetal position, lying as small as possible against the bed of the Bronco. I heard Wilbur roll his window down and speak loudly, "I ain't got much time to gab, Stan. Trying to get over to the other side of the mountain, scoutin' before opening day."

Stan must have stood near, because he sounded like he was in the Bronco with us. I recognized his nasally, high-pitched voice. "Hell, Wilbur, every day is opening day for you. Since when did you ever give a shit about hunting anything in season?"

Wilbur laughed. "Well, I got a pal comin' up from Denver to hunt, wants to do things legal."

"Since when did you have any pals?" snorted Stan.

Stan must have pissed off Wilbur with that jab, because the Bronco revved and rocked, like he was about to take off. I wondered if Wilbur might try to run over Stan's toes.

"Now listen, asshole, get your truck around me. I'm tired of talkin' to ya."

Stan must have stuck his head into the cab, because I heard him smacking his gum. "What's ya got in the back, there, under the tarp? You already jumped the season, Wilbur?"

"Get your fuckin' head outta my rig, Stan. What I got back there is nonya!"

"Nonya?" asked Stan.

"None ya goddamned business." Wilbur laughed at his own joke. "Scat, now, before I lose my patience and whip your ass."

I lay motionless under the tarp, scared to breathe or twitch a muscle. Sweating from every pore, I longed for fresh air. Worse, I fought off a sneeze spurred on by the dusty floor of the Bronco.

"I could make you stop, search your Bronco. I am a deputy——"

"You ain't shit, now move." Wilbur was about to lose his temper. I heard it in his voice, terse and sharp. I hoped and prayed Stan didn't push him anymore.

Stan must have retreated a ways, because his voice trailed off. "I'll let it go this time, Wilbur, but don't think you're foolin' me."

"Stay down, College Boy, he's comin' up to pass us."

A few seconds later, Stan pulled alongside us. Stan must have wanted to talk some more, but Wilbur didn't give him a second chance. The Bronco jumped forward. Once again, we were headed east for the other side of the mountain.

"You can pull that tarp off ya now, but keep low," said Wilbur.

"Holy balls!" I rolled the tarp away, gasping for air. My heart raced. "That was mighty close, Wilbur."

"Don't shit your pants, College, but I think he knows you're back there."

"How do you figure?"

"The whole time we was talking, ol' Stan was looking behind me, toward you." Wilbur sighed. "I didn't have a chance to tell you, but one of your boots was stickin' out of that tarp."

"Shit!" Now I had Wilbur in the doghouse, too. "I'm sorry."

"At least I ain't bored," Wilbur chuckled. He shifted gears and picked up speed. "I'm gonna put a little distance between us, just in case Stan decides to turn around."

I sat up enough to peer through the rear window and over the spare tire and gas can carrier bolted on the back of Bronco. Halfway around the mountain by now, we had about three more miles before I planned to bail out and walk the last half mile up a spur to my place. "I can get out anywhere, Wilbur. You've already cut my walk in half."

"I ain't kowtowin' to that horse's ass. We'll keep going, but I got a little surprise for Stan."

Wilbur still seemed pissed, but he hadn't lost his sense of humor. We drove on until we came to a long straight piece of road. I glassed through the rear window with my binoculars. A truck emerged from the timber, a quarter of a mile behind us. "Is Stan driving a blue Chevy truck?"

"Yep. I see him too," said Wilbur, flatly. He sped down to where the road turned into a thick stand of spruce. When he stomped on the brakes, I slammed into the passenger seat. Wilbur jumped out of the rig and ran around to the back. He opened the rear window and hollered, "Get your pack. I'll pick you up a little ways ahead."

Wilbur grabbed the chain saw and ran down the road while pulling on the starter cord. After two or three cranks, the little beast roared. Wilbur gave it a few moments to warm up while he studied a tall evergreen arching overhead. He cut a shallow notch out of the tree facing the road, then hopped behind the spruce and sawed a foot below the first cut. At the same time, the blue Chevy neared, a hundred yards away, the tree buckled. Wilbur stepped away, making sure to avoid a widow-maker.

As if in slow motion, the waist-thick spruce crashed across the road, bouncing a few times before coming to rest. Wilbur ran to the Bronco, laughing, and threw the chain saw in the back. He took off just as Stan braked in front of the roadblock. Wilbur rolled down his window and flipped the finger in response to Stan's angry honking.

Fifty yards down the road, I stepped from behind the tree where I had watched Wilbur's performance. When he stopped, I jumped into the front seat and hollered, "How the hell you gonna get back to your place?"

Wilbur shifted gears and laughed. "This ain't the only route across the mountain!"

Chapter Eleven

Speeding down the rocky road, I wondered what Wilbur meant about another way across the peak. As far as I knew, he had just cut himself off from returning to his place. Stan was bound to be waiting, maybe with reinforcements this time. I'd spent as much time as most folks on the peak, but the only options I knew were to return the same way we'd come or keep taking this road north all the way to Baggs and make a long loop down Highway 13.

Wilbur enjoyed getting the best of Stan, chuckling for some time after leaving the wannabe lawman talking to himself behind the fallen tree. But as the adrenaline of the chase wore off, I pressed the issue. "No shit, Wilbur, how do you plan to get home?"

"You seen all those assholes runnin' 'round here the last few years with them ATVs, College?"

"Yep." I hated the damned things. I'd been run off the road more times than I cared to remember by the noisy, obnoxious toys. As far as I was concerned, anybody too lazy to walk a little ought to stay at home.

"Well, those sons of bitches have cut enough trails up here, a fella can get about anywhere he wants." Wilbur nodded to his left, toward the eastern flank of the peak. "I spent all summer hikin' around them ridges."

I was sick to think the mountain had been so scarred by off-road travel. But I didn't doubt Wilbur. If anyone could get around on marginal roads, it was him in his trusty Bronco. "Is that why you mounted that new Warn winch?"

"Between my winch and that chain saw, I can get around most any place I want in a pinch. Like now, for instance." Wilbur turned my way. "My turn to ask a question."

"Shoot."

"How come you're stickin' your neck out so far for an old girlfriend? Laurie, right?"

"Laura." I didn't like talking about her, even with Wilbur. But he deserved an honest answer, considering how he was sticking his own neck out for me. "She was my sweetheart in college. She wanted to get married after the Old Man died, but I turned her down."

"I got hitched when I was eighteen," said Wilbur. "Few months later, got sent over to Korea. That was pretty much the end of that."

I never knew Wilbur had been married. "Well, finishing college is hardly the same as going overseas to war, but after my grandfather died, I just didn't want to be with anybody."

"So you broke up?"

"Not exactly. We tried to keep it going for a while, but things weren't the same."

"You getcha a new gal?"

"Nothing serious."

"She got a new fella?"

"She met Tom Tucker this summer . . ."

"He's the pusher you robbed," said Wilbur. "I can see where this is goin'."

"Yeah, he's got her all fucked up on coke."

" 'Course, it takes two to tango—"

"That's true, Wilbur, but when someone gets that monkey on their back, they'll do 'bout anything." Thinking about it pissed me off. "The last month, or so, she's been his slave. Tucker doesn't give a shit about her. She's just a goddamned toy to him. I don't want to talk about it anymore," I said with clenched teeth, turning away.

"So, you're just gonna come sashayin' back, make everything right?"

I ignored the sarcasm in Wilbur's tone. "Something like that."

"What we got here," Wilbur said to no one in particular, "is a real crusader."

We came to the head of a meadow, near the turnoff leading up a steep hill to my cabin. Wilbur stopped the Bronco. "You best bail out now," he said. "Cut across the woods to your road—just in case somebody's watchin'."

I hopped out and fetched my pack from the back. "Appreciate the ride, Wilbur."

"Stay high up on that mountain," said Wilbur, through his open window. "Come around in a few days, we'll talk about that ride to Craig—"

"Wilbur, I believe somebody's heading our way," I interrupted. Stepping away from the rumbling engine of the Bronco, I cocked my ear to the west. "Yes sir, I hear a vehicle."

"Don't worry 'bout me, College Boy." Wilbur shook my hand and sped down the trail.

I watched him disappear around a bend in the road, then hustled up the aspen-covered hillside. Hiding behind a fat tree trunk, I watched a blue Chevy, the same truck, enter the meadow. Through my binoculars, I confirmed Stan was the driver. I had to stay put. The wooded hillside wasn't thick enough to conceal me if I moved.

The truck crept past my position. A hundred yards down the trail, it left the main road and turned up the steep spur leading to my cabin. Wilbur was in the clear, but now Stan was my problem. Fair enough.

I glanced at my watch. Another hour before darkness. I debated whether to stay put or head toward the cabin and keep tabs on what Stan was up to. Low-hanging clouds spit snow. I put on my storm gear and sat against a tree, wondering how the hell I was going to stay out of trouble up here for much longer. Waiting until Stan drove back down the mountain might have been the most cautious play, but the weather was turning to shit. I wanted to get into the dry.

After Stan's vehicle climbed up the hillside, I walked to the spur heading to my cabin. I had to cross the road to reach the cabin, so I'd do that now, hoping the snow covered my tracks before Stan headed back down.

Reaching the rutted trail at the base of the steep hill, I hopped over a couple of rocks, minimizing my sign. I decided to make a big loop to the cabin, staying far from the road. Stan would have to walk a ways to cut my trail. I was betting against that. Walking in a wide semicircle, I heard Stan's truck grinding up the road. With fresh snow on top of the muddy road, the deeply rutted trail had to be slick as greased owl shit. Traveling would be slow. It would be near dark by the time he reached the end of the road.

Chapter Twelve

Shortly before I reached my cabin, Stan stopped somewhere near the end of the road. The snow had let up around sunset. Another thirty minutes of light. Maybe he was just scouting before opening day of deer and elk season, but I wouldn't bet on it. I wasn't taking any chances.

Once inside, I lit the cabin with a single candle. Until I heard Stan coming off the mountain, I wasn't going to light my stove. I cracked open the window facing south, to make sure the rumble of any vehicles carried inside. And I didn't play the radio. If he was going to find my place, he'd have to literally stumble into it. He wasn't going to see camp lights or smell wood smoke.

A little later, while I was eating a cold supper of saltines and Vienna sausages canned in congealed grease, a rifle cracked near the end of the road. I stepped outside, waiting for another round to help pinpoint the location of the shooting. Had Stan jumped the season opener? Did he pot a grouse or a cottontail on the road? When no second shot came, I walked back inside.

Without a fire in the stove, the cabin grew cold. I read by candlelight, a blanket draped over my shoulders.

A couple of hours after dark, I extinguished the little candle lantern and crawled into my sleeping bag. It had been a long day, hiking to Wilbur's, getting chased by Stan. I was worn out, but couldn't sleep a lick. I kept waiting for the growl of that blue Chevy to let me know Stan was crawling off the mountain. Every creak of the cabin, each phantom sound drifting from the woods through my opened window, I imagined to be Stan stalking me.

Sometime before sunrise, when gray against the cabin windows betrayed false dawn, I rose and dressed. Unsure if I'd ever drifted off to sleep, I didn't remember hearing a rig.

I slipped on my pack and left the cabin. I needed to know what the hell Stan was up to. After making a wide loop, I reached the road and headed uphill. The only sign I found was the partially covered tracks from the evening before.

Stan had never come down.

He was still up there.

I walked swiftly through Eagle Grove and beyond the point where I'd flattened Stan and Larry's tire a few days earlier. At every bend in the road, I slowed and raised my binoculars, wondering when the day-old tire tracks would lead to a blue Chevy truck. If I heard a vehicle, I planned to slip off the road to the left, opposite my place. Then, I'd disappear into the timber, leading anyone foolish enough to follow me on a merry chase.

At the very end of the road, where it died abruptly below a rocky outcropping, I spied Stan's truck. Stalking the Chevy like it was a wounded bear, I dodged from tree to tree, watching for any sign of movement. Closing to twenty paces, I was unable to peer into the cab through thick ice on the windows. Was he sleeping inside? I lowered my binoculars and crept to the truck.

Stan wasn't inside.

Walking past the Chevy, I found his tracks, neatly etched in the snow. One set of footprints, leading into spruce and pine. The hair stood up on the back of my neck. Something wasn't right.

Again, I followed. More cautious now that I was tracking a man on foot rather than a truck, I alternately took a step, then paused to look ahead. The rising sun felt warm against my back. A blue sky promised good tracking conditions, with no more snow to hinder my hunt. The pungent scent of evergreens drifted on the morning air.

Slowly, I unraveled Stan's trail. He walked quickly, judging from the length of his steps, through bare aspen. Ahead, where his footprints veered into dark spruce, another set of tracks intersected Stan's. When I reached the junction of signs, I gasped and felt cold sweat run down my back. Lion tracks, as large as a dessert plate, covered Stan's footprints. This cat had lost a toe.

The tracks tell their tale.

I patted my hip for the reassuring bulge of the Old Man's revolver under my coat. Into the spruce I crept, following the cat that had followed the man.

The lion creeps, too, for a few yards, then pauses, gathers its feet, and leaps.

A shiny object on the trail gleamed in the morning sun. A spent cartridge. Seven-millimeter Remington Magnum.

Unscathed, the big tom flies across the snow, four of Stan's steps for each of the cat's. Stan runs, too, but not fast enough.

Ahead of a little rise, a bloody depression in the snow marked their first embrace.

Stan rises, abandoning his rifle, stumbling on past the crest of the path, crawling now, desperate to escape.

I pulled my pistol, walked on.

Over the ridge and behind a tree, Stan lay on a sheet of red ice. Frozen terror etched across his face, his throat shredded, his limbs sprawled grotesquely. And blood sprayed everywhere. Didn't know a man had so much of the stuff.

Cat tracks, lined in crimson, led away at a run. I viewed the tracks through my binoculars, following them until they disappeared into a patch of buckbrush, a hundred yards away.

Confident the tom had fled, I fell to my knees, as if I'd just finished a long race. I retched what little remained in my stomach. Holstering my pistol, I rubbed snow in my face and fought to keep my wits. Since starting my run, I'd seen enough blood and death to last a lifetime.

My head spun . . . and I panicked. Running back to the road, brush lashed my face. Soon, I emerged from the timber, nearly colliding with Stan's truck. Making no effort to conceal my tracks, I ran down the jeep road until I was even with my cabin, then I left the road and made a beeline for home. Bursting inside, I drank a full canteen of water and collapsed on my bunk.

I caught my breath and wits at the same time. I had to get out of there. Outside, I scraped snow from my cache, removing the cash and cocaine, both bone dry, just like the survivalist at the gun show had promised. I stuffed little more than I had arrived with into my rucksack and locked the cabin behind me.

Heading west, I ran to reach Wilbur's place before nightfall.

Chapter Thirteen

"Couldn't have happened to a nicer guy," said Wilbur. "I'm just sorry you had to see it."

As dark as things seemed, I laughed involuntarily at my host's morbid sense of humor. "I feel responsible, again," I argued, "just like when those deputies got shot up—"

"Bullshit." Wilbur rose from his rocker and topped off my tea with a slug of Jack Daniel's. "Totally different. You don't know why the hell that idiot was up there. Maybe scoutin' before the opener tomorrow, maybe lookin' for you."

"But if he was looking for me—"

"Then he got just what was comin' to him, playing the half-assed cop."

I sipped my tea, my mouth and neck tightening in protest of the first alcohol I'd drunk in weeks. On an empty stomach, and dehydrated to boot, the laced tea went straight to my head. I noticed Wilbur studying me.

"Go ahead, College Boy, you need to limber up a little. I'll mash us up some taters from my garden to go along with that slow elk I got roastin' in the oven."

"Damn, that sounds good."

"You bunk on the couch," said Wilbur. "Come mornin', though, we got to get your ass outta here."

"You know, I'm packin' some bad stuff."

"You ain't no dope dealer."

"Yeah, but if we get caught," I slurred. "Get you in a fix."

Wilbur poured another slug of Jack in my cup, which now held more booze than tea. "Like I told ya before, I learned how to dodge folks a long time ago, givin' them slopes the slip in Korea."

"Just get me to the edge of town, I'll take it from there."

"Be a lot of folks about tomorrow mornin'," said Wilbur.

Tomorrow was Saturday, opening day. "Used to be like Christmas, Wilbur. The Old Man taking me out of school to hunt." The booze felt warm and good going down. Made me feel like talking. "Maybe we can go, next season, after I get things squared away."

"You bet, College."

Then the liquor turned on me. I remembered my final hunt with the Old Man. That seemed like a long time ago. In these very mountains.

"You remember season before last, Wilbur?"

"Sure I do," said Wilbur. "Your grandpa's last trip up here."

"I wanted to help get him that cow elk so goddamned bad . . ."

"I know, but he just didn't have it in him no more, Boy." Wilbur sipped his liquor neat, from a G.I. coffee cup. "He still had a time, just comin' along."

I imitated the Old Man's high, creaky voice, "I'll just tend the camp, keep the bears off the meat pole."

We both laughed.

The Old Man passed away when I was in school. Took two days to get the word to me. I hitched a ride home. And who was there waiting for me, wanting to console me, help me get through losing my last living relative?

Laura.

Wilbur brought me back to the here and now. "Traffic's really gonna pick up around here when somebody finds Stan up there." He thumbed toward the top of the peak. "Gonna be a hell of a mess, all the hunters mixing up with the law snoopin' around."

"You think we should get word to the sheriff now about Stan?"

"Hell, no," said Wilbur. "How much deader is he gonna get

between today and tomorrow?" Wilbur finished the last of his drink, his face tightening like he'd bitten into a lemon. "You were right to come down here. After this, you'd have to hole up in a badger den to keep from gettin' pinched."

"What about Stan's wife, though?"

"This is the best thing that ever happened to her, College." Wilbur rose and staggered to the kitchen. Over his shoulder, he said, "She'll get Stan's share of the Ben Franklin, and now, maybe, her boy can come back home." Wilbur washed spuds in the sink and laughed. "Somebody oughta give that damned cat a medal."

"Think he'll attack anybody else?"

"Nah, that ol' tom's in for shinin' times the next few weeks, what with all the wounded game and gut piles gonna get strewn around here."

"You don't think he'll keep killin' men?" Now I was wondering if we shouldn't hunt up that murdering lion.

"What I think he is, College Boy, is an old son of a bitch that's having a hard time huntin' for himself." Wilbur found a knife and started cutting up potatoes with the skin still on, "Rocky Mountain Style" he always called it. He dumped the spuds into a two-quart pot half full of water and placed it on the stove. "Taters'll be ready just ahead of that roast."

I sipped my drink and nodded toward the radio on the windowsill. "Heard any more about the shoot-out?" It was one of those questions you didn't want to ask, but sometimes a lingering suspicion was more unsettling than the truth.

"Oh, damn, I done forgot to tell you," said Wilbur. "They caught that gal, the one you said got shot up." Wilbur grimaced. "Found her stayin' at a ranch a little north of Craig. Lost a lot of blood, don't know if she'll make it."

"Goddamnit," I muttered. I needed her to pull through, to tell the law I wasn't part of the killing, just passing by the wrong place at the wrong time. "What about her boyfriend?"

"They're still lookin' for him," said Wilbur. "As much as they've been snoopin' around here for you, just imagine how hard the law's hunting for that boy."

"What's it gonna be like, trying to get to Craig tomorrow?"

Wilbur pulled a BLM map from a bookshelf and spread it on the kitchen table. He rubbed his chin and considered the expanse of country between the peak and Craig. "We'll leave well before first light, take the county road west to Highway Thirteen."

"Just a couple of guys going hunting."

"Yep, 'cept a couple of hunters wouldn't be driving into Craig at dawn on opening day, College."

"So?"

"So, a few miles north of town, we'll get off the highway, take this ranch road around to the east side of Craig. The game warden usually sets up a check station, here." Wilbur tapped the map. "We don't want to go through that."

I raised an eyebrow. A silent question.

"Lot of times the highway patrol helps out with them check stations."

"I see."

"At any rate, I think I can get you to town," said Wilbur. "But then what?"

"Figured I'd take a Greyhound, you know, '*Leave the driving to us.*'"

"That don't sound like such a good idea," said Wilbur. "You really want to risk stoppin' in every Podunk town between here and Aspen?" He shook his head and looked at a road map of Colorado tacked on the wall. "You got Meeker, Rifle, Silt, New Castle, Glenwood Springs—"

"I'm hoping the farther away I get from Craig, the less they'll be looking for me."

"Jesus Christ, College, think. Two cops got shot. This ain't local."

Because Wilbur didn't sound confident, my confidence was shaken. Did he think I could get my ass out of a sling or not?

Getting to Aspen was only half the problem, too. Originally, I planned to return after the ski season was in full bloom, with every one of the resort town's twenty thousand beds spoken for. In early fall, though, there'd only be a few thousand year-round locals to hide amongst. Hell, even the leaf turkeys would be gone by then. I tried to focus on one problem at a time, but the liquor made concentration fuzzy.

"Well, Wilbur, like you said yourself, I can't stick around here anymore, and I damned sure don't want to hitch any more rides."

Wilbur nodded toward the stove, topped off my drink, and poured the last of the Jack Daniel's into his cup. "Let's sit while them spuds are cookin'." He gave me a toothy grin. "I got an idea I'm workin' on, 'bout how to get you back to Aspen. Lemme sleep on it."

Chapter Fourteen

The distant rumbling of four-wheel-drive vehicles woke me a few minutes ahead of Wilbur's alarm clock. Thick-headed and cotton-mouthed from too much Jack Daniel's, I was grateful, at least, for Wilbur's fine supper that took a little of the edge off my hangover. Using my flashlight, I dressed, pulling on long underwear before I slipped into wool pants and shirt. I pulled my boots on and lit one of the gas lanterns.

Wilbur stirred in the corner of the cabin. "I'll drag my ass out of this bed when I smell coffee brewin'," he said, his voice thin and scratchy.

"Fair enough," I said. "You hear those rigs?"

"Sure, be a lot more, 'tween here and Craig."

I stuffed split wood into the stove, then stepped outside. The frost-covered ground glimmered in weak starlight. Not a cloud in the sky, I noticed with satisfaction. A good day for traveling. The porch thermometer read well below freezing and a tinge of violet colored the eastern horizon. I walked into the timber next to the cabin and pissed on frozen grass. In the darkness of the spruce grove, I listened to vehicles, full of anxious hunters, climb the mountain. Stepping out of the timber, I looked south where the county road wound up from the valley floor. The distant headlights of more cars looked small, pairs of white eyes moving imperceptibly. Then I saw another vehicle bringing up the rear and instinctively reached for my binoculars—still in the cabin.

I hustled inside to fetch my binoculars. Wilbur had abandoned his coffee strike and was dressing in the warming cabin.

"You'd never make it as a waiter, College Boy." He finished tying his boots and ambled into the kitchen. "You want somethin' done right, you got to do it yourself."

I grunted and stepped back outside, ignoring something Wilbur said that sounded like a joke, judging by his tone. From the porch, I looked south, finding the little procession of vehicles nearing the base of the mountain. Now, they were led by a truck bearing red flashing emergency lights. I stuck my head inside the cabin.

"Wilbur, you ought to take a look at this."

He placed a coffeepot on the gas stove and walked to the doorway. "Whatcha got?"

Nodding south, I handed him my binoculars.

"Shit," Wilbur muttered, studying the county road through a gap in the trees.

"What do you think?"

"Looks like somebody already found our pal, Stan."

We stepped back in the cabin. How would this affect our ability to get off the mountain? My mind spun. How could someone have discovered Stan so soon? Must have stumbled into him the evening before.

"Well, let's just see how many pilgrims are coming, College," said Wilbur. "This could be a break for us." He pointed south. "Maybe we'll wait until they get past my place, then slip out of here, behind 'em."

I made myself a cup of tea and returned to the porch. The vehicles coming from the south were out of sight, having reached the timber at the base of the mountain. But now I heard a distant siren floating on a gentle westerly breeze. Should I gather my gear and slip into the brush behind the cabin? Wilbur came outside, still bleary-eyed, a mug of steaming coffee in his hand.

"Got your stuff packed?" he asked.

"Yes sir, ready when you are."

He pointed south. "Soon as that emergency vehicle passes my driveway, we'll get out of here."

"You figured out what route we're taking to town?" The keening of the siren grew increasingly loud.

"We'll take the west road to the highway, head south for a while—"

"Here they come." I pointed toward the end of Wilbur's driveway and raised my binoculars. I glimpsed a white Jeep Wagoneer with emergency lights and a Moffat County Sheriff emblem on the driver's door. "Sheriff just passed and two more trucks."

"Let's get goin'," said Wilbur.

We ducked back inside. I grabbed my pack while Wilbur turned off the gaslights and closed the stove flue. Looking the place over for anything I might have left behind, Wilbur handed me a fluorescent-orange vest and cap.

"Put 'em on, College Boy," he said with a wink. "We're goin' hunting."

Wilbur put on another set of hunter orange, and we stepped outside into growing light. A shot rang out from near the top of the peak, followed a split second later by the unmistakable plunk of a bullet striking flesh. "Somebody just filled his tag." Wilbur nodded wistfully toward the mountain. He locked the cabin, and we walked to his Bronco.

I scraped ice off the windshield and windows while Wilbur started the cold engine. Climbing in, I gestured behind the front seat. "Want me to ride back there?"

"Nope," said Wilbur. "Look suspicious as hell if we get pulled over, having you hidin' under a tarp." He adjusted his rearview mirror and looked my way. "We're drivin' out of here like we own the place."

Wilbur navigated the Bronco through the narrow gateway and

drove another hundred yards to the end of his driveway. Looking left and right, he eased onto the county road, driving slow along the rutted trail. "Anybody comes along, wants to gab, you let me do the talkin'."

Fine with me. I was scared as hell to be riding to Craig in broad daylight. Up to now, I'd done most of my running at night or in the back of a truck where I could bail if things went to shit. Now I was stuck inside the rig, my fate entirely out of my hands. I looked over my shoulder at my pack in the back. Could I still make a dash for the timber if we got pulled over? Soon we'd be out of the forest and into the sagebrush where there wouldn't be enough cover to hide a jackrabbit, much less a man.

A mile down the road, Wilbur snapped me to attention. "Somebody comin' up ahead."

Even in the Bronco, with its suspension stiffer than a log wagon, I was able to use my binoculars. "White pickup, looks like civilians. Two men in orange."

Closing to a hundred yards of the truck, Wilbur pulled off the road to allow the hunters to pass. The driver, a man with a heavy mustache and three-day beard rolled down his window and paused.

Wilbur followed suit, forcing a small grin. "Mornin'."

"You boys are headin' in the wrong direction."

"How so?"

"Hell of a roadblock up ahead." The man spit tobacco juice into a Styrofoam cup and nodded over his shoulder. "'Bout three miles east, right at the property gate, couple of deputies pulling everybody over, checking IDs, askin' a lot of questions—"

"Yeah, real pain in the ass," a younger man I took to be the driver's son, interrupted. "We should have been up here an hour ago," he complained bitterly.

Wilbur twisted his face into a look of surprise. "That so? What's goin' on?"

"Deputies didn't say much," said the driver, "but I overheard some fellas in front of us talking about a man getting killed up here yesterday."

"Well, good thing we're only going down the road a little ways," said Wilbur. "Thanks for the heads-up, though." He nodded and pulled ahead.

"Shit, now what?" I asked. "Think we ought to turn back, try to go another day?"

Wilbur looked into his rearview mirror, then at me. "For all we know, we'd just run into more law on the way back." He shook his head. "Nope, we just need to keep goin', get off this damned mountain."

"Yeah, but what about that roadblock?"

"Buck up, College, we're just another pair of hunters—"

"Heading in the wrong direction," I said, "with a pack of dope and cash."

"What's your idea?" asked Wilbur.

"Let's drive on, scout that roadblock before we commit ourselves. You know they'll be looking over people leaving the ranch a lot closer than hunters coming in."

"Sounds reasonable," said Wilbur.

The road switchbacked through sagebrush hills dotted with little groves of pine and aspen, soon leaving the snow-covered ground behind. Well above the eastern horizon, sun poured golden light on the frosty road, illuminating piles of fallen leaves. Above, a dazzling sky of blue made me wish we really were going hunting, not running. I stole a furtive glance at Wilbur. He looked intense, white knuckles gripping the steering wheel, but alive, too, like he relished excitement above and beyond his routine, nonconformist life. I hoped he didn't end up getting more than he bargained for.

We passed four more vehicles of disgruntled hunters before we reached the base of a low-lying ridge overlooking the ranch boundary. "Let's pull over, have a look at that roadblock," I said.

Taking care not to skyline ourselves, we crept to the top of the sagebrush-covered hill. The road dropped from the rim into an open basin, running a quarter of a mile to a double gate in the fence line. Sure enough, two deputies manned the opening, attending to several vehicles backed up behind a cattle guard. Through my binoculars, I watched the deputies talk with two men in a green Dodge Power Wagon. They checked IDs and handed the driver a flyer, before letting them pass.

"Wilbur, I'm going to bail out here."

"The hell you say."

"I'll loop around the right, meet you back on the road a few hundred yards past that roadblock." I backed off the ridgeline, Wilbur bringing up the rear.

"Where you goin' now?" he asked.

Stripping off my hunter orange, I pointed to the Bronco. "Need to fetch my pack."

"Be easier for you to slip around 'em without it," said Wilbur.

"I'm not letting you drive through that roadblock," I said, thumbing over my shoulder, "with that shit in your car." I studied the hillside that dropped down to the gate in the road. Not a lot of cover, just sagebrush and a few stunted cedars. "I think I can get over that hill without anybody spotting me."

Reaching the Bronco, I slipped on my backpack and shook Wilbur's hand. "Just in case things go to shit, you don't know me."

Wilbur grinned. "You'd have been a good hand in Korea."

"See you on the other side." I turned, ambling toward a thin stringer of orphaned aspen, the last good cover on the hillside.

Chapter Fifteen

I slipped up into the trees, pausing now and then to watch Wilbur drive his Bronco down to the roadblock. By the time he reached the edge of the cattle guard where the deputies waited, I had climbed to the end of the grove. I hid behind the last tree, watching his performance through my binoculars.

A lawman motioned for Wilbur to pull off the road, clearing the way for three trucks to enter the ranch. The deputies inspected the incoming vehicles, checking IDs, and providing some sort of flyer. Sitting behind the wheel, Wilbur poured coffee from his thermos and watched the procession of vehicles enter the ranch.

I glanced uphill, beyond the aspen where I stood. From here on, I'd have to crawl on all fours to stay out of sight. I tied one end of a stout cord to the handle of my pack. To keep a low profile on the sparse hillside, I'd drag my backpack rather than wear it. While I still had the luxury of standing, I surveyed my path across the hillside. The boundary fence, marking the halfway point of my sneak, was about three hundred yards away. I'd crawl at a slight uphill angle until I reached it, slip under the barbed wire, and descend the hillside to the road.

All a hell of a lot easier said than done.

After a few minutes, the deputies had processed the incoming vehicles and turned their attention to Wilbur. I left the security of the trees and dropped to my hands and knees. Prickly pear cactus dotted the open hillside, forcing me to carefully plan my every movement. If I hugged the ground, though, I was out of the deputies' line of sight. I picked out one of the few clumps of sagebrush ahead as my intermediate destination.

A few minutes later, I reached the cover and rose to my butt to spy on Wilbur, two hundred yards below. He was out of the vehicle looking up the hill, while both lawmen searched his Bronco. It was mid-morning now. No other vehicles waited. By this time, I figured most folks were out hunting, not driving to their spot. Through my binoculars, I could swear he was nodding for me to move. I didn't relish the idea of belly crawling for several hundred yards so I checked the deputies once more and gathered my pack.

Bent over double, I rose to my feet, running across the hillside. Heading to the fence, it was easy to watch the lawmen's search of the Bronco. Wilbur must have seen me, because he walked around to the rear of his rig, interposing himself between the deputies and the hillside.

Nearing the fence, the two lawmen finished their search and turned their attention to Wilbur. I chuckled as he ambled in an innocent little loop, causing both deputies to turn their backs to me. Taking advantage of Wilbur's subterfuge, I sprinted for the property boundary, a hundred yards ahead.

Reaching the fence, I slid behind sagebrush and looked directly below me. The deputies returned Wilbur's driver's license to him and gave him a flyer. They motioned for him to head east. For the rest of the sneak, I was on my own.

I lay on my back and wiggled under the bottom strand of barbed wire, pulling my pack through behind me with my drag cord. Back to belly crawling, I made slow but steady progress, slithering from one patch of sagebrush to the next. The deputies took their morning coffee break, sitting together in one of the two white Wagoneers parked next to the gate facing away from me to the east. I considered making a run for the edge of the hillside, another hundred yards away, but decided against it. This close to avoiding detection, I didn't want to take any chances.

Fifteen minutes later, I crawled over the ridgeline and spotted Wilbur, parked off the road, a hundred yards below. I rose and flew downhill on wobbly legs. Halfway to the Bronco, a silver pickup with a pair of orange-clad hunters came around the bend, heading toward the ranch. I slowed to a walk until they passed Wilbur, then hustled the last leg to the valley floor.

Opening the passenger door, I threw my pack behind the seat and barely climbed in before Wilbur spun gravel, getting the hell out of there.

"You did a good job gettin' across that hillside, College Boy," he said, looking ahead as he sped down the gravel road, "but those guys in that truck saw you running down to the road."

Fighting to catch my breath and will my pulse below redline, I gasped, "Think they'll say anything to those deputies?"

"Yep," said Wilbur flatly. "You're not wearing orange or carrying a rifle, so they ain't gonna think you're a hunter. And you was moving like a scalded monkey."

"Shit, I thought we had it made, and then that damned truck showed up out of nowhere."

Wilbur drove faster than I would have, putting distance between us and the roadblock. "I'm lookin' for one of those ATV trails I told you about before," he said. "Ain't no way we're getting to Craig on the highway."

I looked over my shoulder, praying not to see a pursuing Wagoneer with flashing red lights.

"Probably be a few more minutes before they put two and two together, but they're comin'." Wilbur looked in the rearview mirror, then back to the winding county road. He pulled a folded piece of paper from his sun visor and handed it to me. "Pretty good likeness."

I took the flyer like it might bite me. Two pictures adorned the handout. One looked to be a high school graduation photograph of a young man named Jesse O'Dell, the other an artist's conception of a guy who looked a lot like me.

"Deputies told me that O'Dell was the shooter," said Wilbur. "They must have got that info from his gal before she died—"

"That girl didn't make it? Shit, I didn't think—"

"The other guy," said Wilbur, "they ain't sure about, but they'd still like to get their hands on him. They think he's runnin' round the peak somewhere."

I took my eyes off the poster for a moment. "What about Stan, they know 'bout him?"

"Ya, you were right, a hunter scoutin' before opening day found him last night." Wilbur looked in the rearview mirror again. "Good thing you got the hell out of there, one of the deputies said they got a helicopter coming in today."

"Sweet Jesus." For the first time since I'd gotten myself into this mess, I no longer had the luxury of thinking two or three steps ahead. The same thought kept circling round and round like a broken record: how were we going to escape from the law sure to be coming any minute? Not much cover on the south side of the road, but if I could reach the first hillside I might find someplace I could hide until dark. Hell, I could always walk to Craig.

"Wilbur, let me out of here," I barked. "No sense in both of us getting caught. You've done enough already."

"Easy, College, we're just about there," said Wilbur. He glanced into an empty rearview mirror and flashed me a slight grin. "I got an idea."

Another hundred yards east, Wilbur slowed, downshifting into first gear. Then we stopped on the shoulder of the road. "Get out and lock the hubs, College."

While I engaged the front axle into four-wheel drive, Wilbur bailed out of the Bronco and ran to the fence paralleling the north side of the road. He opened a gate I had never noticed before and hustled back.

"Close that gate after I get through," he hollered.

This was no time to ask questions, but I thought we were escaping on the wrong side of the county road. How were we getting any closer to Craig by running north?

Wilbur drove through the narrow gap in the fence and waited while I struggled to hook the tight loop of wire over the fence pole. I got a lot stronger when I heard a distant siren coming from up the road and finally managed to close the gate. Wilbur drove onto the prairie slowly, careful not to leave any more signs than necessary. We wove through sagebrush for a hundred yards, slipping over a low-lying ridge. Out of sight from the road, Wilbur shut down the Bronco.

We both got out and crept back to the crest of the hill as the siren neared, blaring loudly across the sagebrush flat. A few minutes later, one of the white Wagoneers came blazing past the fence gate.

"Stupid bastard," said Wilbur. "He's got no idea we left the county road."

"Yeah, we dodged him—for now," I said. "But sooner or later he's going to realize we're not in front of him."

"By then, we'll be a long way from here."

"Wilbur, how do we reach Craig without getting back on that county road?"

"New plan, College," said Wilbur as he headed back to the Bronco. "We ain't going to Craig."

Chapter Sixteen

For a couple of miles we drove north, down in a dry streambed. The west flank of Baker's Peak loomed to our right. That's where I figured we were headed, but I didn't want to bother Wilbur. He had his hands full, keeping us from getting stuck in the sandy arroyo. When the creek bottom opened up into a grassy pasture, Wilbur picked up speed until we came to a fence line. Then he really crossed me up, turning left, away from the peak and straight toward the state highway.

"Jesus Christ, Wilbur, where the hell are we going?"

"Well, College Boy, I been thinkin' things through——"

"And?"

"We can't get to Craig, not now that they'll be lookin' for my Bronco."

"That's true——"

"And I don't think we could make it back to the peak, even if we wanted to."

"So?"

"So, I'm going to take you to L. Q. Preston's place." Wilbur pointed ahead. "Just a few miles west. You've driven by it a hundred times. He's got that spread right off the school trust land next to Highway Thirteen."

"You know him?" I asked. "He's a friend of yours?"

"Hell, yes, we hunt coyotes together."

"You're going to ask him to put me up for a while?" I didn't want to get anybody else involved in this mess.

"Naw, he ain't gonna put you up, College Boy." Wilbur chuckled. "I'm gonna see if he'll take you to Aspen."

"Shit, you figure?" I couldn't imagine asking anyone to risk their neck, hauling me nearly two hundred miles to Aspen. I was still considering setting off for Craig by foot. I could make the fifty-mile walk in two or three days. Take my chances from there. I hadn't shaved in a couple of weeks. Had a pretty good beard started. Maybe that would throw off anybody studying that damned wanted poster. I'd just slip on a Greyhound and pray for the best.

"College Boy, you willing to part with some of that cash to get out of here in one piece?" Wilbur took his eyes off the trail running along the fence line and looked my way. "I think L.Q. will do it, if the money's right."

"Hell, yes, I'll pay." I'd been guarding the stolen cash pretty carefully, but it wasn't going to do me—or Laura—any good if I got pinched.

"What'd be a fair bargain, Wilbur?" I asked. "Think he'd take me for a couple of thousand?"

"That'd probably get it done, but I wouldn't dicker—or tell him too much 'bout what you're haulin'," said Wilbur. "Let's just talk it over with him, I'll help you fellas work somethin' out." Wilbur added, "Oh, I nearly forgot, L.Q.'s got him a wife, Darlene. We don't want her in on this."

"How's that?" I asked.

"L.Q. inherited this ranch from his daddy, along with a pile of bills. He married Darlene 'bout ten years ago. Adopted her boy, too."

"Sounds like a good man," I said.

"Yeah, but the thing is, right after they got hitched, Darlene started managin' the books, put L.Q. on a budget, got the ranch back in the black."

"What's wrong with that?"

"Nothin', 'cept L.Q. has to hide his fun money from her or it's gone faster than you can say 'savings account.' Darlene don't abide L.Q.'s hobbies or fun, for that matter."

"What sort of hobbies does he have?" I asked.

"You'll see." Wilbur pointed ahead as we reached the top of a grassy swale. "There's his place, on the next ridge."

Like Wilbur said, I'd driven by the ranch every time I took the west road to the peak. But I'd never taken the time to study the place. Out in the middle of a flat basin of sagebrush, a double-wide trailer sat in the shade of the only trees for miles in any direction. A World War Two-vintage Quonset hut stood behind the little grove of cottonwoods. Otherwise, the ranch headquarters had the trappings of all the other spreads dotting the prairie in Moffat County, derelict vehicles in varying stages of decay, obsolete farming implements, a pipe corral and handling chute, and a half dozen dogs of mixed descent, resting and scratching themselves.

When we came even with the cottonwoods, Wilbur crept over a cattle guard in a gap of the fence and drove past the trailer without stopping. A short, stocky woman I took for Darlene stood at the doorway, hands resting on her hips. She gave us a barely perceptible smile, then stepped back in the double-wide.

"Wilbur, how do you get along with Darlene?"

"She tolerates me, that's 'bout it. Thinks I'm a bad influence."

We drove through the cottonwoods, neatly planted decades ago into parallel rows. The Quonset hut stood at the end of the trees, a hundred yards from the trailer. Nearing the building, a tall man with a thin, craggy face and long blond hair flowing from the back of his Massey Ferguson baseball cap stepped out of a crack in the two huge sliding doors. I guessed his age at around thirty-five or forty. He wore grease-stained coveralls and held a wrench in his hand. Moments later, a short, chubby kid, maybe fourteen or fifteen, followed.

Wilbur grinned and stood on his brakes, raising dust as we slid to a stop. The boy laughed and waved. We got out of the Bronco, Wilbur shouting, "How come you boys ain't out huntin'?" Before they could answer, he followed with, "L.Q., Billy, this here's my ol' huntin' buddy's grandson. Call him College Boy."

I shook L.Q.'s hand. He had a firm grip and a little grin that might have been a smirk. His eyes sat close and were a little crossed. He was an inch or two taller than me and thin as a scarecrow.

"This here's my boy, Billy," L.Q. said in a high, western drawl.

I nodded at the lad as Wilbur broke the ice. "Ol' College Boy's got himself a problem," he said. "Needs to get to Aspen. Yesterday."

L.Q. squinted. "That so?" He studied me, like he was trying to place my face. "We met before?"

"I don't think so," I said. "I got a place up on the peak, but I've never had occasion to come by here."

"You sure look familiar."

"At any rate, I was thinkin' maybe College Boy could hire you and the Champ," said Wilbur.

I wondered who the hell the "Champ" was.

"Could be—if the money's right," said L.Q. He gave me that ironic grin again. Hell, he'd already figured everything out.

"I guess you're just too busy to take him yourself," L.Q. said to Wilbur. "'Course you'd lose all kinds of time, going through all those check stations and roadblocks."

Before Wilbur could answer, L.Q. nodded Billy's way. "Buddy, how's 'bout grabbing three beers outta the shop fridge and a pop for yourself."

L.Q. halted the boy before he slipped in the Quonset hut. "Oh, and turn off that police scanner, too."

"Wilbur, we ought to get your Bronco out of the sun, don't you think?" L.Q. looked my way. "Pard, help me open up the Quonset."

L.Q. and I leaned into one of the doors, sliding it the full length of its track. Light poured into the enormous shed, shaped like a half-pipe. Inside, a fire-engine red Ford F-350 stood next to a pristine Willys CJ-2. Another rig, an Oldsmobile 442 without an engine, waited for attention. I was starting to see what Wilbur meant about L.Q.'s hobbies.

Wilbur parked on the side of L.Q.'s fleet. "Not a bad idea, gettin' this rig outta sight," he said to L.Q. No bullshit between two old friends.

Billy appeared from the recesses of the hut, his hands full of drinks. L.Q. took the longneck Budweisers from him and motioned toward a little cubicle built into the left front corner of the Quonset. "Step into my office, boys."

L.Q. took a seat behind his desk, covered with stacks of gun and automobile magazines, while Wilbur and I sat on a couple of folding metal chairs, sipping the cold beers. Billy, still silent, leaned against the wall, chugging his Mountain Dew. L.Q. asked, "So you want me to haul ya to Aspen?"

"I'd like to hire you——"

"Would you settle for Basalt?"

"Sure, I'm really headed to Woody Creek, anyway." Basalt was only fifteen miles north of the trailer park where I lived. Still, I wondered why he was reluctant to travel all the way to Aspen.

"See, they're kind of a pain in the ass at Aspen Airport," said L.Q. He winked at Wilbur. "Basalt's more do-it-yourself friendly."

Confused, I asked, "Why do we need to go to an airport?"

"'Cause we're flyin', pard," snorted L.Q. "I can land on a road, need be, but I'd rather not, 'specially up in the mountains."

"Flying?" I asked

L.Q. raised his eyebrows and looked at Wilbur. "Didn't you say he wanted to hire me and the Champ?"

Wilbur laughed, slapping his thigh. "Gotcha, College Boy."

Chapter Seventeen

My face reddened. The joke was on me. "What the hell is a Champ?" I asked.

"Well, I'll show ya," said L.Q., rising from his chair. "Follow me."

Leaving the makeshift office, we walked to the rear of the Quonset. "Billy, turn on the back lights," hollered L.Q.

A tiny single-engine airplane rested in the recesses of the hut. It had high wings hanging over a narrow cockpit and tail-dragger landing gear. The plane's fabric skin was painted plain white, cut by a red racing stripe on each side of the fuselage interrupted by *LQ-1* in black lettering behind the rear windows. I stooped under one of the wings and peered into the cockpit. Seating was tandem, with the pilot's chair ahead of the passenger's.

"She's a beaut, ain't she?" beamed L.Q. "Nineteen forty-six Aeronca Champ."

"Shit, Wilbur," I said, through clenched teeth. "You didn't say anything about flying."

"I didn't say anything 'cause I thought you might back out," said Wilbur. "But this is perfect and, besides, L.Q.'s a hell of a pilot."

Suddenly, another red flag popped up in my spinning mind. "L.Q., what'd you mean before," I asked, "about Basalt being more 'do-it-yourself friendly'?"

"Pard, I don't have a pilot's license."

"What? You let it expire?" I asked.

"Nah," said L.Q., with a nonchalant wave of his hand. "Never had one. You might say I'm self-taught."

I gasped and almost choked on a swallow of beer.

"College Boy, you should have seen ol' L.Q. learning how to fly," said Wilbur. Fighting laughter, Wilbur pointed toward the county road. "He'd taxi back and forth out there, day after day, until he finally got the nerve to pull the stick back."

"Jesus, L.Q.," I said. "You never took any lessons?"

"Oh, well, to be honest, I did get some pointers from the guy I traded with to get the Champ—"

"Swapped an old truck and two horses for it," Wilbur snickered.

I stared back at the little plane in disbelief. Was this really safer than driving or hitching a ride to Aspen? I scratched my head, squinting at the Champ. There'd be no check stations or road-blocks, though.

"Whatcha got for luggage?" L.Q. eyed me suspiciously. "How much you weigh?"

"Just have my pack. I can get it down to maybe forty pounds. Dressed, I probably weigh one seventy."

"We'll be a little heavy," said L.Q. "Might have to stop once for fuel."

I winced.

"Don't worry 'bout that, though," he said. "She runs on regular car gas. We'll just put her down on a county road, taxi to a station."

"L.Q., what'd be fair recompense for a round trip to Basalt?" asked Wilbur.

"My momma didn't raise any fools," said L.Q., glancing my way. "I'll take a guess and say you need this ride pretty bad."

"Two thousand get it done?" I asked.

"That's a little more than I was gonna hold out for," said L.Q., "but I'll take the extra."

"How about a thousand up front and the balance when we get there?" I asked.

"Done. But I could really use the up-front money right now."

"No problem." While L.Q. and Wilbur gabbed about the Champ, with Billy silently listening, I slipped to the back of the Bronco. Making sure no one watched, I dug into my rucksack and cut open the tightly wrapped package that held the cash. I pulled out one bundle of bills and returned the container to the bottom of my pack. Ambling to the back of the Quonset, I handed the money to L.Q., stopping his chatter in mid-sentence.

"Well, look at that," he said. "Do I need to count it?"

"Can if you like."

"Don't worry," said Wilbur. "College Boy's a straight shooter."

"Billy, come here," barked L. Q. He counted five hundred dollars from the bundle and took it from the rubber band. "I want you to get on your trail bike and take this over to Mr. Hiner's place. Tell him it's for the COD I'm expecting from JC Whitney."

Without saying a word, Billy stuffed the wad of bills in the front pocket of his jeans and turned to leave the Quonset.

"Billy, come back here, son." L.Q. pulled a twenty from the remaining stack of bills and handed it to the kid. "That's your cut, now get going." L.Q. winked at Wilbur. "Hush money."

"Wilbur tell you anything about my wife, Darlene?" asked L.Q., his beady eyes aimed my way.

I didn't know what to say. Didn't want to betray a confidence, get my old pal in trouble.

Wilbur bailed me out. "I told him she was careful 'bout money."

"Careful?" scoffed L.Q. "She's tighter than wallpaper."

"Got you outta debt," Wilbur chided.

"Can't argue about that, but here's how we're gonna handle this," L.Q. said, returning his attention to me. "Too late to leave today." He pointed toward the Champ. "She doesn't have lights, and I don't know how to fly by instruments, so we'll leave tomor-row mornin'.'"

"Sounds good," I lied. It sounded damned risky. A cross-eyed, unlicensed pilot in a plane so small that two skinny passengers and forty pounds of rucksack might overload it. If I weren't so desper-ate with the law closing in, I would have run from the Quonset hut and never looked back.

"You're hiring me for a full day of coyote hunting. Got that?"

"Okay."

L.Q. counted another three hundred dollars from the dwin-dling bundle of bills and handed it to me. "It's real important that you pay me this tonight at supper—in front of Darlene."

"No problem," I said, putting the money in my wallet.

"She'll confiscate it, put it the bank, and I'll pocket the rest."

Wilbur laughed. "I guess what she don't know won't hurt her."

"Hell, yes," L.Q. whined, "I got an operation to manage here." He motioned toward his fleet of vehicles as well as an elaborate reloading bench I noticed for the first time along the back wall. "Soon as I get a couple of those projects done, I'll double my money selling them to some sucker."

Out of L.Q.'s sight, Wilbur winked at me and shook his head.

"Anyways, pard, plan on staying in here tonight. You too, Wilbur." L.Q. pointed back toward the office. "Got a couple of cots in there, and some blankets." He took a deep breath and ex-haled slowly. "I'm gonna go tell Darlene about our plans. You boys come up for supper in an hour or so." Before leaving the Quonset, L.Q. stopped and turned our way. "Remember, keep our story straight or there'll be hell to pay."

Chapter Eighteen

At dusk, Wilbur and I left the Quonset hut for L.Q.'s trailer. Walking through the cottonwoods, I glanced to the west as the sun slipped behind sagebrush hills overlooking the ranch. A red sky portended good flying weather in the morning, but I was still unsure of this plan.

"Wilbur, can L.Q. really handle this?"

"Hell, yes. You ought to see him chase coyotes with that little plane," said Wilbur. "That's a hell of a lot more dangerous than flying you at fifteen hundred feet to Basalt."

"How so?"

"Shit, I'm using a shotgun on them dogs. We're maybe a hundred feet off the deck before I shoot."

All the same, I was nervous as hell about getting in that plane. I'd never really liked heights, passed on a number of chances to climb Colorado peaks with my college buddies. Wilbur brought me back to the here and now.

"Listen, this supper's more dangerous than your trip tomorrow. Just follow my lead with Darlene and, remember, you're up here for a coyote hunt."

"What about a name?" I asked. "I don't want to tell her who I am."

"Hell, just tell her to call you 'College Boy,'" said Wilbur.

"That won't do. She's gonna want to know my name."

"Well, hell, make up an alias," said Wilbur. "But you might tell me what it's gonna be."

Nearing the trailer, I asked Wilbur, "Think Darlene ever read Hemingway?"

"Shit, I don't know—probably not."

"Okay, well, tonight my name's Nick Adams, then."

"You can call yourself 'Rumpelstiltskin' for all I care, College Boy. Let's go get something to eat."

Walking up the porch steps, Darlene met us before Wilbur knocked on the door. Maybe thirty-five, she was a short, busty red-head, dressed in jeans and a western shirt with metal buttons. Her hair was pulled back into a tight ponytail, revealing all the creases and wrinkles in her face that had seen much wind and sun. She looked the part of a brook-no-nonsense, hardworking rancher's wife.

"Wilbur," she said flatly, "haven't seen you in while."

I got the impression it hadn't been long enough.

"Who's your friend?" she said, sizing me up from head to toe.

Rather than taking a chance on Wilbur's memory and social graces, I extended my hand. "Evening, ma'am, I'm Nick Adams." I waved my thumb at Wilbur. "He calls me 'College Boy' so much, I think he forgets my real name sometimes."

Looking me in the eye, she shook my hand as hard as any man. "Nick, come on in." Almost as an afterthought, she added, "You too, Wilbur."

Inside, the double-wide was neat and organized. From what little I knew of Darlene, I'd have expected no less. A color TV sat against the end wall, sandwiched between two big mule deer shoulder mounts. A coffee table covered with hunting magazines and the local rural electric monthlies revealed the couple's reading pleasure. A beat-up couch, camouflaged by a crocheted afghan, and L.Q.'s throne, a Naugahyde recliner, completed the living room décor.

"L.Q.'s on the back porch, cooking on the grill," said Darlene. "Would you fellas like a beer?"

"Sure," we said in unison.

Darlene stepped into the open kitchen, midway between the living room and the bedrooms at the opposite end of the trailer. She grabbed two more of those longneck Budweisers from a refrigerator plastered with pictures and Billy's school work. I saw a lot of A's circled in red on tests and homework assignments.

Trying to break the ice, I said, "Looks like your son's a good student."

"Whenever I can wrestle him away from L.Q., I do my best," Darlene said. She tried to hide it, but I could tell she liked talking about Billy. It was the first I'd seen her smile.

Wilbur slipped out the door to visit with L.Q. I stood awkwardly at the edge of the kitchen. "Where does he go to school?"

"Moffat County High," said Darlene. "He's a freshman."

"Mind if I look at those papers?" I asked, nodding at the refrigerator door.

"Be my guest."

I sipped my beer, reading an essay about his first hunt with L.Q., while Darlene hovered over my shoulder, studying me studying Billy's work. He had shot an antelope earlier in the fall. Reading the story, I felt like I was on the trip with him and his dad. Billy wrote of pungent sagebrush, warm September days, clouds piled high and white against the blue sky of late September.

I whistled low. "That boy can write."

"What do you do for a living?" asked Darlene. "By the way, do you want me to call you Nick or 'College Boy'?"

"College Boy's fine." It didn't make me feel as dishonest. "I graduated this spring from Mesa," I said, nodding south. "I had a construction job this summer in Aspen, but I'm taking some time to see the sights this fall."

"What'd you study?"

"English."

"Me too," she said.

"Where'd you go?" I tried to keep a poker face, but knew I'd been busted.

"Greeley." That meant University of Northern Colorado, the state's biggest teacher's college. "I taught school in Baggs, seventh and eighth grade, before I quit to marry L.Q."

Darlene opened the back porch door, releasing the thick aroma of searing beef. I overheard L.Q. tell her another few minutes before the steaks were cooked.

"College Boy," she said, "we've got a little while longer before dinner, I want to show you something."

I followed her out the front door, down the porch steps, and a ways toward the Quonset, before she stopped abruptly, turning my way.

"Those two always think they can pull the wool over my eyes," Darlene said, nodding back toward the trailer. "But I wasn't born yesterday."

She paused, but I didn't know what to say.

"Something's not quite right here," she said, looking at me with her arms crossed.

I said nothing.

"I don't think you're hiring L.Q. to go coyote hunting, and, really, I don't care as long as he stays out of trouble and doesn't get hurt." She motioned toward the Quonset hut and the pasture beyond. "We love living here. L.Q. may be a rascal sometimes, but he's a good husband and a fine father. He gave his name to Billy." She looked my way. "I'll play along with this, but you're accountable."

"I won't let him get himself in trouble." A promise I wasn't sure how to keep.

Darlene looked at me, waiting to hear more, but all I said was, "It's for a good cause. I'm trying to help someone else."

She forced a small smile and nodded once. "Let's go eat."

Returning to the trailer, L.Q. placed steaks on our plates while Wilbur stood behind his chair, eyeing me suspiciously.

"College Boy," he asked, "you fetch that money for your hunt tomorrow?"

"Oh, yeah," I said. The sham felt ridiculous now, but I played along, for the benefit of Wilbur and L.Q. more than for Darlene. I dug the three hundred dollars from my wallet and grinned. "Who do I pay?"

"Just give it to Darlene," said L.Q. "She's the boss."

When I handed her the money, she said, "That was easy."

"Hey, Mom, what were you and College Boy talking about?" asked Billy.

"Just visiting, hon," said Darlene. "Nick was telling me all about fishing the Big Two-Hearted River."

The reference to Hemingway's short story nearly caused me to choke on my beer.

"All right, everybody," said L.Q., "supper's on the table. Let's eat."

How the hell was I going to keep L.Q. out of trouble?

Chapter Nineteen

The big meal and beer should have provided a somnolent effect, but it didn't slow my racing mind for long. I awoke in the darkness to the rhythm of Wilbur's buzz-saw snoring.

Two hours until first light, according to my Timex, I turned over and punched my lumpy jacket into a different-shaped pillow. My heart already drummed at the idea of flying. I shut my eyes and concentrated on other thoughts to distract my too-busy mind.

Hard to believe I'd be in Aspen, or at least Woody Creek, that day. Never planned to return so soon, less than a month since I had robbed Tom Tucker. Was he back on his feet? Out $75,000 of his own cash, he was probably accountable for over ten pounds of cocaine. Or was that the other guy's loss? Either way, I'd made at least one enemy for life. But if trouble was looking for you, the Old Man always said to meet it halfway.

So I was coming.

I'd been running so hard the last few weeks, I hadn't thought much about the future. Now it stared me in the face. First, I'd slip back to my little place at the Woody Creek Trailer Park. Hopefully, there'd be no ominous notes tacked on my door. I'd have to check my mail at the Woody Creek Store and Post Office, too. I couldn't forget ol' Chance's story about an APB out for a guy who met my description. Why were the cops involved?

I found it ironic, the law being Tom Tucker's best friend. Because the cops would be the only thing keeping me from putting the dope-dealing son of a bitch out of business for good. In the back of my mind, a plan had been forming ever since I'd decided to hold onto the cocaine.

I needed to find Tom Tucker. Stalk him—again. This time I wouldn't steal his money or his dope, just his freedom.

Then I'd save Laura.

I'd been searching my soul ever since Wilbur had asked me why I was risking my neck for an old girlfriend. It was a damned good question. I was worried about Laura, seeing her fall into the clutches of a monster. I was doing this for her, her family, too. But what about me? Was I just trying to protect her, or win her back? Ever since my freshman year, when I'd been lucky enough to meet her in Delta, we'd been together. I missed her, wanted to be with her. I had to be honest with myself. But even if we were never a couple again, I could still live with all my mistakes if I helped her make a new start.

I checked my watch again. One hour before first light.

"Goddamn, College Boy, you been tossin' and turnin' all night," said Wilbur from across L.Q.'s office. "What the hell time is it?"

"Time to get up," I said. "L.Q. will be down here before you know it. Said he wanted to get an early start."

While Wilbur postponed the inevitable, I rose and dressed in damned near every piece of clothing I had. L.Q. said the Champ would be cold as an icebox up at nine thousand feet. The little plane's heater worked like the half-assed units in Volkswagens. No fan, just freezing air forced over the manifold. Not very effective.

I turned on L.Q.'s desk lamp. "Better be getting up, Wilbur." I looked through the window facing the double-wide. "Lights are on up at the trailer. L.Q. said he'd bring coffee."

"College, I'm getting too old for this bullshit," said Wilbur, kicking away his blankets.

"Just a little while longer, then you can get back to your hidey-hole. If the cops let you, that is."

"Don't worry 'bout me," Wilbur chided. "Far as what happened yesterday, you was just a hitchhiker I picked up." He paused for effect and looked me in the eye. "Otherwise, I don't know a damned thing 'bout that guy on the poster."

Dressed, I packed my gear. I removed another bundle of cash for L.Q.'s final payment and stuffed it in my wallet. The rest of the money remained in the bottom of my pack along with the cocaine. I covered the contraband with my raingear. I hefted the Old Man's Smith & Wesson revolver.

"Wilbur, something I want you to have."

"Nah, I'm not taking any money," he said. "You don't owe me nothin'."

He must have seen me getting L.Q.'s cash. I knew better than to try to pay Wilbur for his help. That would have been an insult to his honor.

"This is what I want to give you." I handed Wilbur the revolver, cased in the moose-hide holster. "I think the Old Man would want you to have it."

Wilbur sat on his cot, boots still untied. He examined the piece fondly, wide-eyed and hopeful. Then a frown crossed his face. "I can't take this, College Boy. You're gonna need it a lot more than me."

"No, sir, that's yours," I said, with an air of finality.

"Yeah, but what about that Tucker fella, ain't you gonna need this to finish—"

"I'm going to finish him all right, but not with a gun."

We both heard L.Q.'s footsteps outside.

"Go ahead and put that away now, Wilbur. Don't want to spook my pilot."

L.Q. barged into the Quonset, singing an off-key rendition of the Bellamy Brothers's "If I Said You Had a Beautiful Body Would You Hold It Against Me?"

Wilbur winked at me and laughed.

Undeterred, L.Q. crooned louder.

"I'm glad somebody had a good night," Wilbur scoffed.

"You betcha boots, pard," said L.Q. He sipped from his steaming coffee cup and placed a thermos and two plastic mugs on his desk. "That's for you, boys."

Wilbur tied his boots, then poured himself a cup. I passed, watching L.Q. study numbers scribbled on a pad of lined paper.

"What's that?" I asked.

"Did some calculating last night, about our weight and balance," said L.Q. "I figure we can take on about sixty pounds of fuel, tops."

"How much is that?" My stomach knotted. The reality of getting in that flying orange crate stared me in the face.

"About nine gallons, give or take."

"Will that get us there?" I asked hopefully.

"Be close," said L.Q., "but one way or the other, I'm gonna have to refuel to get back home."

"That'd be easier while you still got College Boy with you," said Wilbur between sips of coffee.

"True," said L.Q. "On the other hand, my cargo won't be as hot flying home." He nodded my way. "Heard some pretty interesting chatter on the radio this morning."

Ever since we'd met, I figured L.Q. knew the score. I was glad he did. At least I wasn't hoodwinking him into giving me a ride. He knew what he was getting himself into for two thousand dollars.

L.Q. took a seat behind his desk, studying a map of Colorado tacked to a cork bulletin board. "Got us about a hundred and eighty miles. Two hours or so."

"Hell, you'll be back home for lunch," said Wilbur.

L.Q. glanced out the window. The first hint of dawn crept across the eastern horizon, a pink band below the velvet sky. "We'll leave at sunup," he said. "We'll have more lift in the cold, make up for being a little heavy." He looked at the map again.

"Do you have to file a flight plan, or anything?" I asked.

Wilbur and L.Q. looked at each other, both grinning. "Hell, pard, I don't even have a radio in the Champ."

"How do you navigate?" I asked. "How do you keep from getting lost?"

"I fly IFR."

I didn't know what the acronym stood for, but I remembered what L. Q. said the day before about flying after dark. "I thought you said you didn't know how to fly by instruments?"

"I-F-R," L.Q. said slowly. "I. Follow. Roads."

Wilbur and L.Q. laughed at my expense.

"Good enough," I said. "I just hope you can see them."

"Don't worry, partner," said L.Q. "It's clear as a bell out there."

We moved the vehicles from the Quonset, then pushed the Champ outside. By the time L.Q. fueled the plane, the sun was creeping above the mountains to the east.

"Reckon I ought to show College Boy how to start this thing?" asked Wilbur.

"Might as well, it'll make things simpler if we have to take on gas before Basalt," said L.Q. He shook Wilbur's hand, then climbed in the front seat. He tinkered with some switches and opened his window. "Go ahead, pull her through."

"Follow me, College Boy," said Wilbur. We walked to the front of the plane. "See, this ol' plane ain't got a starter motor." He pointed to the two-bladed wood propeller. "You got to hand prop the engine."

As if I wasn't already nervous enough, now I had to learn how to start this damned plane.

"He ain't got the magneto switched on yet, College," said Wilbur, turning the prop one revolution. "This is to prime the engine."

L.Q. barked through the open window, "Clear."

"Okay, now he's got the ignition on," said Wilbur. "The trick to starting one of these things is to sorta lean into the prop as you turn it, then rock backward—all in one motion. Be careful or the damned thing will cut your arms off, or maybe your head." Wilbur placed both hands on one blade, stood on his toes, and pushed downward. The engine popped and sputtered as the propeller rotated unevenly. White smoke blasted from the exhaust pipe on the bottom of the cowling. In a few seconds, the engine picked up rpms, running smoother now. It sounded like a big sewing machine.

We stepped away from the plane as L.Q. warmed up the engine. "All right, College Boy," said Wilbur. "You best climb in. Don't forget your pack," he laughed.

I shook his hand. "Thank you, Wilbur. Thanks for everything."

"Don't be a stranger," he said. "Come back and see me after you get everything straightened out."

L.Q. opened the door and leaned forward, allowing me to slip into the back. I placed my pack behind me, then buckled my seat belt. L.Q. looked over his shoulder and handed me a headset. "Put it on, partner," he hollered over the engine blare, "so we can talk."

I adjusted the headphones to fit over my stocking cap and swung the microphone near my mouth.

"Put this intercom in myself," said L.Q. "It's voice activated, just speak into the mike."

"Can you hear me?" I asked.

L.Q. nodded his head. "Try not to bump that stick between your legs, and keep your feet off the pedals. Roger that?"

"Roger."

"All right, we're gonna taxi over to my runway."

L.Q.'s "runway" was a hay meadow behind the Quonset. He pushed in the throttle and the Champ bumped along the road. From my seat in the back, I couldn't see over the engine cowling but could view most of the sparse instrument panel. To gauge our progress, I looked out the side window. The little plane was tight, but provided a hell of a view with the entire cockpit sided by windows. Soon we reached the edge of the recently mowed field and L.Q. braked the Champ to a stop.

"I'm gonna do my run-up." He pushed in the throttle, racing the engine to a busy whine. Twisting a switch on the door between us, he said, "Checking the magnetos. Looks good." The stick between my legs moved in box pattern as L.Q. looked through both windows. "Checking the elevators and ailerons."

He pulled the throttle back and studied the instrument panel for a few seconds, then looked over his shoulder. "You ready, pard?"

"You bet," I lied. My heart raced faster than the little engine.

"Okay, I'm gonna give her the onion." L.Q. pushed the dash-mounted throttle all the way in and released the brakes. The Champ lurched forward, slowly picking up speed. The plane rocked along the uneven field while he used the rudders to keep us heading straight. When the airspeed indicator bounced around forty miles an hour, L.Q. pushed the stick forward, raising the tail off the ground. The Champ gained lift, and a few seconds later he pulled back on the stick, propelling us into flight. I held my breath, nervous as hell about crashing.

Off the ground, the ride was smoother. We kept a westward bearing for a few minutes while the Champ slowly gained altitude, then banked to the south. I looked back toward L.Q.'s place. Through my binoculars, I watched Wilbur driving toward the county road in his yellow Bronco. From a thousand feet, everything looked small, like a model. I recognized Highway 13 below us, a ribbon of concrete bisecting the prairie.

"How you doing back there, pard?"

"I'm good." I meant it. I was actually enjoying the flight. I'd never seen the country between the peak and Basalt from the air.

"Can't have any more fun than this—with your clothes on," L.Q. laughed.

I glanced at my watch. With luck, I'd have a late breakfast in Basalt.

Chapter Twenty

Thirty minutes later, we reached the north edge of Craig. Looking south, I saw a cloudless horizon. A fine day for flying. Smooth sailing all the way to Basalt. With an airspeed of eighty miles per hour, we easily passed the few vehicles traveling on Highway 13.

I spotted the white roof of the City Market grocery store, the lumberyard and the county courthouse. From our cruising elevation, the town looked like a Matchbox play set, complete with the little cars I had played with as a kid.

We veered southwest, picking up Highway 13 again, south of town. Crossing the Yampa, I watched the muddy river curve away to the west on its run to the Colorado. The Williams Fork Mountains rose east of us, their snow-clad peaks looming above us. Now I understood why we had to follow the low-lying valleys rather than cut across to Glenwood Springs.

L.Q. remained silent, letting me enjoy the panoramic view from the Champ. I always hated garrulous tour guides, showering folks with arcane facts instead of allowing them to soak in the experience.

Between Craig and Hamilton, the ride got bumpy. L.Q. spoke for the first time since we'd settled into our course above Highway 13.

"Picking up some wind from the west, pard." He moved a lever to the left of the instrument panel. "Gonna have to work again—just trimmed her out a little more."

Heading south toward Hamilton, the growing wind shoved the

little plane sideways. We crabbed along, the Champ flying obliquely, like a car out of alignment. Watching my stick and pedals articulate, I could tell L.Q. was working his ass off to keep us on course. Not bad for a cross-eyed, self-taught pilot. A few miles past Hamilton, the highway turned west. The plane straightened out, the ride not as rough.

Studying the highway, I noticed we were losing ground to westbound traffic. The airspeed indicator bounced around eighty miles an hour. Had we hit a stretch of road without the ubiquitous Colorado Highway Patrol?

"Those cars are hauling ass down there," I said.

"Nope, I don't think so, pard." L.Q. tapped the gauge. "That's airspeed, not ground speed."

"What's that mean?"

"Means we're probably moving around fifty miles an hour— ground speed. We got a pretty stiff headwind, maybe thirty miles an hour."

Now I was spooked. "We gonna be all right?"

"Oh, yeah, but we're burning fuel a hell of a lot faster than I planned."

I always hated that word, "but."

Studying the instrument panel, I didn't see anything that looked like a fuel indicator. "Where's the gas gauge?"

"You can't see it from back there," said L.Q. "It's mounted on the cowling, in front of the windshield."

"Shit," I muttered. Up to now, watching those gauges had given me some relief. A false sense of control. As long as the needles stayed in the black and the wings were level, I knew we were okay. Now I had to worry about running out of gas. Sort of like watching the end of a close football game without seeing the clock.

Forty-five minutes after passing Hamilton, we reached Meeker. Studying the little cowboy town, I spotted an airport. "Think we ought to gas up down there?" It was the first I'd spoken since L.Q. apprised me of our fuel problem.

"Nah," he said. "We got enough to make Rifle. More user friendly."

"Really?" How was the Garfield County Airport going to be any more hospitable to an unlicensed pilot than Meeker?

"I'm headed to a private strip, not the airport."

Passing over Meeker, I looked back longingly at that lovely airport. How far was L.Q. pushing our luck? The wind hadn't let up and was still doing its best to shove us off course. Studying a Colorado highway map, I realized once we reached Rifle, we'd have a tailwind the rest of the trip to Basalt. No choice but to trust L.Q.

A few minutes later, L.Q. pulled back on the throttle, I assumed to conserve gas. It didn't work. With less power, we were quickly blown toward a long ridge east of the highway known as the Grand Hogback. After a few miles, he put the balls to the wall, fighting to get back over the highway.

"We ain't gonna make it, partner."

My heart skipped a beat. "Sweet Jesus." I panicked. "We're going down?"

"Nah," L.Q. laughed. "We ain't gonna make Rifle."

That sounded a little better. My heart slowed down to normal.

"What are you gonna do?"

"Get some gas in Rio Blanco."

I looked at my map. "They got a strip?"

"Nope."

"Where the hell are you going to land?"

"Little field on the edge of town."

"You landed there before?" I asked hopefully.

"Nope, but it's always looked like a good spot," said L.Q. "Right across the road from a Texaco."

At a gap in the Grand Hogback, L.Q. banked the Champ,

making a wide arc into the wind. Heading west, I spotted the little town. Just a few scattered buildings and half a dozen streets. We began our descent, surrendering hard-fought elevation.

We were committed now.

"Make sure your seat belt's tight, partner."

Across the highway, I spotted L.Q.'s makeshift runway. "Is that gonna be long enough?"

"Hell, yeah, I can make this plane kiss my ass."

"What about all those cows?" I asked.

"They better git," laughed L.Q.

A power line ran parallel to the highway, smack in the way of our approach. Our wheels nearly scraped the wire-braided cable. I gasped. L.Q. pulled back more on the throttle, dropping us near the tawny field.

"Looks good," he said. At an airspeed of forty miles an hour, we descended onto the pasture, stampeding the terrified cattle to the west. We bounced a couple of times into the air before the Champ landed for good.

"Thank God," I muttered, wishing I could kiss the ground.

We taxied to the edge of the field, then turned right toward the Texaco, a quarter of a mile away. Halfway to the gas station, the Champ sputtered and died. L.Q. removed his headset and looked back at me, a sheepish grin plastered on his face. "Guess we'll have to walk the rest of the way."

"What happened?" I asked naïvely.

"We ran out of gas, partner."

"Holy shit, L.Q."

"Yeah. I know."

We fetched a plastic gas container from the rear of the plane and hoofed it to the station. A small crowd of customers and the station attendant gathered, watching us. We jogged across Piceance Creek Road and made a beeline for one of the two gas pumps. Ignoring the onlookers, L.Q. filled the five-gallon container with premium gas.

"How much we gonna put in her?" I asked.

"Let's go with two of these," said L.Q. "Ten gallons will get us there and then some, 'specially once we pick up that tail wind."

"Okay, well, how about you take that first five back to the plane and I'll go pay for the gas."

"Sure, partner," said L.Q. He had lost a little edge to his normal cockiness, having nearly killed us with his fuel management. "I'll be right back to get the second five."

I felt bad for him as he walked away. "Hey L.Q.," I shouted, "good landing."

He gave me a thumbs-up and trotted toward the Champ.

I braced myself for some crap, walking to pay for the gas. Nearing the double doors, a couple of teenaged boys, maybe Billy's age, laughed. "Hey, dude," one of them said, "you guys always land in hayfields?"

"Yeah," the second kid said. "How come you ain't using an airport?"

Brushing by them, I muttered, "Didn't have enough gas to make Rifle."

As I walked to the counter, the attendant hung up the store telephone and looked my way, shaking his head. "You know, you just can't land that damned thing any ol' place you please, Jack."

The man was around forty, balding with a big gut and a beet-red face. His jeans were cinched with a hand-tooled belt with a silver rodeo buckle he probably claimed to have won. A green Texaco jacket over a Denver Broncos orange jersey completed his outfit.

"Well, I'm sure sorry about that, sir," I said. "We wouldn't have landed there, but we were out of fuel." I pulled out my wallet. "It was an emergency."

"I don't give a shit. You're not supposed to land there." He pointed toward the field. "You could have hit my cattle."

"Well, I'm sorry, we'll get out of there as soon as we gas up," I said. "We need ten gallons." I handed him a twenty.

"I'll take your money, but I'm still making a complaint."

"Are you the owner of that pasture?" I asked.

"Damn right," he said. "That's my property."

My heart quickened. "We'll sure get out of there."

"You sure as hell will."

I took my change from the angry fellow and left the station. Outside, one of the two teenagers approached me. "Hey, dude, he called the highway patrol on you guys. You better get out of here, Captain Kirk." Both boys laughed.

Looking across the road toward the Champ, I saw L.Q. lolly-gagging back for the second can of gas. I gave him an earsplitting whistle and waved frantically. He broke into a jog, then a run as I kept motioning for him to hustle.

A few minutes later, he arrived at the pump, pale and breath-less. "Shit, partner, where's the fire?"

"The guy who owns that field called the police," I said. "We better get this gas and go."

Chapter Twenty-One

We ran back to the Champ, taking turns carrying the plastic jerry can. I had considered taking off with only the five gallons L.Q. had already put in the plane, but that would have required another stop somewhere before Basalt. I didn't want to make any more hayfield landings, thank you.

L.Q. poured the gas into the plane while I nervously paced, praying we got off the ground before the Colorado Highway Patrol arrived. I didn't doubt that teenager's tip for a second. The station attendant/landowner had been mad as hell. I was just glad he sold us the gas. Then again, we didn't give him much choice, pumping it ourselves.

Finally, L.Q. finished fueling the Champ and stowed the can away. "All right, partner," he said, climbing into the plane. "Let's see if you can hand-prop ol' *LQ-1*."

"Damn." I had forgotten about my new chore. I approached the job with trepidation, remembering Wilbur's cautions. I tried to remember the instructions verbatim.

L.Q. hollered through his open window, "Pull her through."

This was the easy part, magnetos off, no chance of losing any appendages. A dress rehearsal. I turned the prop a full revolution to prime the engine.

"Clear," L.Q. shouted.

Magnetos on, a live performance. Holding one of the blades with my fingertips, I stood on my toes and pushed downward,

while rocking away from the propeller. The engine sputtered hopefully for a moment, then died.

"Shit," I screamed.

L.Q. laughed through the cab. "Clear," he said. "Twist her again."

Walking back to the front of the Champ, something caught
my eye to the north, in the direction of the Texaco. A patrol
cruiser, its emergency lights flashing red and blue, pulled into the
gas station. L.Q.'s grin hardened to a grimace when I nodded toward the law.

"Get this son of a bitch going," he shouted.

I rocked into the propeller once more. The engine popped and
coughed. L.Q. gave me a thumbs-up as the propeller spun, picking
up rpms. My elation at starting the Champ without losing any dig-
its or limbs was short-lived. Over the din of the racing engine, I
heard a siren. Glancing toward the Texaco, I was stunned to see
the patrol car, a black-and-white Plymouth Fury, had veered across
the field and headed toward us.

L.Q. opened his door, furiously motioning me to climb aboard.
Slipping behind him, I didn't even have a chance to take my seat
before he taxied away from the oncoming patrol car. He led the
cruiser on a spirited chase, but the patrolman cut us off from the
long axis of the field. We couldn't get enough run to liftoff.

Without the headsets, which we hadn't had a chance to put
on, I shouted over the whining engine, "Now what?"

"Hold on," he hollered, "we ain't caught yet."

We made a big loop in the field, the patrol car right behind us.
I realized L.Q. had given up trying to take off from the meadow.
With the cruiser in tow, he motored along the west fence, heading
straight toward the Texaco.

"What the hell you doing?" I shouted.

"Gonna use the road for a runway," laughed L.Q.

"Shit," I hollered. But my pilot's swagger buoyed my confidence.

Nearing the county road, my spirits soared. The patrolman, in his zeal to apprehend us, had not closed the barbed-wire gate. L.Q. pulled back on the throttle and taxied the Champ through the narrow opening, the plane's high wings clearing the fence poles by inches. He turned left onto the road, heading west, directly into the wind.

I opened my window and looked behind us. The Plymouth followed, lights flashing, siren whining. "Better get going," I shouted. "He's on our ass." I worried the patrolman might ram the tail of the Champ. Mirrored Ray-Bans hid the officer's eyes. He wore the same campaign hat as Teddy Roosevelt's Rough Riders and a blue shirt with epaulets and lots of brass. He looked like a very tough guy.

The plane's little four-banger was no match for the V-8 of the cruiser. But every time the Smokey tried to pass us, L.Q. veered in an S-shape pattern. The thirty-five-foot wingspan of the Champ stymied the patrolman's attempt to get around us. As we accelerated toward takeoff, the cop seemed satisfied to track us from the rear. Looking ahead, I discovered the source of his patience. A series of overhead wires spanned the two-lane road, preventing L.Q. from taking off for as far as I could see.

When the airspeed indicator reached fifty miles per hour, I felt the lift of the Champ growing. It wanted to fly, spurting into the air with each bump in the road. L.Q. pushed the stick forward, raising the tail. Dancing on the rudders, he ran on the front wheels, poised to takeoff. The patrolman responded, narrowing the gap between us to a few feet.

Then I looked ahead of us, fear robbing my breath. An 18-wheeler headed in our direction, a half mile away. "Sweet Jesus, what are you gonna do?" I asked over the discordant harmony of the Champ and the patrol cruiser.

"Got a plan," he shouted. "Fasten your belt—say your prayers."

At seventy miles per hour, L.Q. pulled back the stick imperceptibly, the plane lifting a few yards off the road. Another overhead wire passed by, barely clearing our wings.

"Goddamn, that was close."

"Just one more. Then I'm gonna shoot the gap."

The truck loomed in front, its lights flashing us now. Behind, the cruiser met our pace, nearly touching our tail. Couldn't the patrolman see the truck bearing down on us?

Spying the next overhead wire, I wasn't sure if we'd reach it before the truck smashed head on into us. L.Q. kept the Champ airborne, our elevation perhaps ten feet.

One hundred yards.

Fifty yards.

Twenty-five yards.

We slipped under the wire, then L.Q. yanked the stick back. The plane rose, fighting for elevation. The next wire grazed the bottom of our front tires. We cleared the truck's trailer by mere feet.

We made it.

The patrolman wasn't as fortunate. His view obstructed by the Champ, he didn't see the truck until it was too late. Turning sharply to avoid a head-on collision, the Smokey drove his cruiser into the barrow ditch, like a teenager pissing in his pants, losing at a game of chicken. Flying out of the shallow gully, the Plymouth plowed through a fence and bulldozed into the sagebrush flat. Coming to a stop, the rig's hood flew open, white smoke erupting from the engine, mingled with prairie dust.

L.Q. circled, making a big loop over the wreck. We both watched the patrolman extract himself from the battered cruiser. The nattily dressed officer stumbled on wobbly legs, shaking his fist at us.

"No Christmas card from that ol' boy," L.Q. hollered, as we

headed south, climbing to our cruising elevation. He tipped the Champ's wings in farewell, one last act of defiance.

With shaking hands, I followed L.Q.'s lead and put on my headset. "How 'bout some music for the last leg of our trip?" he asked.

"Sure. You bet." I breathed deeply, collecting my wits. I had nearly broken my promise to Darlene. When would I stop running? At this rate, sooner or later, I'd roll snake eyes.

L.Q. inserted a tape into the dash-mounted cassette player. "I wired this into the headsets myself," he boasted. A few seconds later, I tapped my foot to Lester Flatt and Earl Scruggs, picking the hell out of "Foggy Mountain Breakdown."

Chapter Twenty-Two

South of Rio Blanco, Highway 13 veered to the southeast, paralleling a dogleg in the Grand Hogback. Still recovering from our brush with the highway patrol, I gazed at the White River National Forest below and the Flat Tops farther to the north. In better days, I'd hunted elk and mule deer with the Old Man in this country. Years later, I'd guided Laura on some of the same trails. Brushy south-facing slopes gave way to bands of aspen and evergreen. At timberline, tawny parks crowned by rocky peaks beckoned. Would I ever return to the high country? Would Laura and I ever return?

I'd had a hard time getting her off my mind the last couple of days. After robbing Tom Tucker, I'd left everything behind on my run to the peak. Keeping one step ahead of the law consumed me, helped me block the need for remembering, the need for guilt, the need for dread.

Now that I was returning, it was all coming back. Leaving Laura behind to go it alone, letting her fall prey to Tucker. I hoped I wasn't too late. Beyond rescuing her, I wasn't even sure what I wanted. Better figure that out. I owed her the truth. When the time came, I hoped I'd know.

At Rifle, we headed due east, following I-70 and the Colorado River. Still no needless chatter from L.Q. I had caught my breath and enjoyed the last of the fall colors. Most of the aspens were bare, but the cottonwoods and willows still shimmered in the wind, showering the Colorado with their restless leaves, yellow and red.

The muddy river sparkled in the morning sun, a brown ribbon running to the sea.

At the edge of Glenwood Springs, we changed course again, flying south toward Highway 82. When we reached the Roaring Fork Valley, my old stomping grounds, L.Q. gave Flatt and Scruggs a rest, speaking for the first time since escaping from Rio Blanco. "Look familiar, partner?"

"Oh, yeah." I looked toward the Roaring Fork River, with its long blue pools and foamy-white rapids. "Coming up on one of my favorite fishing holes." They'd be biting on hoppers, still, I thought. Maybe Panther Martins and Mepps, too, especially the big browns. Wouldn't be any time for fishing on this trip, though. Maybe next spring.

"Listen, partner," said L.Q., "Darlene doesn't ever need to hear about that scrape with the law, right?"

"As far as I'm concerned, we've been coyote hunting all day," I said. Did he really think he was fooling her?

"Yeah, well, all the same," L.Q. stumbled, "whatever we did, we didn't get chased by the fuzz."

"Secret's safe with me." Who knew when I might be back at the peak? If I did make it, though, I'd like to see L.Q. again, maybe even hire him for a real coyote hunt. Wouldn't mind spending some time with Darlene and Billy, either.

If I made it.

At the edge of Carbondale, we left Highway 82 and flew south to a county road across the river. "Got your bearings, partner?"

"Yeah, we're over Catherine's Store Road."

"That's right—maybe five miles from Glen-Aspen."

A few minutes later, we circled a long dirt landing strip running east-west in the middle of a rolling pinon-juniper flat. The remoteness appealed to me. Not a soul in sight. L.Q. took us in from the east, descending into the wind. After the hayfield behind his

Quonset and the pasture at Rio Blanco, this looked like a real run-way.

L. Q. put her down smooth, slick as ice. Plenty of strip left for his takeoff. "I ain't gonna shut down," he said, as we slowed to a stop. "Need to be getting back or Darlene'll get worried."

I didn't want her fretting. Didn't want to hand prop the Champ again, either.

"You got enough gas to get home?" I hoped L.Q. didn't get into another brush with the law.

"I'm planning on landing at my buddy's place outside Rifle," he said. "Got plenty of fuel to get there."

I pulled a wad of bills from my wallet. Final installment on a hell of a flight. I retrieved my pack and crawled out of the plane, sliding past L.Q.'s seat. "Here you go," I said, handing him the money.

"Do I need to count it?" He laughed, offered his hand.

"You were right," I said over the idling engine, "you really can make this thing kiss your ass."

"I do my best."

"Well, you do pretty well." I shouldered my pack, gave him one more look. "Say hello to your family, keep an eye on Wilbur."

L.Q. waved as I backed away from the Champ. A few minutes later he was off the ground, tipping his wings before banking to the north.

I walked along a two-track service road, aiming to reach the frontage road across the river from Highway 82. Hitch a ride or walk to Emma, then slip into Basalt, all told around fifteen miles to the east.

I felt a little safer, now, nearly two hundred miles from Moffat County. But I still carried enough stolen cash and dope to get my throat cut or be thrown in prison. And now I was on my own again—returning to the scene of the crime. No more old hands like Wilbur and L.Q. to bail me out. There was a lot more to being a criminal than I'd realized. I didn't figure to make it my career, though. One more job in Aspen, then I'd retire from the profession.

Chapter Twenty-Three

An hour later, I walked along Catherine's Store Road, trying to catch a ride to Basalt. Gazing north toward Red Table Mountain, I noted the snow line around 9,000 feet. Below the demarcation line separating winter from fall, the country was still dry. Along the Roaring Fork, it almost felt like summer. The heady aroma of sweet cottonwoods reminded me of fishing trips with the Old Man. In quiet eddies, mallards chortled, and trout rose in the slanting sunlight of late morning.

The third vehicle heading my way, a sixties'-vintage Chevy truck with Pitkin County plates, stopped a hundred yards past me, raising a cloud of dust on the shoulder of the gravel road. A waving arm beckoned. I ran ahead, my pack jostling against my back.

"Where ya headed?" asked the driver, an old man traveling alone.

"Basalt."

Before I could volunteer to hop in the bed, the man nodded toward his right. "Come aboard. You can throw your pack in the back."

"Thanks, appreciate it." I walked around the front of the truck and climbed in, stuffing the pack at my feet. "Carrying some fancy photography equipment, don't want to let it bounce around too much."

"Suit yourself," he said.

Driving along the Roaring Fork, I feigned interest in the river to study my host. His face was vaguely familiar. Bushy eyebrows hooded intense gray eyes, squinting in sunlight reflected off the water. White hair flowed from the back of his canvas baseball cap and wire-rimmed glasses rested upon his hawk nose. He wore a tan down vest over a red flannel shirt. I guessed his age closer to seventy than sixty. We sat in silence for a mile or two, mutually content to share the warm October day with our own thoughts.

I looked over my shoulder to view the truck bed. His cargo included a couple of spinning rods, an old metal Coca-Cola cooler, and a folding chair. He might have dressed plainly and driven an old truck, but something told me he was a man of means. Maybe it was his perfect posture or his hands, smooth and bony, like those of a musician, not a laborer.

Figured I might as well break the ice, be sociable. "How's fishing?"

"Good, good," he said, "already caught my limit."

That meant eight fish. "Rainbows?"

"One big German brown, maybe twenty inches," he answered, "the rest, stockers."

"Stockers" meant hatchery-reared rainbow trout. "That's a good morning. Where'd you catch 'em?"

"In the river." He took his eyes off the road for a second, glanced my way, laughed. "I might give you a ride, but I'm not telling you where my fishing hole is."

"I don't blame you," I said. A man needed to protect his spots for himself and maybe a tight-lipped friend or two. "What'd you catch 'em on?"

"Salmon eggs—worms later on in the morning." He leaned away from me a little, like he might catch a scolding.

"I was guessing hoppers." If he thought I was a snob about my fishing, he was mistaken. I'd have used a pitchfork if that's what it took to catch a mess of trout for the pan.

"So, you're not a dyed-in-the-wool fly fishermen?" he chuckled. "I thought all you youngsters were purists these days."

"Not me. I just like to catch fish, whatever it takes."

"Are you from around here?" he asked.

"No," I said, clinging to a loophole in the truth, "just passing through, going to see a friend up in Aspen." Normally, I'd have introduced myself by now, but I didn't want to share that information. I had an alias ready, though.

"Would that friend be a young lady?" he asked, a wry smile crossing his face.

A lucky guess. Weren't all young men looking for a girl? "Yeah, how'd you know?" For a ride, I'd play along.

"In my line of work, a fellow gets a sense of these things. Learns to read people."

"What do you do?"

"I'm a writer," he said.

"What kind of writing do you do?"

"Started off reporting for a newspaper, when I was about your age," he said. "Worked nearly twenty years for the *St. Louis Post-Dispatch*. I made my bones writing novels, though."

I studied his face more carefully. "Are you Michael Davis?"

"In the flesh," he said with a smile, "but my friends call me 'Doc.'"

Only in the Roaring Fork Valley, I thought, would I have hitched a ride with one of the most famous novelists in America. I had read his books, mostly detective and mystery stories, since high school.

"My grandfather loved your stuff," I said, "passed along every book to me."

"A favorite come to mind?"

"I must have read *True Justice* ten times," I fawned. "Bet I've given four or five copies away to friends."

"Well, I'm grateful." He patted the cracked dash of the Chevy. "Bought and paid for by my readers." He looked my way. "Now you know a lot more about me than I know about you."

"Just call me C.B.," I said, taking a page from Wilbur's book.

"What do you do for work, C.B.?"

"Unemployed college graduate."

"Ah, those were the days," he mused.

I laughed, a famous writer pining for my sorry milieu.

"Where'd you go to school, what'd you study?" he asked.

I couldn't believe Michael Davis was interviewing me.

"Mesa College, Grand Junction." I looked his way, boldly winked. "English major."

"A kindred spirit."

"Yeah, right." I laughed again.

"Everybody's got to start somewhere," he said. "Believe it or not, only seems like yesterday when I graduated from the University of Missouri."

We drove through the tiny hamlet of Emma, took Highway 82 the rest of the way to Basalt. Waiting for the stoplight at the turnoff to the Frying Pan Road, Davis checked his watch. "How about some lunch?"

I was in a hurry to get to Woody Creek, but it seemed like a lifetime since I'd eaten last. L.Q. and Darlene's dinner, to be specific. "Well, I am hungry."

At the green light we crossed the highway, drove along Basalt's main and only street. A few hundred yards into town, we parked in front of the Midland Bar and Café.

I grabbed my pack and opened the door.

"Oh, you can leave that in the cab. I'll lock it up."

"That's all right, I got my wallet stuffed in it. I'll bring it in with me."

We entered the joint, narrow and long. The bartender, a burly, bearded man in a plaid Pendleton shirt, hollered over the din of the midday drinkers, "Hey, Doc, how's fishing?"

"Caught my supper, Noah."

"There you go."

Slipping between the patrons seated at the bar and a row of small tables against the opposite wall, we reached the back where the café served food. A good-looking blonde, maybe thirty, tall and shapely, rushed to greet us. "Doc," she said with a smile. Her eyes flicked across to me, returned to Davis. "Two for lunch?"

"You bet, Linda."

She led us to a corner booth, across from the kitchen. I slid my pack under the table and took a seat against the wall. By now, a force of habit.

Davis sat, handed me a menu. "Good eats, here. I recommend the pork chop sandwich, best I've had."

I'd enjoyed the double cheeseburger the couple of times I'd eaten here, but played dumb.

Within minutes the blonde brought us silverware, doting on Davis like he owned the place. "Regular, Doc?"

"Yes, ma'am."

She nodded my way, pencil poised.

"I'll have the same."

"What to drink, boys?"

"Coffee," said Davis.

"Iced tea for me, please."

"I'll be right back with your drinks."

As she walked away in her snug Levis, Davis shamelessly watched every bounce of her tight ass. He turned my way, winked. "If I was thirty years younger—hell, make that twenty."

Out of curiosity, I glanced at his left hand, didn't see a ring. I knew he'd had a bunch of wives, but had no idea of his present marital status.

"So, what are you going to do with this English degree, C.B.?"

"Haven't had a chance to give it much thought." A true statement. I'd been scheming, running for most of the last two months.

"Teaching?"

"Haven't got the patience."

"Public relations?"

"I'm no snake-oil salesman."

Davis laughed. "Something must have inspired you to get that degree." He cleaned his glasses with a red bandana. Without his specs, he looked older, big bags under his eyes.

Our waitress brought our drinks, temporarily rescuing me.

"Thank you, Linda," Davis said, a big smile on his face.

Turning back to me, he continued, "What's your next move? Got anything in the works?"

Yeah, Doc, I'm gonna rescue Laura, and put a low-life scumbag of a dope dealer out of business.

I drank my tea, shook my head. "One of my profs told me to go on for an MFA. She said she'd write a good letter for me."

"What's wrong with that?" he said. "Sounds fun."

"Don't know if I can stomach any more school for a while."

"You want to get some life experience, get your hands dirty," he said. "I understand that, too."

"I want to see the world, write stories about it." It was one of the first honest things I'd told him.

"I see—a freelance writer." He sipped his coffee, pondering my career goal. "Of course, you'd have to have some interesting experiences and a unique perspective."

It occurred to me that I was getting a leg up on both requirements.

"Okay, here's the deal, kid," said Davis. "You just passed your first job interview."

I said nothing, didn't know what the hell he was talking about.

"You're a perfect fit, just what I'm looking for."

"Which is?"

"I need a guy like you to do legwork for me. You know, research stuff in libraries, courthouses, go to places I'm writing about, take photos and the like."

The last thing I had expected to receive was a job offer. Davis measured my interest, trying to read me like we were in a poker game.

"I just lost my last helper," said Davis wistfully, "young guy like you, got married, kid on the way, had to settle down."

Not meaning to look a gift horse in the ass, I still asked, "What makes you think I'd be good at this?"

"You don't have anything else you want to do, for now, and this work would be great experience for your own writing—"

Davis stopped in mid-sentence when the waitress brought our food. Then he nodded at me. "Besides, someday you can tell folks you worked for Michael Davis."

He pulled a card from his wallet, handed it to me. "Think on it and give me a call after you find that friend you're looking for."

"Thanks, Doc, I sure will." Sounded interesting. Might have to consider it if I was still in one piece when the dust settled up Aspen way.

Chapter Twenty-Four

I hopped out of Davis's pickup along the shoulder of Highway 82 across from the turnoff to Woody Creek. I'd been lucky in more ways than one. He'd been heading back to his digs up Maroon Creek, so I didn't have to hitch another ride out of Basalt. I was well fed on his dime, and then there was the matter of a job offer. I placed his card in my wallet and shouldered my pack, watching the old Chevy scratch gravel toward Aspen.

I shot the gap in traffic, running across the two-lane highway. Gazing north, across the Roaring Fork River, I eyed my little trailer. My Jeep was still parked where I'd left it a month before. I counted that as a good sign. Imagining a worst-case scenario, I'd envisioned the law or Tucker confiscating or stealing it in my absence.

Walking down the winding path to the valley bottom, I crossed the bridge over the river and headed left on McClain Flats Road. My pace quickened as I neared the park. Most of the folks living there were working stiffs. Early afternoon, on a weekday, the place looked quiet. That was good. I wanted to slip into my place as discreetly as possible.

It was a small trailer park, around fifty units, spread out for a half mile south of the confluence of Woody Creek and the Roaring Fork River. The entrance passed a general store and U.S. Post Office. Debating whether to check my mail first or get to the trailer, I took the easy way out, stopping at the little log-sided building.

I entered the deserted office with satisfaction. I'd only lived in the park since June, so I didn't know too many of the locals. But I still didn't want to run into anybody until I figured out what was what.

I scooted over to my box and peered through the little glass window. I had mail. Dialing the combination on the lock, I prayed for no official-looking letters. With shaking hands, I pulled out the letters and magazines crammed into the tiny box. Turning my back to the door, I nervously sifted through the correspondence. Everything seemed harmless until I came to a pink slip for a package.

I walked over to the Dutch door, half opened, that served as the office counter. An old lady with white hair and thick glasses puttered around the cluttered room, sorting mail, stuffing it in the boxes. I coughed, but she didn't hear me.

"Excuse me, ma'am," I said, waving my claim.

"Oh, sorry, son, didn't see ya there."

With bony, liver-spotted fingers, she took the slip, then disappeared into an opened closet. I heard shuffling of paper for a time before she emerged with a brown manila envelope.

"We've had this a while," she said, more like a question than a statement of fact.

"I forgot all about it," I said. "Hope it wasn't an inconvenience."

Once again, I held my breath, reaching for the envelope. Before I read the label, she smiled, spoke softly, "Congratulations."

It was from Mesa College. At the bottom, it read in bold, darkened caps, "Please do not fold, spindle or staple—diploma enclosed."

I'd gone through Mesa's graduation ceremony in June, receiving an empty black diploma cover. The dean explained they had to make sure none of us new, upstanding graduates had stiffed the college on any bills or flunked any courses our last semester. I was still disappointed to have gone through that dog-and-pony show for nothing but pomp and circumstance. Looking at that envelope, realizing I finally had that diploma in my hand, I wished for someone to celebrate with.

Someone like Laura.

I left the post office and ambled toward my trailer a hundred yards away at the rear of the park. I kept my head down, studying my mail. If I ran into anyone, I planned to ignore them.

Reaching my place without seeing anyone, I looked over my Jeep, a green '58 Willys CJ-5 with a black canvas top. No slashed tires, no notes on the windshield. Everything looked in order.

I walked up the steps to the porch and opened the screen door. A small, folded piece of paper fluttered to the deck.

Shit.

I gathered the note, glanced furtively in both directions, and unlocked the door. I slipped inside the tiny trailer, cold and musky from my long absence. I locked and bolted the door behind me, took a deep breath, then read the note.

It was from Laura.

> *Slim,*
> *Where are you? Been looking for you every day. Gotta talk.*
> *I'll keep trying to find you.*
> *L.*
> *P.S. Don't come to Aspen*

Oh, Goddamn, now what?

My heart raced, my mind spun. I must have reread Laura's note ten times, always coming to the same conclusion: Tucker had figured out I ripped him off. I sat, thinking things through. Maybe his knowing wouldn't affect my plans that much, anyway. He was going to find out sooner or later. I only worried about Laura, didn't want her getting in the middle. Tucker didn't love her.

Then I gasped, realizing the danger I'd put Laura in if Tucker knew who I was. Tucker would throw her to the wolves to catch me, get his stuff back.

I took a deep breath. I wasn't going to lose my nerve now, not after everything I'd already been through. Had to keep busy, shove panic away.

Flying to Basalt, I'd made a mental to-do list. The first order of business was to stash the dope again and most of the money. Sure as hell couldn't keep it in my cracker box of a trailer. I had a place in mind a few miles up Woody Creek.

I left the trailer and went to start my Jeep. Dead as a doornail. Figured. Hadn't run it in over a month.

How the hell to get my rig going?

I had a charger, but that would take several hours before the battery was strong enough to crank the engine. I was in a hurry, didn't want to burn daylight. If I left now, I had enough time to drive up into the forest, stash my contraband. But I needed to find another truck to jump my Jeep.

Maybe I could catch someone coming or going from the general store or post office. Then I remembered the trailer park maintenance man, Juan. Hell, yes, he'd give me a jump.

I slung my pack over one shoulder, walked to Juan's little trailer, as small as mine, on the south end of the park.

I'd met Juan a couple of times since I'd moved into my trailer back in June. First, when he walked me through the place, checking the boxes off on a rental agreement, verifying the plumbing and heating were in good order, the refrigerator worked, the place was clean.

In Juan's broken English, I barely understood his instructions, but nodded knowingly, figuring I could make sense of everything on my own.

Our second meeting came when I couldn't figure everything out on my own, like lighting the pilot to the little furnace when we got a freak snowstorm in late July.

"Joo gotta learn dis for jourself, man," he gently scolded.

Juan perked up when I tried my three years of high school Spanish on him. "*Muchas gracias. ¿Tu quieres una cerveza?*"

We split a six-pack, laughing off the July snow as the furnace strained to heat my trailer. Between his crummy English and my half-ass Spanish, we had a hell of a good chat.

Somewhere around thirty, he'd been working in Colorado for a couple of years, saving money to bring his family up from his hometown in Chihuahua. Whether or not he was in the U.S. legally was open to question. One way or the other, I didn't give a shit, just hoped our fellowship from that snowy day in July would get me a jump.

Nearing Juan's trailer, I heard country music drifting from the workbench built off one side of his place. In the afternoon sunlight, he worked on a small engine, probably for a lawn mower. When he saw me coming, he grinned, exposing a gold front tooth, and shouted over the radio, "*Hey, amigo, qué pasa?*"

"*Nada mucho, Juan.*"

Before I could remember how to ask for help, he laughed, peeked in both directions. "Hey, there's a beautiful woman been lookin' for joo." He laughed again, then feigned a serious look, shaking his finger at me. In a deep voice, he asked, "Where joo been?"

"*Norte,*" I said, pointing toward Wyoming. "When was she here last?"

Juan looked confused, then nodded. "Toodaay."

"Shit!"

"*Sí,* joo need to find her."

I glanced toward his truck parked in the carport built off the other side of his trailer. "I need a jump," I said slowly, squeezing imaginary alligator clips in my hands.

He studied me, cocked his head to the side. "*No comprendo.*"

I pointed toward the truck, twisted an invisible key in my hand, and made the sound of an engine barely turning over.

"*Oh, oh, sí,*" he said. "*Batería muerta.*"

I nodded at the late model Ford. I assumed it belonged to the trailer park, hoped it was okay for him to help me with the company vehicle. "Can you give me a jump, ah—*puente de batería?*"

He wiped his hands on a rag, "*Sí, por qué no?*"

I pointed toward my trailer and turned to walk away, when Juan spoke again in a hushed voice. "Been some other hombres looking for joo."

Shit. Tucker's guys.

Behind me I heard Juan start his truck, then I rounded a curve in the trailer park road, and looked down the way toward my place.

Laura's red Volkswagen Beetle was parked next to my Jeep.

She jumped from the driver's seat and ran my way.

Chapter Twenty-Five

Sprinting toward Laura, I saw she'd shortened her shoulder-length hair to a pixie cut. And she had a half-cast on her right arm. I slowed as I neared her, unsure of myself, uncertain how to greet her. She didn't pause, though, nearly knocked me over in her embrace.

"Where have you been?" she sobbed. "Everything's crazy."

I held her, felt her heavy breathing, and sensed her terror.

I heard Juan's truck, glanced over my shoulder, and shook my head. He nodded, backed away.

I looked at Laura. "What's this?" Beneath one of her teary eyes was a faded black band. I held her close again, kissed her head.

"He did this to me, went nuts," she said, fighting for her breath.

I thought she might faint. I glanced around, saw no one. "Let's get in the trailer, Laura."

"No! It's not safe, we gotta go, we gotta go now, he knows everything, he'll kill us both."

I held onto Laura's arms, studying her. Her eyes darted about, like a beautiful wild animal caught in a trap. Right off, I saw she'd lost weight. Her face was gaunt. Her jeans hung loose around her waist and her arms were thin and toneless. Was she stoned?

"Come inside," I said, trying to stay calm for both of us. I wasn't going anywhere until I learned what had happened to her. But I was already grateful I'd left the peak early. Looking at Laura, I knew she wouldn't have made it to the New Year.

I led her into my place, locked and bolted the door behind us, mostly for show, then I slipped off that damn pack that had become my albatross. "Sorry about the mess," I said, glancing around my cluttered digs, "Just got home." I walked her to the couch and sat next to her.

"I know, you fool," Laura whispered. "I've been looking for you every day since—" She paused, cried inconsolably.

Nothing ever disturbed me more than a woman crying, always had a tough time with it, always wanted to do something to make things better, right now. But some inner voice, maybe just experience, told me to keep quiet, let her have her cry, let her get it out.

"He knows you ripped him off, so he beat me, broke my arm, gave me to his friends—they hurt me." She buried her head against my chest, cried again.

My heart sank. I bowed my head, felt like I'd been shot in the stomach. What had I done? What to tell her? Sure as hell couldn't say everything I'd done was for her. What a damned mess I'd made of everything. A broken angel crying in my arms.

I thought she might sleep, but after a few minutes she took a deep breath, raised her head, and rubbed her eyes. "We've got to go. He's looking for us, him and his friends."

"When did this happen?" I asked. "Where've you been staying?"

"Last week," she said, her voice soft and quiet. "One of his friends is a cop. I think he helped Tom figure things out."

She didn't need to tell me everything right away. I didn't press her. She could take all night to tell her story.

But she went on, "After his friends were done with me, they left me tied up at his place. I managed to get loose when they left the house."

I lightly touched her cast. "You go to a doctor?"

"Aspen Valley. They put the cast on, wanted to call the cops, make a report. I slipped out of there, thought he might come looking for me. Been staying with some of the other waitresses from *La Cocina*, just hiding all day. I spent the last couple of nights in my car. I didn't want any of the girls getting hurt."

"Why didn't you go home?" Her mother and big sister lived in Delta, around a hundred miles away.

"I couldn't leave. I had to find you, make sure you didn't get blindsided."

"He really broke your arm?" I winced and bit my lip.

"Cracked my wrist. Hurt really bad, and I told him."

"Told him?"

"Said he'd kill me if I didn't tell him who you were." She gazed into my eyes, "Will you forgive me?"

I squeezed her against my chest, chuckled lightly. "Forgive you?" I asked incredulously. "Nothing to forgive you for. Thank God you told him." A lump grew in my throat, my eyes watered. I wanted to be strong for her, but now I wept. "I hope someday you'll forgive me."

"I'm so tired—so tired—got to sleep."

I rose, cradled her in my arms and carried her into the bedroom. Laying her on the bed, I pulled off her cowboy boots, helped her out of her jeans. The trailer hadn't warmed up much yet, so I grabbed a sleeping bag from the closet, got her zipped up in it, put a pillow under her head.

"Sleep, baby," I whispered into her ear. "I'll be in the other room. Nothing else is gonna happen to you. Just sleep."

I closed the bedroom curtains on the setting sun and eased the door shut. I went to the closet off the living room and fetched the Old Man's Winchester Model 12, hidden within the sleeve of a coat in its canvas breakdown case. I pulled out the gun, took it to the kitchen table. I removed the plug required for duck hunting that limited the magazine capacity to two shells.

There were no restrictions for shooting a snake.

I assembled the pump shotgun, scrounged through a few half-empty boxes of shells and came up with a handful of 2-shot, meant for geese. Not a bad load for a man, either, especially in the confines of a trailer park. Wouldn't have to worry about piercing the walls of another trailer, hurting an innocent person.

I loaded four rounds in the magazine. Shucked one in the chamber, loaded one more in the magazine. Left the safety on.

Please come to me, Tom Tucker. Your friends are welcome, too. Save me the trouble of hunting you down. I'll wait all night. Come whenever you want.

Chapter Twenty-Six

For the first few hours after Laura came, I had a hell of a time concentrating on anything but wondering when Tucker and his boys would come looking for her and me. I paced the trailer, carrying my shotgun and looking out the window for any sign of trouble.

A tense moment happened when a Chevy Blazer stopped in front of my place, a little after dark. Peering through a slit in the front window curtains, I saw a man in the passenger seat looking at my trailer. Could have been some of Tucker's friends or maybe just guys lost in the park.

Otherwise, I spent a long night trying to slow my spinning mind riddled with unanswered questions. Was Laura still on drugs? Could I get her the help she needed? Could she recover? Stay clean? Was there a future for us?

I tried to shove away my dread, puttering around the trailer. I straightened up the place, swept away weeks of dust, tidied up the kitchen, and cleaned out the refrigerator. I removed Tucker's cash from my rucksack and hid it in the crawl space of the trailer. With my identity revealed, I gladly shaved off my scratchy beard. I went out to Laura's Beetle, packed all her clothes, books, purse, everything else in a suitcase I found in the front trunk. Brought it all inside.

Every once in a while, I cracked my bedroom door to check on her. She slept through the night, only waking once, when I heard her rise to use the bathroom. I was already figuring out how to get her home to her family in Delta. Before I went for Tucker, I wanted her safe, away from the mess I'd made.

When sunrise finally came, I knew the son of a bitch wasn't coming. At least, not for now. I turned my thoughts to resupplying the trailer.

I didn't have any fresh food or anything else to make life easier for the next few days. I made a list: milk, eggs, bacon, bread, peanut butter, coffee, soap, shampoo. The general store stocked everything I needed, but I wasn't leaving Laura alone for one minute.

Around seven thirty a.m., I heard some kids playing outdoors, waiting for the school bus. I stepped outside, waved to a young boy, maybe ten or twelve. He looked my way warily, like he'd had that lecture from his parents, the one about not talking to strangers.

Finally, he came over with a couple of his pals. Safety in numbers.

"Hey, buddy," I said, "how'd you like to make ten bucks?"

His friends perked up, but he frowned. "Whad'I gotta do?" he asked in a suspicious tone.

I took the list from my pocket, pulled out my wallet. "Take this to the store, give it to the lady, pay for it, and bring everything back to me. Think you can handle that?"

"Yeah."

I gave him the list and plenty of money. "Hurry up, partner, don't miss your bus."

The boys turned, ran to the store.

Fifteen minutes later, they were ten dollars richer, and I had a cardboard box full of food and supplies. Laura still slept, but I hoped some good smells from the kitchen might perk her up.

I was in a fix. She needed rest, but I wanted to get that rucksack out of my place, especially considering a dirty cop was involved.

I made coffee, fried bacon, toasted bread. I laughed lightly when I heard her rise and open the bedroom door.

"That's not fair, Slim," she said, walking into the kitchen, wearing my bathrobe. She already looked better, but I knew she'd been through hell. It would take a long, long time to make things right. Still, her cheeks were more pink than ashen, and her dark brown eyes were clear, no longer bloodshot.

"Little darlin', sleep okay?"

She yawned, stretched her arms. "Good, you get any?"

"Yeah, a little," I lied.

"Hey, no more Grizzly Adams," she said, pointing toward my clean-shaven face. Then her smile faded when she noticed my shotgun resting by the door. "Anything happen last night?"

"I don't think so," I said. "Somebody came by after dark, a white Blazer. Ring any bells?"

She frowned, shook her head. "No."

"You want a shower before breakfast? I got some soap, shampoo or you can eat first." I pointed toward her suitcase next to the couch. "I brought in your stuff last night."

"I think I'll eat first, I'm starved."

I poured her coffee, scrambled half a dozen eggs for us. Waiting on her breakfast, she walked over to the little kitchen table, pored through my mail. "Look at this—Joe College." She waved the manila envelope from Mesa.

I didn't make a big deal of it. "Just a piece of paper."

"Yeah, right," she scoffed, opening the envelope. "Bachelor of Arts, English."

I walked behind her and looked at my degree. "It ought to have your name on it, too," I said. "Wouldn't have finished if it hadn't been for you." True. I'd almost dropped out when the Old Man died in the middle of my junior year. Laura talked me into staying in school. I no longer had any living kin. She said we should get married, she'd be my family. But that sort of commitment scared the hell out of me. Was it the mistake of my life?

We ate breakfast. She must have noticed my concerned interest in her appetite.

"I know, I know," she said, "I'm a wreck. I want to get better. I can straighten out, now, getting away from—him."

"Laura, I gotta ask—are you still on—"

"I haven't had any coke since he beat me, gave me to his friends," she said. "Last night was the first real sleep I've had since—I need to rest. I knew you'd take care of me."

I had a lot of other questions, but I figured they'd wait. Laura didn't need to be interrogated after the hell she'd been through.

"I want to get you away from here, Laura." I reached across the table and held her hand. "I'll take you home, back to Delta."

"Don't you want me here?" She put her fork down, lowered her head.

"I want to keep you safe—"

"What makes you think I'd be safe back home?" She looked at me, pleaded, "I feel safe with you, besides, I don't want that bastard coming anywhere near my big sister or my mother."

"Well, this trailer park's a pretty secure place," I shrugged. "Be awful bold of him or his friends to come around, with all the eyes and ears around here." I said that only to reassure her. I had no illusions about Tucker's ruthlessness when his money and drugs were concerned. That reminded me about the rucksack full of cocaine. "Feel up to getting around a little today?"

She looked around my trailer with no TV, no phone, just a bunch of books and gear piled about, and asked, "Leave all this?"

I laughed. "We need to run a few errands, go to Glenwood Springs and get some stuff."

"We'll be okay leaving?" she asked.

"Yeah, just for a while," I said, with false conviction. I figured Tucker's people watched all the time, but as long as we stayed on the beaten path I didn't think they'd risk coming after us or breaking into the trailer in broad daylight.

An hour later Laura and I ran down Juan for that jump, then we hit the road in my Jeep, a sack of dirty laundry in the back along with my pack full of contraband. I'd given up the idea of burying the shit up Woody Creek. With winter coming on, the road to my hidey-hole might get snowed under. I needed to be able to retrieve the stuff at will, once I set my trap.

After Laura, my '58 Willys was the second love of my life. Built the same year I was born, it was the only car I'd ever owned. Bought and paid for from all my summer earnings, mowing lawns, painting houses, dishwashing for the grill at the local drugstore. The Old Man found it for me, overhauled by a mechanic he knew. I learned how to maintain the rig, taking vo-tech classes in high school. I didn't fancy myself a great mechanic, but I knew that Jeep inside and out.

We didn't try to talk much over my noisy ride, just soaked in another clear fall day. Laura covered herself with the wool blanket I kept in the back and slept all thirty miles. On the north end of Glenwood Springs, I pulled into a coin-op laundry, leaving the Jeep running. When Laura drowsily opened her eyes, I told her to hang tight.

I ran inside, stuffed all our clothes into three machines. Didn't sort colors, underwear, socks, any of that bullshit, just set all three washers on "permanent press," poured a little box of Tide in each and the requisite quarters.

Next stop was Bill's Sporting Goods. I needed another pistol. Not like the popgun I'd given Wilbur, a big one. Once again, I left Laura in the Jeep, not wanting to scare her. I kept an eye on her through the shop window. I made a beeline to the gun counter and found what I was looking for. Five minutes later, I was the proud owner of a brand new Smith & Wesson Model 19 .357 Magnum.

I drove on to the train station along I-70. Laura raised her eyebrows, panicked a little. "You trying to get rid of me?"

"Nope, but you got to come in with me on this one."

I locked the pistol in the storage compartment under the passenger seat, retrieved my pack from the back. We walked through the station terminal, holding hands like a sad couple about to part. At the end of the long, narrow building, I found a bank of rental storage lockers. A month for four dollars. I shoved my rucksack into one, fed coins into the slot, closed the door, turned the key. Two minutes later we were driving to the grocery store.

I took Laura inside on this stop, too. We raced up and down every aisle, throwing food and supplies in our cart like a couple in one of those shopping contests. Half an hour later I was out two hundred dollars, and the back of my Jeep was half full of brown paper bags. We were just about done, I thought.

We'd reached the northern edge of town, and turned around, heading back south. Driving over the Colorado River, we passed Glenwood Hot Springs with their sulfurous stench and came to the heart of the little city. Laura pointed toward the storefront.

"Would you take me there?"

"Which store?" I asked, double-clutching down into first gear.

"The beauty salon."

"Sure."

I got lucky and pulled into a parking spot in front of the shop. Laura looked into my rearview mirror, ran her fingers through her hair.

"I did this myself," she said, studying her work.

"Really?" I didn't know a damned thing about women's haircuts. I had thought her hair looked a little uneven, but figured that must be the style.

With little expression, she turned my way. "I cut it right after I escaped from Tom's house, after his friends—"

"You don't have to say anything else," I said, holding her hand.

"I want to."

"Okay."

"When they were done with me, I felt so dirty. After I left the hospital, I went to a friend's house. I must have spent an hour in the shower, even after the hot water ran out."

I stared into Laura's eyes. If she could go through this ordeal, I could sure as hell listen, as painful as it was. I knew then she'd need a lot more help than I could give her. But I'd be her bridge.

"I scrubbed myself 'til I was raw, cut all my hair—"

I pointed toward the shop. A sign hung over the sidewalk, "Kitty's." "Let's go inside, they'll fix you up." I didn't know if I should say this, but I did anyway, "You look great with short hair. You've got the face to pull it off."

She smiled. "Let's go, then."

We entered the shop to the familiar smells of peroxide and ammonia. The little parlor was staffed by an older lady, probably the owner-operator, and a girl around Laura's age. The young gal gave a customer a shampoo in one sink, while the owner used a blow dryer on another woman's new "do."

Laura sat by the front window, grabbed a magazine, and waited her turn. I walked to the back of the shop, under the guise of using the bathroom and nodded at the manager. I motioned for her to follow me.

Slipping through a curtain of beads, I whispered to the beautician, "You see that young lady sitting in the waiting area?"

The woman, a redhead around sixty with an open, friendly face, pulled the curtains apart, studied Laura for a moment, turned toward me. "Yes, son, pretty girl."

"Well, she's had a tough time of it the last few months," I said. "She needs some TLC today."

"I hope you're not the rotten egg that hurt her."

"No ma'am, I'm trying to be the good guy."

The redhead peeked again at Laura, looked at me. "What'd you have in mind?"

"The works, haircut, manicure, pedicure, you name it."

"Well, we're not too busy right now. I have to set Shirley and put her under the dryer." She glanced at a pink neon clock on the wall. "My helper needs a lunch break, though."

"How about I order a couple of pizzas?"

"Are you serious?"

"Yes, ma'am."

"This might be kinda fun," she said, "but it'll cost a pretty penny. Can you afford it?"

I handed her a fifty. "That ought to get you started."

"What's your friend's name?" she asked.

"Laura. And I bet you're Kitty."

"That's right, son, and what's your name?"

"Just call me Dillon, Kitty."

Chapter Twenty-Seven

Two hours later, we motored south toward the laundromat. I couldn't keep my eyes off Laura. Some short hairstyles seemed harsh to me, but Kitty had given Laura a soft, feminine look. Her dark-brown hair was parted on the side, swept back, and tapered gently in the neck. It highlighted her big brown eyes and high cheekbones. Once, when we waited at a stoplight, Laura laughed, glanced my way, nodded ahead. "It's not gonna get any greener." She could be a real smart-ass.

We'd had only one bad moment at the beauty parlor. After the young assistant gave Laura a shampoo, Kitty took over, seating Laura in a padded chair facing a large mirror. As Kitty combed out her wet hair, tears came to Laura's eyes, starting down her cheeks in two big drops. I put down a dog-eared, year-old issue of *Sports Illustrated* and rose from my chair. I pulled up short when Kitty looked my way, smiled, then gestured for me to stay put. She stepped around the chair, whispered in Laura's ear, and got a small laugh. Laura remained smiling for the rest of the appointment.

I had fun, alternately watching the two beauticians dote on Laura and reading about the latest styles and how to manage men in *Mademoiselle*, *Vogue*, *McCall's*. We ate pizza, listened to the Rolling Stones, Def Leppard, AC/DC. I figured the young assistant chose the music.

Leaving the beauty parlor, Kitty pulled me aside, nodded toward Laura, who had already stepped outside. "You take care of that girl, son, she's a keeper."

When we reached the laundromat, Laura held out her hand, asked for my quarters. "I've seen how you do laundry before," she said. "Let me sort our clothes into the dryer." I pointed toward the washing machines I'd used, and five minutes later we were back on the road.

By now it was mid-afternoon, and Laura was running out of steam, her face slack with fatigue. Still, I had one more stop, at least as important as any of the others we'd made. I needed a helper. I hadn't slept in two days. Nor could I leave the trailer, even to check mail, buy stuff at the general store, or jog, for fear of leaving Laura alone and unprotected.

A few miles south of Glenwood Springs we took a county road east, pulled up to an open gate in a fenced compound, drove under an overhead sign, GARFIELD COUNTY HUMANE SOCIETY.

"What's going on?" asked Laura.

"We're about to get a new employee," I said. "Did I ever tell you there're two kinds of dogs—"

"Yeah, yeah," interrupted Laura, spoiling my joke, "family members and employees."

We sounded like an old married couple, her finishing my sentences.

"Okay, well, how 'bout this one, all dogs fit into one of two groups—"

"Workers and eaters," she blurted. "But, seriously, what are we doing here?"

I parked in front of the one-story, cinder-block shelter and turned toward Laura. "Trust me on this one."

We left the Jeep and walked to the front door, serenaded by a choir of barking dogs. I followed Laura inside, stopped at an office off the side of the narrow hallway. Two employees rose from behind their desks, an enormous man, maybe thirty years old, with "Archie" embroidered on his shirt, and a tiny woman, "Betty," probably close to seventy. In a cavernous voice, Archie asked, "What can we do for you today?"

"We're looking for a dog."

"Well, you came to the right place," he answered.

Betty asked, "Puppy or adult?"

"Definitely an adult dog." I needed help right now, not in a year or two. The two employees smiled, perked up. I knew adults were harder to place than puppies.

"Family dog, house dog, outside dog, what are you looking for?" asked Archie.

"We live in a little trailer park," I explained. "We're a short walk from a nice creek bottom where we can exercise the dog, but it'll be staying in a trailer." I paused while Archie rubbed his chin in thought. I added, "We'd like something pretty big, provide us with some security."

"Uh-huh. You all have any children?"

"No," I said, while I snuck a peek at Laura, "not yet." She blushed, studying her newly painted nails.

Archie came out of the office, with Betty in tow. He stood a full head higher than me, and looked about twice as wide. He considered our needs for a minute. "We have around forty dogs here, right now, but I'm thinking about three or four that might work for you."

Betty was bursting at the seams to go in the kennel, pacing and fidgeting. Finally, she said, "Let's go look at some dogs, for heaven's sake."

When Laura and I entered the double doors of the pound, every canine in the joint came in from the outside, stood on hind legs to inspect us. My ears rang from all the barking. The place was clean, though, didn't stink at all, just smelled like, well, dog. We walked down a long concrete walkway, bordered on both sides by chain-link fencing, partitioned into little kennels, each with its own door.

The first kennel held a beagle. Laura dropped to her knees, rubbed the little hound's face through the fencing with her left hand. "Oh my, what a sweetie you are," she said, then turned to me, "How 'bout this one?"

Over the beagle's baying, completely out of proportion to its size, I said, "Gee, I was hoping for something a little larger. Let's keep looking."

"We won't have any problem finding a home for her, miss," Archie said. "Everybody loves a beagle."

Slowly, we worked our way down the kennel, Laura stopping to admire each inmate. The problem was she wanted every one of them, but I hadn't seen any prospects that suited me yet.

Halfway through the tour, we came to our first real candidate, an eighty-pound hound, probably plot and redbone. "Now, here's a good one." said Betty. "We call him Ol' Blue." Laura was a sucker for his sad eyes and wrinkled face, but I was worried he might be too friendly to strangers. We kept looking.

Our next candidate was a collie. "Here's one of the dogs I was thinking about," said Archie. "It's just about the smartest animal in the place right now, sweet as can be, very gentle, make a great pet."

Laura liked it, asked, "What's his name?"

"Well, it's a *her*, miss," he chuckled, "and her name's Suzie."

We made a mental note, walked on.

All the dogs in the kennel barked sporadically during our tour, but one voice stood out in its urgency, ferocity. I recognized the source of the howling when we came to the kennel of an enormous black dog with a head as big as a bear's. I guessed it was a cross between a Labrador and a Newfoundland.

"Good lord, Slim," gasped Laura, "He's bigger than I am." She knelt against the wire, gazed into the beast's coal-black eyes.

Betty said, "Oh, that's Jaws—"

"You mean Duke," Archie gently scolded. "I wasn't thinking of him for you folks, he's been in a little trouble."

That piqued my curiosity. "What'd he do?"

"Jaws—um—Duke, was abandoned in someone's backyard, he may have been abused, too," explained the man. "He treed two control officers who tried to rescue him. We had to tranquilize him to get him here. Anyway, he's very aggressive."

Near the end of the row, we came to the prettiest dog in the place, a medium-size German shepherd. "Here's a dog that might really work for you," said Archie, "his name is Oscar. He's smart, trainable—"

"Oh, he's my favorite," gushed Betty. "He might have a loud bark, but he wouldn't bite a soul. He'd be a great companion, be good with kids someday."

"He sure is handsome," said Laura, patting his head.

"But he's got so much more going for him than just his looks," said Betty. "He's loyal, intelligent…he's just the bee's knees."

"Yeah, he fills the bill, folks," said Archie. "This is the one you want."

Having seen all the dogs, Betty pointed toward the office. "Let's go back if you folks are ready."

"Sure," I said, then stepped out of their hearing and spoke quietly to Laura.

When we reached the office, Archie and Betty were all smiles. "Let's do the paperwork for Oscar," said Archie.

"No," said Laura, "we want Jaws."

Archie walked close to me, said in a low voice, "I hope you're not biting off more than you can chew. He's definitely not for the casual owner."

The same sentiment had crossed my mind. Laura ran to Jaws's kennel, stuck her face near his. "We're gonna be best friends, boy. I'll take real good care of you." Jaws licked Laura's nose through his cage, a friendly grin spreading from ear to ear.

Watching her reassure the monster buoyed my confidence. "I think this is gonna work out," I said to Archie, "besides, I've never done anything casually in my life."

We had a hell of a time fitting Jaws into the back of my Jeep, with all our other stuff crammed back there. Laura maintained constant surveillance, keeping him out of our groceries. I fetched our dry laundry, and we headed back to Woody Creek. Watching Jaws and Laura, I wondered, could they help heal each other?

Chapter Twenty-Eight

Nearing Woody Creek, I noticed low-hanging clouds up the valley toward Aspen. The temperature had dipped below freezing, forming frost on the windshield. I'd lived in the valley long enough to know Indian summer was over. Snow was on the way.

Pulling up to the trailer, I helped Laura tie a length of rope to Jaws's collar. While she took him behind the place to heed nature's call, I unloaded our groceries and supplies. Inside the trailer, I unpacked my new revolver, loaded it with Remington Kleanbore ammunition, then hid it inside my boot. Stepping outside to check on my two new roommates, I saw Juan walking down the road.

He must have felt winter coming on, too. He looked cool as hell in a wool poncho, like the ones the badmen wore in spaghetti westerns. He nodded with a grin that faded to a worried look. "Been someone looking for joo, amigo. Same men."

"Oh, is that so?"

"*Sí*, two men."

"You talk to them?"

"No, they just drive around, stop, look for a while."

"*¿Carro blanco?*"

"*Sí, Sí.*"

"Shit."

"I keep lookout, amigo, *buenas noches.*" Juan headed back to his trailer.

When I turned around, Laura stood by the door, holding on to Jaws.

"What'd Juan want?" she asked.

I'd always tried to be straight with Laura, didn't like to bullshit her. But I didn't want to scare her either. Before I could think of what to say, she said, "I heard something about a white car."

"Yeah, sounds like that white Blazer might have come around today."

"No one's gonna mess with us," she said, patting her new bodyguard's head.

I was glad Jaws gave Laura confidence, but I didn't overestimate his utility. He was only a first line of defense, an early warning system. While intimidating and dangerous, he could still be taken out with a poisoned steak or a gun.

I followed them inside, glancing in both directions before I locked and bolted the door. I made a pallet on the floor next to my bed for the dog, found a bowl for water, another for his food. The pound had given us enough for a few meals. I planned to buy a fifty-pound bag in the next couple of days. While Laura played with Jaws, I made his supper, a bowl of dry chow sweetened with an egg and warm water. I'd get his dull, dingy coat shining like a jaguar.

"Laura," I called, "you should always feed him. You'll bond faster that way." I pointed toward the linoleum floor in the kitchen corner. "Let's feed him here, keep his water here, too."

She took the bowl, Jaws right behind her. When she placed it on the floor, he pounced on it, like a wolf on a kill. Laura stepped back, watched in awe.

"You think that's why they named him Jaws?"

"Nope."

"What do you think?" she asked, as the dog inhaled the last bit of his food.

"I think they called him Jaws because he took a hunk out of somebody's ass—like the shark in the movie."

We both laughed.

Then I saw a white Blazer pull up to the front of the trailer.

"Why don't you take him into the bedroom?" I said, amusement jumping into alarm.

"Wait a minute," said Laura. "That's the car that's been coming around here, isn't it?"

I ignored her question for a moment, watching the driver boldly park behind my Jeep, blocking my exit.

I heard a low, guttural growl behind me. Jaws sensed our tension.

"Laura," I said, with an edge, "you need to go the bedroom, take the dog."

She peered over the front window curtain, shaking her head. "I think I've seen them before."

The Blazer idled off the road, thirty feet away. Both men stayed inside. I placed my arm around Laura's shoulder, led her into the bedroom. Jaws followed.

"I won't be long," I said, then closed the bedroom door.

By now, I'd seen a lot of action, running across Wyoming and Colorado. I didn't panic, wasn't scared, thought calmly. The dope was stashed in the train station locker and the money concealed between the floor joists of the trailer. I pulled the revolver from my boot, stuck it in the front of my pants, put on my down jacket.

Stepping outside, I walked slowly to the Blazer, using the Jeep to screen myself. A man with a narrow, pockmarked face rolled down the passenger window. His eyes were beady and wicked, like a rat's. He had long sideburns and wore his hair in a ponytail.

"So you're the guy started all the trouble," he said, then nodded toward my trailer. "Where's Laura? We'll take her off your hands, if she's too much for you to handle."

I flexed my knees, ready to duck if he pulled a gun. I couldn't see the driver, but heard him laugh. I unzipped my coat, revealing the pistol stuck in my jeans.

"Now you see it, now you don't." I covered the revolver with my coat. "But you know it's there."

The man's eyes widened, like he wasn't armed himself, or at least didn't expect trouble. I heard a second voice, the driver, speak lowly, "Let's get the fuck out of here." I eased ahead, peering into the Blazer. The driver was a big man, with a bushy beard, lots of hair, huge hands wrapped around the steering wheel.

"What do you want?" I said, not much louder than a whisper.

"Just checkin' things out, making sure somebody's keeping an eye on Laura," said the man riding shotgun, ol' Rat Face.

I looked up and down the trailer court, saw no one about. I was emboldened by their lack of resolve. In one fluid motion, I slipped around the Jeep, pulled my revolver, stuck it in the taunting man's scarred face.

I cocked the pistol, pressed the muzzle against his jaw. "Open up," I hissed, sticking the barrel into his mouth. The man's eyes crossed, staring down at the pistol in my hand. "How do you like being threatened?"

"Hey, man," said the driver, his hands raised in submission, "we just came here to deliver a message."

"I'm listening." A car approached, one of my neighbors. I lowered the hammer, pulled the pistol from the rat's mouth and raked the front sight of the barrel across his cheek.

"Goddamn," he shrieked, covering his bloody face.

"Tom Tucker wants to meet you," said the driver, his eyes wide and fearful. He handed me a folded piece of paper.

"You've delivered the message, now get the hell out of here and don't come back."

I stepped back quickly, nearly getting my toes run over when the burly driver backed up, then tore away. I made a mental note of the license plate, walked back to the trailer. Laura stared at me through the opened front window, her mouth agape.

I stepped inside, brushed past her, and walked to the kitchen. With shaking hands, I dampened a paper towel with cold water and cleaned the blood off my revolver. I sprayed another towel with a shot of WD-40 and oiled the piece. I heard footsteps behind me, followed by the tapping of toenails on linoleum. I tried to hide my adrenaline crash and relief at avoiding disaster. I wanted to be strong for her.

"You okay?" Laura asked. She placed a hand on my shoulder. "That was crazy."

I turned around, forced a smile, and glanced at my watch.

"Want to go to the general store?" I asked. "Buy a box of dog biscuits?"

"No," she said, flatly. She took my hand, led me toward the couch. "I wanna talk."

I slowed, nodded toward the bedroom. "I bet you're worn out. We overdid it today—"

"No, no," she said, "you're not getting out of this one, not this time. You're gonna sit down with me. I'm worried about you."

You're worried about me?

I guess Laura saw something in me I hadn't been able to see myself, through all the weeks of hitchhiking, running, fear, and violence. I held her with both arms and told her about robbing Tucker. I told her about the Wyoming deputies, running across the prairie to reach the peak by sunrise, getting chased around the mountain by a half-assed lawman until he got himself killed by a lion. How Wilbur and I had slipped through the roadblocks, how L.Q. and I dodged the Highway Patrol after we ran out of gas, flying to Basalt. By the time I was through, the sun had set.

"You did all that for me?" she asked through her tears.

I sat forward, covered my face. "Yeah, that's why I did it." I was afraid to look at her, afraid she'd reveal her contempt for me. "I'm sorry, Laura, I was trying to help you."

"Were you jealous?"

"I was worried."

"Were you jealous?"

"I was worried, scared for you—and jealous."

She leaned against my back, wrapping her arms around me. I felt her cast against my belly. "You wanted to save me. You knew he was a monster, before I did." I felt her warmth, her breath against my neck. "The last few days—it's the first time I've been clearheaded in a long time—look at me, Slim, look at me."

I turned Laura's way, gazed into her pleading eyes.

"You saved me, we've both been hurt, but you still saved me."

We're not out of the woods, yet.

I held her in the dark until she fell asleep in my arms. I carried her into the bedroom, tucked her in. Jaws followed, and when I closed the door, I heard him climb onto the bed. I chuckled. The Old Man would have rolled over in his grave, but he never had to save the woman he loved from Tom Tucker.

Chapter Twenty-Nine

Sometime around midnight, I heard Jaws scratching the bedroom door. I rose from the couch, pulled on my boots, and let him out of the bedroom. We were lucky; he was housebroken. Before I closed the door, I glanced at Laura. She slept peacefully in my sleeping bag.

I put on my stocking cap and jacket and tied a length of cord to Jaws's collar. We stepped outside into ankle-deep snow with more softly falling from the sodden sky. I led him around the trailer to his new favorite tree. He raised a leg, sounding like a racehorse pissing on a flat rock. Then he wagged his ass, prancing, like he wanted to play. I had other plans, though. I dragged him back inside, dried off his paws with a dirty towel, and let him back in the bedroom.

I left the trailer again, locking the door behind me, and moseyed over to the general store.

Enclosed in a wooden box, a pay phone was bolted to the outside of the building, under a neon light. I fed the phone coins, pulled Tucker's note from my pocket, and dialed his number. I breathed deeply, trying to slow my racing heart.

On the second ring, he answered, a liquid voice, deep and Texan.

"Howdy. Tom Tucker here."

"How's your pal doin'," I asked. "I think he shit his pants over at my place today."

"Well, lookee here, 'ppreciate you getting back to me so fast."

Tucker chuckled. "I think you did scare the shit outta ol' Merle. Nasty cut on his face, too."

"That was just a kiss. Improved his looks."

Tucker laughed. "I like it."

"Know what I like about you?" I asked.

"What's that?"

"Nothin'."

"Seems to me, I'm the aggrieved party," said Tucker, calmly, as if asking for a cup of coffee. "You ripped me off, remember?"

"Yeah, I remember," I said. "I remember you crying like a baby, choking on that mace."

"Ah, hell, pard," said Tucker, "kin shouldn't carry on like this."

"Kin?"

"Yeah, we're kinda like husbands-in-law."

I said nothing, but stiffened at the thought of us ever having shared Laura.

"Got you there, didn't I?" he said. "How is the lovely young lady?"

"She's doing better, not that you give a rat's ass."

"Oh, I do, though," he said, "I do."

"You really think she helped me rip you off?"

"Laura?" Tucker scoffed. "Hell, no. She'll snort a rail with yah and suck a cock or three, but she's no thief."

"Why'd you do it then? Beat her, let your boys have their way with her?"

"I didn't do it to hurt Laura, sonny. I did it to hurt you."

Tears stung my eyes, but I fought to hide them and the growing lump in my throat from Tucker.

"Bet that mace didn't hurt near as bad as what I did to Laura. What do you think, pard?"

"I think you're a rotten son of a bitch," I hissed. If Tucker had been in my presence, I would not have spared him as I did Rat Face.

"I've heard that before, too, but how do you see all this ending?"

"Badly—for you."

"I'm not the one runnin', though, am I? Looking over my shoulder every day, worried about the law and Tucker's boys comin' for me and my woman."

"We'll get by."

"I can make this all go away," said Tucker.

"You want your shit back."

"You still got it?"

"Yeah, took real good care of it, too," I said.

"I'll want it back, and more."

"I need a few days," I said. "I want to take care of Laura, clean up your mess."

"Nobody ever said Tom Tucker's an unreasonable man. I'll give you some time. Just don't make me wait too long. I'd hate to have them folks up Wyoming way come lookin' for you."

"I'll call you next week," I said, anxious to be rid of the devil.

"You're gonna sleep with one eye open 'til you do." Tucker laughed, hung up on me.

I walked back to the trailer, numb to the descending blizzard. The snow had already covered my tracks.

Why are there men like Tucker, men who treat others' loved ones like garbage, men who enjoy others' suffering?

Chapter Thirty

I didn't rise until mid-morning. Hadn't slept so long in weeks. Jaws scratched on the bedroom door when he heard me stir. I let him out, careful not to wake Laura. This day, she could sleep as long as she wanted.

I dressed in wool pants and flannel shirt, then retrieved my Sorels from the living room closet. Leading Jaws outside, we walked into a new, bright, perfect world. From the valley floor to the ridges east and west, a mantle of fresh snow buried the country. Overhead, the sun shone in a dazzling blue sky.

Jaws pulled me through knee-deep drifts to the trees behind the trailer. Circling tightly, he glanced my way, self-consciously, as he squatted, begging for privacy. I laughed and turned my back. A minute later he ran past me, nearly pulling the lead from my hands. Cooped up in that cage for God knows how long, he needed exercise. Thinking on plans for the day, I led him back to the trailer.

I kept busy for a couple of hours, going through the gear I had hauled to the peak. I sharpened a couple of knives on the Old Man's Ouachita stone, waterproofed my Vasque boots with Sno-Seal. Then I got real ambitious and paid my bills for the last month, trailer rent, utilities, student loan. Since graduating, I had kept my overhead low, no phone, no TV, no extra bullshit. I had a feeling my expenses were about to rise, caring for Laura and Jaws. Whether Tucker liked it or not, he was going to finance whatever medical help she needed. I scooped up my mail and walked to the post office.

Heading back to the trailer, I ran into Juan. He left little doubt he'd figured out I was in trouble.

"Hey, amigo, lot of bad hombres comin' round here, no?"

"I sure appreciate you keeping an eye out for us."

"*Policia*...they come too."

"*¿Cuando ocurrio?*"

"*Ayer por la mañana.*"

"Shit," I muttered. It sounded like Tucker's crooked cop was keeping an eye on us, too.

I thanked Juan and headed back to the trailer.

When I returned, a little after noon, Laura was still in the bedroom. I decided to check on her. Cracking the door, I heard her crying. I wasn't sure if I should leave her alone or try to help. I decided she'd been on her own enough the last few days.

"Laura," I said softly, "you okay? Can I come in?"

When she didn't answer, I took one step inside. The room was still dark with the shades down. Shortly, my eyes adjusted to the light. She lay on the bed, looking up at the ceiling.

"Laura?"

"What do you want?" she said through her tears, rolling away from me in the sleeping bag.

I stepped closer, then sat on the edge of the bed. When I lightly touched her shoulder, she flinched and cried even harder.

"If you'd just married me, when I wanted, none of this would have happened..."

I bowed my head, not knowing what to say. Her words cut like a knife. I still wasn't sure we should have been married after the Old Man died, me still being in school and her working fifty miles away in Delta. At the time, I wondered if I was bad luck. All my loved ones had died. I didn't want anything to happen to her. I wanted to go it alone for a while. I'd made a mistake. I damned sure shouldn't have given her the cold shoulder after all the support she'd given me.

"Laura, I'm hoping you'll forgive me, someday. If you give me a chance, I'll make it up to you. You'll see." Through the sleeping bag, I softly rubbed her shoulder.

She sniffled, cleared her throat. "But everything that's happened now. What I've done—what they did to me—things will never be the same. You'll never look at me the same way."

She didn't fight me when I gently pulled on her shoulder, rolled her over on her back. I leaned over her, gazed into her eyes. I fought a lump in my throat. "When we get through all this, things aren't gonna be the same, Laura—they're gonna be better. Nothing matters to me, but helping you, being with you." I didn't know what else to say.

"You mean, you still want—"

I pressed my finger against her lips, kissed her forehead. I whispered in her ear, "I want to take care of you. We're gonna get through this together."

Laura slipped partway out of the sleeping bag. She hugged me, cried against my chest.

Earlier in the fall, days before I robbed Tucker, I'd gone to the Pitkin County Library, dug up everything I could find about cocaine. I knew Laura had been using for a couple of months, not much longer, as near as I could figure. I expected her to be tired as hell for a few days, but that damned cocaine monkey would be on her back a lot longer. Now I was wondering how to get her some help beyond my support and love.

I rubbed Laura's right hand, felt her cast. "When do you need to go back in, let 'em take a look at this?"

"Any day, Slim," she said, pausing as she rubbed her forehead. "They told me to come back in ten days. They might be able to put me in a splint."

"That'd be great," I said, "No more wearing a garbage bag to bathe."

"The day after this all happened, I went to Dr. Johnson at the Aspen Valley Hospital. He set my arm, and we talked about what happened to me."

I held Laura, felt her tears come again. "It's okay. You don't have to fight it."

She sobbed a bit, fought through it. "He said they'll test me, when I come in, maybe again in another couple of weeks, see if I have VD."

I remembered robbing Tucker. *I should have used a gun instead of mace.*

"I don't know what I'll do if—"

"You'll take the medicine they give you, get better," I said, trying to reassure her.

"I know, but VD?"

"You didn't do anything wrong, baby—"

"I don't know how I'm gonna pay for all these bills, I'll be waiting tables forever."

"That's the easy part," I said. "Tucker's paying for everything, and then some."

"The money you stole?"

"Damn right."

"I thought you were giving all that stuff back to him."

"I'm giving him back the coke, not the money—"

"He'll never go for that," she said.

Tough shit.

"Where he's headed, they don't let you bring that kind of stuff, anyway," I said.

"Where's that?"

"Jail or hell."

"I bet you're wondering how I ever got mixed up with him."

"I guess so," I said.

"Last spring, around the time you and I quit seeing each other much, he started coming to the restaurant."

My heart sank.

"He'd always talk to me, even if I wasn't waiting his table," Laura said. "He was funny, charming, always told me how pretty I was." She paused, rubbed her eyes. "Slim, after we broke up, I was so blue, didn't have much confidence. It was really exciting to have someone pay attention to me."

I wanted to tell Laura what an idiot I'd been to push her away and not realize then how much she really meant to me. But I bit my tongue, let her go on.

"After a couple of weeks, he asked me out," said Laura. "It was fun. I thought it was cool, seeing an older guy. He had his own house, knew everybody, treated me great. He gave me little gifts and flowers. We went out to eat at nice restaurants and went to movies."

It hurt to hear about another man, especially that son of a bitch Tucker, dating Laura. But I didn't have anyone to blame but myself.

"One night he took me to a party with a bunch of people I didn't know. Everybody was smoking pot. I didn't really want to do it, but felt out of place, so I took a couple of hits." Laura laughed softly. "I hadn't had any since the time you and I smoked some, when I came up to stay with you during Christmas." She poked me in the ribs. "Remember?"

I remembered. I had gotten ahold of a couple of joints from one of my buddies on the cross-country team. I thought it was an odd habit for a runner, but my pal said we'd have a great time. Laura and I got high, went to see *Kentucky Fried Movie* and laughed our asses off. We went back to the little crib I shared with two other guys, both out of town for the holidays. We made love all night, slept in until early afternoon. I woke up with a murderous headache, though, and swore off weed.

"Anyway," said Laura, "sometime later in the evening after we got high, he asked me if I'd ever tried coke." She inhaled deeply, sighed. "Everybody else was doing it. I thought it'd be okay. I trusted him, didn't think he'd let me do anything dangerous."

I already didn't like where this was going. Laura's father was a drunk who died early. She was a prime candidate for addiction.

"Slim, as long as I live, I'll never forget the first time I tried it." She looked away, shook her head. "I loved it, made me feel so good. I think I knew right away I was in trouble."

"But you were happy before you discovered that stuff," I said. "You know you can enjoy life again without it." I didn't want to preach. I wasn't in any position to judge.

"After that first night, he just kept giving me more, Slim." Laura's eyes filled with tears again. "Soon, we stopped going out, doing all the fun stuff."

I took her hand, squeezed it.

"The more I did it, the more I wanted it," she said. "He got mean, made fun of my cravings, made me do things."

Laura's words hurt, but I braced myself and let her talk.

"Oh, Slim, you should see how amazing you feel, breathing the air, seeing the mountains, feeling their vibrations and moods when you're high. It makes everything just so—so—intense. I feel so alive and in tune with nature." Laura paused for a moment, as if to catch her breath from the rapid-fire babbling. Then she must have caught an expression of concern on my face because she instantly changed her tone. "Oh, Slim, I'm so sorry—I didn't mean—I mean, it's wonderful to be with you. I shouldn't be talking about awful things like getting high. I'm just so confused and mixed up. I mean, I'm not confused about being off coke. I'm going to, I'm going to—it's just that sometimes the memories jump back in my head and everything gets all twisted around and mixed up and—" Her eyes filled with tears and she turned away from me.

I hugged her from behind, as if by holding onto her, I could prevent the cocaine from stealing her back.

Did Tucker have a talent for judging likely prospects to hook? Laura had made a mistake, dancing with the devil, but didn't an older guy have some obligation to look out for a young woman, not take advantage of her naïveté? Mark me down for thinking he was a first-class bastard. Bringing him to his knees would make all my running worthwhile.

Chapter Thirty-One

Over the next few days, Jaws and I maintained a constant guard over the trailer. I didn't expect Tucker to back off for a minute, despite his self-proclaimed reasonableness. Laura slept a lot. I jogged in the trailer park, caught up on some correspondence with my college buddies. Afternoons, we jumped in my Jeep and drove up Woody Creek Road, beyond the ranches and trophy homes. I sat on the lowered tailgate, holding Jaws's lead, while Laura drove slowly on the snow-packed gravel road. He loved the exercise and attention, grinning like a possum eating bumblebees. One day we snuck into Basalt, bought dog food, a stiff wire grooming brush, and a stout leather leash.

Laura brushed out Jaws's thick, wavy coat on the porch in the late afternoon sun. She ended up with a pile of hair big enough to stuff a small sofa. Jaws enjoyed Laura's attention, nudging her with a paw if she stopped to visit with me or rest her arm. They were definitely bonding, helping each other keep their minds on good thoughts. Healing.

Friday morning, I had to take Laura into Aspen for her doctor's appointment. As long as we were going up valley, I wanted to see Michael Davis, talk more about that job offer. I rose at first light and walked to the general store. Doc told me he did all his writing in the early morning before rewarding himself with fishing and lunch. I pulled his card from my wallet, gave him a call. I nearly hung up, when he answered, short of breath, on the fifth or sixth ring.

"Hello?" he asked, with a tinge of annoyance. He didn't sound tired, but edgy, like he was on his fifth cup of coffee, smack-dab in the middle of a murder scene.

I lowered my voice, bit my lip to keep from laughing. "Is this Michael Davis, owner of a green '66 Chevrolet pickup?"

"Um, yes, it is."

"Mr. Davis, this is Wildlife Conservation Officer Johnny Dobbs. Good morning, sir."

"Good morning, Officer." Now, he sounded a lot more accommodating.

"Sir, the reason I'm calling is because I received a complaint this week about a man fishing illegally on the Frying Pan River. My informant recorded a license plate number that matches your vehicle."

"Well, Officer, there must be some mistake, I haven't fished that—"

"No, sir, no mistake," I interrupted, "they witnessed you fishing with worms and salmon eggs in the artificial flies-and-lures-only water. What kind of goddamn fisherman are you, anyway?"

I heard nothing on the other end of the line for a few seconds, then he broke into a belly laugh. "Who the hell is this?" he asked.

"Doc, I met you last week, you picked me up hitchhiking—"

"Kid!" he blurted. "I've been wondering if you were ever going to call."

"Yes, sir."

"Find that girl you were looking for?"

"I sure did."

"Your tone—this sounds serious."

"Could be."

"Oh well, like I always say—life is just a series of marriages." I laughed.

"When do I get to meet this young lady? See you again?"

"How 'bout today?" I asked. "We're coming up to Aspen."

"Early afternoon work for you? I'll be going fishing 'til after lunch."

"Perfect," I said.

"Know how to get to my place?"

"Yes, sir." Anybody who'd been up Maroon Creek knew where Doc lived. He owned a damned palace up there. Not huge, but the nicest looking log home you'd ever seen, on a bench above the creek overlooking a vast network of beaver ponds.

"All right, see you all then."

"Thanks, Doc." I hung up, walked back to the trailer.

We left a little after nine. Laura's appointment was at 9:45 a.m., but she was nervous as hell about being late. I smiled her way, assured her we'd get there on time. I understood the real reason she was on edge, waiting to be tested for a host of unspeakable diseases. Jaws rose from the back of the Jeep, butted his head against her shoulder, grinning with his tongue hanging out. The cab filled with dog breath.

Driving up Highway 82, I glanced over at Laura. She looked great, her tomboyish best, dressed in jeans and hiking boots, with a sky-blue wool sweater over a white turtleneck. The last remnants of her shiner were gone, and I still loved that haircut. She wore a pair of plain, gold stud earrings and a simple gold necklace, one I'd given her. That was my favorite part of her outfit.

She was quiet, engrossed in her thoughts, I figured, as she absentmindedly massaged behind Jaws's ears. My instincts told me to hush up, let her be alone for the drive. I turned on the radio to The Marshall Tucker Band's "Heard It In a Love Song." Laura tapped her toe. I guessed she didn't mind a little music.

A few miles south of Woody Creek, we passed Sardy Field, the site of my heist in September. I thought back to the gray, cloudy evening when I'd started everything. How would this crazy cat-and-mouse game turn out?

We crossed the Castle Creek Bridge, reached the west end of

town. We doglegged right, then left at the Hickory House. We drove down Main Street. The base of Aspen Mountain—Ajax—rose to our right. The slopes wouldn't open until Thanksgiving, but a meridian of snow already separated the east- and west-bound lanes of the highway. Not many tourists were in town. But the locals were about, preparing for ski season. We passed the library, Paepcke Park with its little gazebo, and turned left at Mill Street.

Dropping down to an undeveloped area, we crossed the Roaring Fork River and climbed a steep hill, ending at Aspen Valley Hospital. Laura guided me to visitor parking. I killed the Jeep and turned her way.

She shrugged, saying softly, "I hate this place."

"Yeah," I said, "but it's gonna be okay today."

I waited until she left the Jeep before removing my pistol from a small duffel bag in the back and locking it under the passenger's seat. I didn't want Laura to know I was packing the gun wherever we went. Jaws rested under a tarp in the back. He was good about keeping quiet and sleeping when we left him behind on our errands. But I wouldn't want to be the fool who woke him from a nap.

I jogged to catch up with Laura before she entered the lobby. She took my hand and led me through a maze of hallways within the sprawling, one-floor clinic. When we reached Dr. Johnson's office, she checked in, then we took seats in an empty row of chairs.

Only a couple of other people waited, a mother holding a sleeping toddler with rosy cheeks in her arms. I hoped for a short wait so Laura could get this over with. I passed on a pile of outdoor magazines, holding her hand, trying to reassure her.

"Just think, no more knitting needles to scratch your arm," I teased.

Movement behind the desk caught my eye. A middle-aged

man appeared, dressed in a white coat over a blue shirt and red tie. He had gray hair and was deeply tanned. He looked our way, spoke to a receptionist, then disappeared. A few minutes later, a young nurse emerged from the office.

"Hi, Laura," she said, with a big smile, "come on back."

I rose with Laura, hugged her, and watched her walk away.

I noted the time, then nervously flipped through a stack of fishing and backpacking magazines. Mostly looking at the pictures, I was too restless to read. Forty-five minutes later, I left the office and paced the hallway. I came to a kiosk loaded with pamphlets on drug addiction, therapy, relationship counseling. I pulled a few from the display, stuffed them into my coat pocket, and moseyed back to the doctor's office.

When I walked inside, the receptionist smiled, rose from her desk, and came into the waiting room.

"Dr. Johnson would like you to come back to his office."

My pulse quickened. *Why did he want to see me? Was Laura okay?*

She held the door open, then led me past examining rooms with scales, tables, illustrations of human anatomy. At the end of the hallway, we came to an oak door, not quite closed. I thought I heard Laura laughing. The receptionist knocked on the door, then stepped into the office without me. My heart raced, I wanted to know what the hell was going on.

A moment later, she motioned me to enter as she returned to the front desk. I stepped into the office, turned, and saw Laura sitting on a couch against the wall. She smiled, waved her right arm, now wrapped in an Ace bandage. Dr. Johnson was on the phone and motioned for me to take a seat. I sat next to Laura and carefully held her arm.

"I told you."

She hugged me, whispered in my ear, "Things went great. He thinks I'm going to be okay."

I slumped in the couch, breathed a huge sigh of relief. I over-heard Dr. Johnson say goodbye and turned his way when he hung up.

"I wanted a chance to tell you what a fine job you've done, tak-ing care of Laura."

Before I could think of anything to say, he glanced at an open file on his desk.

"She's gained over ten pounds, her morale's a hundred percent better. There are a few other things here I'll let her tell you about."

I said nothing, just smiled, squeezed Laura's hand.

"Before I let you two leave, do you have any questions?"

"Come back in a month?" asked Laura.

"That's right," said Dr. Johnson, rising from his seat. He walked around the desk, led us to the door. "See the receptionist for that appointment."

I followed Laura to the hallway and turned when I felt a hand on my shoulder.

"Laura's going to be fine, son, but she needs a lot of reassur-ance right now. I'm counting on you. Keep helping her."

I nodded and headed for the front desk. I listened to Laura make her next appointment, then interrupted the receptionist when she raised the issue of installments on Laura's medical bills.

"Excuse me, ma'am, but we'd like to take care of that now."

"Yes, sir, like I was explaining to Laura, we can put you on a payment plan—"

"No, ma'am, I want to pay all the bills...now."

She looked a little surprised, raised her eyebrows and smiled. "Credit card, check, or cash?"

"Cash, thank you."

A few minutes later, Tom Tucker was another thousand dollars or so lighter. I waited outside the hospital pharmacy while Laura picked up a couple of odds and ends. Then we escaped the hos-pital.

Stepping outside, we looked at each other and shared the same alarm, hearing a dog bark like hell. We ran around the building to my Jeep, slowing when we saw a man standing next to the open front door, blood dripping from his arm. Jaws stood on his hind legs, his head extending over the passenger's seat, barking, his teeth gleaming in the sunlight.

The man, dressed in a wool sweater and jeans, pulled out his wallet and displayed a badge: DEA. "Goddamnit, get your dog under control!" He grimaced, turned my way, and pointed toward a white Wagoneer parked next to my Jeep.

"Bobby Lee," he barked, "get your ass in there."

Chapter Thirty-Two

"Billy McComb, Sam Cook, Slim Tucker, College Boy, Nick Adams, Jim Pettigrew." Special Agent Clyde Parker, DEA, shook his head, wagging his finger at me. "You've got more damned aliases than Jesse James." He cleaned the blood off his forearm with a handkerchief, revealing two puncture wounds oozing blood. "Now, I'm gonna have to get a fuckin' tetanus shot," he said, a hint of the South in his voice.

"Oh, well," I said, "at least we're already at the hospital." I was scared as hell, but pissed, too. What the hell was he doing, rummaging through my Jeep? Then it occurred to me, he might haul my ass to jail. "I've got a first-aid kit in my vehicle. Want me to patch that up so you don't bleed all over the place?"

"Like you patched up Chance?"

I glanced sharply his way, but said nothing.

"Oh, yeah, Bobby Lee," he said, "I know more about you than you do." He pulled a spiral notebook from his coat pocket and flipped through the pages. "Robert Lee Shelby, born 1958, Roanoke, Virginia, only child of Walter and Martha Shelby. Family moved to Carbondale, Colorado, in 1971. Parents killed in automobile accident, 1972. Raised by maternal grandfather, John Lofland, who died of natural causes in 1977." He closed his notebook. "Want me to go on?"

"No. That's enough." I felt like I'd been stripped naked. I was a private person, had guarded my background, and didn't want everyone to know I was a goddamned orphan.

I studied Agent Parker, measured the man who held my fate in his hands. I guessed his age around forty, taller than me, at least six three, six four, and a hell of a lot heavier. Still had all his dark-brown hair, but graying at the temples. A face like a soldier, craggy, chiseled chin, fierce gray eyes, ironic grin.

"Do you have any idea what a pain in the ass you've been?" He shook his head. "I was this close to pinching Tucker."

I smacked my forehead. "Shit!"

Agent Parker must have seen me rob Tucker and his pal.

No wonder the law had been looking for me.

He pointed toward a bench near the entrance of the hospital where Laura sat with Jaws lying at her feet. "By the way, that sumbitch has been vaccinated for rabies, right?"

"Yes, sir."

"Okay. Where the hell did you go after you ripped off Tucker? That's the only thing I haven't been able to figure out."

"I hitched a ride to Fort Collins, hung out at CSU for a couple of weeks, camped at Horsetooth Reservoir, blended in with the students, even went to a couple of lectures," I said. "I caught another ride to—"

"Rawlins," interrupted Parker. "Then you hitched another ride to Baggs, and we all know what happened after that."

"Yes," I said softly.

"I bet you didn't know that crazy punk who shot the deputies got killed the day before yesterday, did ya?"

"Jesus."

"That's right, Bobby Lee, he's deader than shit, shot to death by a Wyoming Highway Patrolman." Parker chuckled, nodded north. "They don't fuck around up there." He gave me a shit-eating grin. "They're still looking for that hitchhiker—"

"The one who stuck around, stayed with Chance, patched him up," I said.

"That's about the only reason I haven't stuck a boot up your ass." He laughed, startled me with his sudden transformation. "How 'bout that little turd who got himself killed by a lion? I bet you don't know anything about that, either."

I shrugged my shoulders, kept quiet.

"You know what I'm trying to tell you, Bobby Lee?"

No one had called me "Bobby Lee" since elementary school in Virginia. Parker must have really done some digging.

"That I'm in a lot of trouble?"

"Close," said Parker. "What I'm really telling you... your ass is mine."

"What do you want?"

"Same thing you do. Put Tucker away. I'm also cuttin' you some slack for her." He nodded toward Laura, still sitting on the bench, watching us look at her. "Just don't go thinkin' you're the fucking Lone Ranger."

Parker took a binoculars from the dash, studied Laura. "Oh, shit. She's crying." He lowered the glasses. "Go talk to her, tell her you'll be along in a little while, then get your ass back here."

I bailed out of the Wagoneer, ran to Laura.

She rose, held me. "Is he gonna take you away, arrest you?"

She looked scared. Her beautiful face had turned to softness. I didn't want her to lose the confidence she'd gained over the last few days.

"No, sweetie," I said, trying to calm her. "How 'bout we load up Jaws, get you in the Jeep. He said I can leave pretty soon."

"What's he want?"

"Same thing I do."

I put my arm around her shoulder, led her to my Jeep. After I got her in, I took Jaws to the back. Passing the Wagoneer, he stood on his hind legs and lunged at Parker. The only thing separating the agent from another mauling was a pane of glass. I jerked Jaws's lead, lowered the tailgate, and loaded him in.

Returning to the Wagoneer, Parker glared at me, then nodded

toward Jaws. "I don't know who's more dangerous—you or that fuckin' dog."

I had never considered myself dangerous. My look of confusion must have shown.

"I saw the stunt you pulled the other day with that lowlife, Merle Larsen."

I stuck a pistol in his mouth.

I said nothing.

"You know what I'm talking about."

"Have you been watching us this whole time?"

"Pretty much. I'm not here by myself," said Parker. "Now let me ask you a question."

"Okay."

"Just how in the hell were you planning to get Tucker, anyway?"

"He wants me to give him his stuff back," I said. "I was gonna get the Sheriff's Department to bust him. Can't use the police, there's supposed to be a crooked cop—"

"How do you know Tucker doesn't have anyone from the Sheriff's Office on the payroll?" interrupted Parker. He gave me another smirk. "That's right. You'd have been fucked with that plan. Bobby Lee, this ain't Pop Warner, it's the NFL."

Parker rubbed his forearm, bruised and bloody, went on. "So when you give him back the dope and money—"

"He's not getting the money. Neither are you," I said.

"Excuse me?" Parker asked, his voice high and tight.

"I'm keeping it . . . for her," I said, nodding toward Laura. "She's gonna need more help, especially if something happens to me." I pushed it, knowing Parker needed me as much as I needed him.

"Hmm," mused Parker, "and what about the cocaine? You didn't fuck with that, did you? Use any of it, sell any, or whatever?"

"Hell, no," I said. "But I did think about dumping it in the Roaring Fork, getting every goddamned trout in the river high."

"Good thing you didn't do that, you need that shit for bait—Tucker bait, not fish bait."

It sounded like I was still in the game.

"Okay, Bobby Lee, here's the deal. I don't give a shit about the money. I want Tucker." Parker grinned. "I'm a southern boy, too. I want to get the fuck outta here, don't like all this cold and snow, don't like living in that smoggy-ass Denver, either."

I didn't consider myself a Southerner, but if it made us kindred spirits, I'd go along with him.

"I want to get down to Atlanta, maybe Miami. You already cost me one chance to bust Tucker. That would have been my ticket back home. Bobby Lee, you better not fuck up again."

"What do you want me to do?"

"You owe Tucker a phone call, right?"

The son of a bitch has tapped the general store telephone.

"We're gonna set up a meeting."

"Okay, you're gonna have that meeting, all right—on my terms," said Parker.

"What's that mean?"

"Means you're not gonna give him any phone call, you're just gonna find him in town," said Parker. "That way, he won't know it's coming, won't be ready with his stooges."

"What about her?" I asked, pointing my thumb at Laura.

"I'll take care of your girl, she'll be safe."

"You're asking me to trust you—with everything."

"I have to trust you, too, Bobby Lee. Trust that you won't go to the train station in Glenwood Springs, fetch that dope and run."

He knows everything.

"You know why I believe in you, Bobby Lee? Why I'm willing to risk my career, my chance to get the hell out of here, on a kid like you?"

"Why's that?"

"Because you're the only sumbitch I know hates Tucker more than me."

Parker took out his notepad, scribbled a phone number and a list of clubs in town. He tore out the page and handed it to me. "Here's where to look for Tucker. You won't have any problem finding him. Start looking tomorrow. When you do meet him, don't make any promises or plans. Just tell him you want to get his shit to him. Y'all will figure out the details later." Parker studied his arm, glanced toward the hospital. "All right, Bobby Lee, get the fuck outta here, take care of your gal." He shook his head. "I gotta go get my arm fixed."

Chapter Thirty-Three

We left the hospital and headed back to Main Street. Laura asked me a million questions about Parker and what the hell was going on. Between bites of sandwiches we'd brought with us, I explained the deal to her. Her eyes widened as I described the setup. I had considered keeping my mouth shut, not telling her anything. But I owed her the truth.

Somewhere along Main Street, I picked up a cop, tailing me a car or two behind in his red Saab. *Only here would cops use cruisers like that.* I kept tabs on him in my rearview mirror. Might just be a coincidence.

We passed the Hickory House, zigzagged right, then left, neared the Castle Creek Bridge. The Saab still followed, now right on my ass. The city limit loomed, a few hundred yards ahead.

A little past the bridge, along a wide spot in Highway 82, just before the turnoff to Cemetery Lane, the policeman pulled me over with a single blast of his siren.

"Good grief, Slim," said Laura, "now what?"

I dug my driver's license out of my wallet and unclipped the Jeep's registration from the steering wheel column.

More confident now, in my new role as DEA cooperator, I said to Laura, "Don't worry, baby, we're not flying solo anymore." I glanced in my rearview mirror, saw the cop leave his vehicle and walk toward us. I opened my door, ready to get out, like the Old Man had taught me to do.

"Stay in the car, Shelby," the policeman barked.

I closed my door and unzipped the vinyl window. When I glanced behind the seat, Jaws met my stare, his neck hair raised, his massive head hovering inches from Laura, a low growl rising from deep in his chest. He'd already bitten one cop today. Looking into those coal-black eyes, I swore he was thinking, *why not make it two?*

The policeman reached my door and looked into the open window. He ignored the license and registration I offered. Looking past me, he said, "Hi, Laura. Long time no see."

A look of terror flashed across her face. Jaws's growl deepened, like a bear with its paw in a snare.

I leaned forward, blocking the cop's view of Laura, and waved my license and registration at him again. "What can I do for you, Officer Doherty?"

He looked my way, took off his sunglasses. "I don't need that," he said, pointing toward my paperwork. "Since you had the balls to come into town, I just wanted to remind you about that date you owe Tom."

Tucker's crooked cop. I shook my head, took my measure of the man.

"Aspen's finest—protect and serve."

"That's right, dude," said the cop. He wasn't much older than me, couldn't be thirty. He had a long, dirty career ahead of him.

"Your mother must be proud."

"Don't get smart with me," he hissed, "or I'll drag your ass to the crossbar hotel."

"No, you won't," I scoffed. "That's not what your boss wants."

He sneered, spat on the road. "You just settle things, get this fucking mess cleaned up with Tom, then we'll talk." He straightened and walked back to his patrol car.

Oh, I'm gonna settle things, all right.

"He's one of Tucker's helpers," said Laura, snapping me from a vengeful trance.

"Did he . . . hurt you, Laura?"

"No, baby, but he'd do anything Tom told him to do. He'd kill you without blinking an eye."

I took Laura's hand. "You had such a great doctor's appointment, now all this."

"I'm hanging in there. I'm more worried about you than me."

"Let's go see my new boss."

A mile outside of town, we turned off Highway 82 and came to a fork in the road. One way led to Castle Creek, the other up Maroon Creek. Jagged ridges crowned both sides of the valley, leading to twin pyramids hovering above the rest of the world, the Maroon Bells.

The two-lane road passed the high school, where I'd often visited to watch basketball and football games, and entered a steep and narrow canyon. Maroon Creek, clear and fast, ran along the road. A few miles past the school, the valley opened a bit, home to sprawling willow flats and beaver ponds. I'd fished a lot of this water. Most of the country belonged to the Forest Service, but there were a few precious inholdings, too. Bare aspen rose from the valley floor, greeted partway up the mountain slopes by fir and pine. Like the Maroon Bells to our front, all the high country was blanketed in snow.

I glanced at Laura, and we both smiled, awestruck by the valley. We drove in silence, taking in the enormity of the Bells. Five miles past the school, we reached Doc's place.

I slowed, turned off the main road to a gravel driveway. From the valley floor, only the top half of his cabin was visible. The private road snaked through a thin stand of aspen, scaled a low-lying ridge and, quarter of a mile later, ended at an enormous two-floor log cabin perched above Maroon Creek. Massive stone chimneys rose on each end of the cabin. Most of the first floor was ringed by a covered porch. A detached garage, built of the same huge, hand-peeled logs, stood to the left of the main home. Davis's beat-up Chevy truck rested outside, oddly out of place with the custom-built home.

Laura gasped, covered her mouth, giggled. "The guy that owns this place wants to hire you?"

"That's what he says."

"Can you believe you met him hitchhiking?"

"Destiny, Laura—just like you and me."

Chapter Thirty-Four

We got out of the Jeep and stretched our legs. Jaws whined softly, but we decided to keep him in the back until we got the lay of the land. Nervous, maybe a little intimidated by Davis's digs, Laura took my hand. When we reached the base of stone steps leading to the double front doors, our host emerged.

"Hey, kid, you made it."

At the top of the steps, he shook my hand before turning his attention to Laura.

"Now I know why he took so long to call me," Doc said, clasping her hand with both of his. "I'm Michael Davis—call me Doc."

"Doc, this is my girl, Laura." I hadn't cleared that one, yet, but I felt bold, thought I'd take a chance.

"Come inside, you two."

We stepped into a huge living room with a cathedral ceiling. The far wall was almost all glass, providing an unobstructed view of the Maroon Bells and miles of willow-framed beaver ponds in the foreground. My senses were overwhelmed—like the first time I met Laura.

"What can I get you guys to drink?" asked Davis. "I've got just about everything."

"I'll have a Coca-Cola, if you have one, please."

"Me too, please," chimed Laura. She walked to a wall underneath the stairway leading up and waved for me to follow. While Davis retreated to the kitchen, I joined Laura and studied the framed photographs on the wall. I also noted the log furniture, the wooden floor with its blend of pale hues and dark streaks accenting the rough-cut siding on the interior walls, the paintings and prints of fish and wildlife scattered throughout the house.

"Look at this," said Laura. "Isn't that Barbara Streisand and Doc?"

"Yeah, I think she was in a movie they made out of one of his books."

"How 'bout this one," she said. "That's him and Robert Mitchum."

"One of those film noirs," I said.

I glanced at the other pictures. He'd had tea with the Dalai Lama, deep-sea fished with Lee Marvin, attended bullfights in Spain with beautiful women. Hell, he'd smoked a cigar with Fidel Castro.

"Yeah, I've been pretty lucky, got to see a lot of the world," Davis said, walking up behind us, carrying our drinks. "Let's sit by the fireplace."

We followed him through the living room, around another stairway leading up, to the end of the house, where the stone fireplace rose like a fortress. He took a seat in a wingback chair next to the fire after Laura and I sat on a couch bound in the same red leather. He was dressed in a denim shirt and worn tan corduroys. Like his truck, Davis didn't look like he belonged in his opulent pad.

"Good to have you here," Davis said. "How long have you two known each other?"

"Four years," blurted Laura, "give or take."

"Oh, great," said Davis. He winked at me. "You've already exceeded the half-life of my average marriage. You're off to a good start."

I laughed, glancing at Laura. She looked confused and asked, "Are you married, Doc?"

"No, ma'am, I'm an old bachelor, married to my writing, now." He turned the tables on us again. "How'd you meet?"

Laura and I looked at each other and blushed. "I met Laura my freshman year at Mesa. My pals and I drove down to Delta for a pheasant hunt. Laura was waiting tables at a little restaurant—"

Davis smiled, chuckled. "And you had the nerve to ask for her number?"

"Something like that."

Laura rose and stepped to the window overlooking a beaver pond next to the house. "Slim, those trout are rising. Look at that."

I sensed her stock had just gone up a hundred points with Davis. He left his chair and joined Laura. "How'd you like to catch a limit for our dinner?"

"Really?"

"Sure, follow me."

We walked downstairs to the ground floor of the house, past more paintings, furniture and rugs, until we reached a little room off the guest quarters stuffed with fishing tackle. A rod rack ran the length of one wall.

"Laura, what's your pleasure?"

"Spinning rod, and give me some spinners, Panther Martins if you got 'em."

Five minutes later Laura caught her first fish, a ten-inch brook trout, still aflame in spawning colors. She unhooked it, stuffed it in an Arcticreel, moistened from a dip in the beaver pond. After she scrubbed her hands in the snow, she dried them on her jeans. Laura turned our way and waved.

"Good lord, kid," mused Davis, "all the money in the world can't buy that."

"I know." *Why the hell do you think I've risked my neck to save her from that bastard, Tucker?*

Sitting on padded lawn chairs, we watched Laura fish. The late afternoon sun did its best to keep us warm, but I got chilled.

"Doc, I need to go check on the dog, get a coat."

"I'll follow you. I have an empty kennel if you want."

Walking around the house, I paused, then offered my hand. "By the way, Doc, the name's Shelby, Lee Shelby."

"You mean it's not C.B., Slim?" he laughed.

"And I'm in some trouble, too."

"No shit, kid," he snorted. "I knew that two minutes after I met you."

"And you still want me to work for you?"

"If you can get your ass outta whatever sling you've got it in, yeah." His smile faded, he studied me. "I don't like conformists, people who live by all the bullshit rules, never take chances, never follow their hearts, their dreams." He glanced back at Laura, fighting another fish, and looked at me. "That ain't you, kid, is it?"

"I never thought about it that way, just did what I thought was right, trying to help her—"

"Laura's been . . . hurt, hasn't she?"

I knew Davis had a trained eye, but, shit, I felt like he'd been reading my mail.

I snapped on Jaws's lead, before letting him out of the Jeep. He sniffed at Davis, wagged his tail.

"He's usually not that friendly to strangers," I said.

"He must be a good judge of character," said Davis.

I laughed, thinking of Jaws's earlier reaction to Parker and Doherty. After the dog relieved himself in a snowy patch of willows, Davis led us to a row of kennels behind the garage. Grudgingly, Jaws entered the first door, circled a couple of times, and lay in the sun.

"My last wife wanted to raise Labrador retrievers, train 'em right here."

"Be a good place," I said, looking at all the water surrounding Davis's home.

Davis dismissed the notion with a wave of his hand. "Let's go see how Laura's doing."

We walked back to the lawn chairs and watched Laura. She

had worked her way around the pond to the base of the dam, about as far she could go without waders. Hiding behind the huge pile of woven willow branches, she knelt in a thick overgrown area allowing no room for a back cast. Undeterred, she pinched the treble hook of the spinner with her free hand and trapped the line in front of the reel with her forefinger. She stretched the rod in front of her, creating a big bow in the shaft. Releasing the spinner and the line at the same instant, the lure sailed into the middle of the pond. V-shaped ripples followed the Panther Martin. Seconds later, a hooked trout thrashed on the surface.

"Damn! That's the old bow-and-arrow cast," said Davis. "I could watch Laura fish all day. She reminds me of me."

"She's good, and that's with a cracked wrist."

"You teach her?"

"No, Doc, her dad did—before he drank himself to death."

"You be good to her, kid."

"I'm sure trying."

"Lee, tell me about this trouble you're in."

I was about to recount a wild and illegal month to an old guy I'd just met, but youth needed experience. "Well, Doc, it all started when I robbed a couple of coke dealers—"

An hour later, Davis shook his head and grinned. "Someday you'll have to tell that story."

Writing a book was the last thing on my mind. I just wanted to be done with Tucker and get Agent Parker's blessing to get on with my life. I wanted Laura along for the ride, too. I knew we had a lot of work to do. We needed to make things right after what we'd both been through and still needed to finish. Watching her circle the pond, bringing her catch back to the cabin while the last bit of sun slipped behind the Bells, I vowed to finally share with her how I really felt.

Davis broke me from my trance, pointed toward Laura. "You want me to clean 'em, or you got it?"

"No, sir. Laura can take care of 'em."

We watched her pull a Swiss Army knife from her pocket, kneel next to the edge of the pond, and gut a fat brookie. She tossed the entrails in the willows for the mink, used her thumbnail to remove the kidneys, washed the trout in the pond, and threw it on the snow behind her.

"If I'd had a daughter——" Davis mused. He shook his head and chuckled. "Hey, I've been thinking about the pickle you're in."

I turned and waited.

"Well, there's no getting around your dealing with that Tucker fellow. That's just going to be a dangerous piece of work, no avoiding that. But——"

"What . . . what do you think, Doc?"

He nodded toward Laura, still cleaning fish. "I'm worried about her. She could be in more danger than you."

"Parker said he'd protect her, and he's damned sure got that trailer court covered," I said. "He knows what's going on there better than I do. Must have some men hidden somewhere——"

"The question is whether he'd tip his hand to protect her, Lee."

"I don't follow."

"When you're working Tucker, the bastard will assume Laura's unprotected," said Davis. "If I were in his shoes, and thank God I'm not, I'd send my boys to get her the instant I knew you weren't with her. She'd make a helluva bargaining chip."

"So?" I asked. "If Tucker does that, Parker's men will protect her."

"Maybe, maybe not," said Davis. "If Parker does, Tucker will know you're not on your own, and the jig'll be up."

"Jesus, you think he's using her for bait? You think he'd let something happen to her?"

"I don't know, but he didn't help you with that rat-faced fellow. That could have gone either way if the little bastard had been packing heat." Davis stopped, rubbed his chin. "The bottom line is whether Parker thinks it's more important to protect Laura or catch Tucker."

And that good ol' boy, Parker, really wants to go back to the Southland.

"Shit." I rose from my chair, paced the porch. "I'm willing to risk my neck, but not hers. But Parker won't let me off the hook 'til I help him pinch Tucker." I shook my head, felt trapped, no place to go. "What the hell am I gonna do?"

Davis watched Laura clean her last fish, then turned to me. "Bring her here, Lee. I'll guard her like she was my own daughter." He laughed softly. "Any woman who can fish like her and clean their own catch deserves my help."

Chapter Thirty-Five

Nearing Woody Creek, I glanced at Laura sleeping in the front seat. She'd had a long day. Between her doctor's appointment and two brushes with the law, I knew she must be played out. But we still had a lot of fun at Davis's place. Doc dusted the brook trout in seasoned flour and fried them in peanut oil. With a salad he threw together and fresh bread from Little Cliff's Bakery, we had a great dinner. Laura agreed to stay at Davis's when I hunted Tucker. My new boss even promised to let Jaws room with her in the guest quarters downstairs.

My hunt for Tucker would start tomorrow night, like Agent Parker had ordered. I'd spend the day getting my gear organized and bring Laura back to Davis's. I took him up on his offer to swap rigs with him the next day so I could take his old Chevy into town. That'd help me get the drop on Tucker. No early warning from that crooked cop, Doherty, or anyone else, for that matter. I wanted to get this whole goddamned mess behind me. Besides, tomorrow was Saturday, a big night of partying for the locals. Tucker was sure to be about, peddling his wares.

Laura stirred when we pulled into the trailer court. I pulled the pistol from under the seat and got Jaws out of the back. Before I let him wander behind the trailer to do his business, we entered the trailer and searched the place, room by room, just in case. When I was satisfied, I waved Laura inside.

"I'm gonna take a shower, clean that fish smell off me," said

Laura. She grabbed my arm as I stepped back outside. "I need to talk to you before I go to bed, though."

"Sure."

I led Jaws outside and let him ramble in the moonlight. On the long lead, he ran from tree to tree, until he found that one splendiferous spot. His piss raised steam on the cold fall night. To his chagrin, I dragged him inside, begging off playtime on my own fatigue. Before I closed the door, I heard a man call me from the street.

I turned and recognized Juan, nearing my Jeep.

"*Camión noches*," I hollered, stepping back outside.

"Hey amigo," said Juan. "Some people, they come today, looking for joo."

"*¿Huerto blanco?*" I asked, stunned that ol' Rat Face would have the balls to come back after eating my pistol during his last visit.

"No, no," said Juan. "They, ahh, *federales*? They talk to me, ask questions, I got to tell or they *deportar*, no?"

Parker's men, strong-arming Juan to find out more about me.

"Juan, you tell them whatever they want to know," I said. "Stay out of trouble—*estancia fuera del apuro*." I shook his hand. "*Muchas gracias*."

Juan shuffled on, taking a walk around the park. I returned to the trailer, not surprised to have learned of Parker's snooping around. Maybe he would keep Tucker's boys at bay, but I still didn't trust the wheeler-dealer lawman.

I stepped inside and heard the shower running through my bedroom door. I sat, pulled off my boots, stripped to my T-shirt and boxers, and lay on the couch, with Jaws resting on the rug in front of me. I read by the light of a table lamp. After a short while, I turned off the light and pulled the blankets to my chin, worn out from a long day.

Somewhere between consciousness and sleep, I heard the bedroom door open and footsteps head my way. A sliver of light escaped from the room, just enough to illuminate Laura. She sat on the edge of the couch, wearing one of my flannel shirts.

"Are you up, Slim," she said, her voice satiny and low. She reached over me and gently rubbed my shoulder.

I shook my head and cleared my throat. "Yeah, sorry," I chuckled, "just laid down."

I rose to sit next to her. "What's up?" Her damp brown hair was brushed straight back and her skin glowed from the warm shower.

"I'm not sure where to start." she said, "It's about you and me, what Dr. Johnson told me today, stuff like that."

"Okay."

Laura looked nervous, her eyes flicking about, like she didn't know where to begin. She'd always been the one to take the initiative when we needed to talk. But I remembered the promise I'd made to myself earlier in the day. I wanted to show her I was willing to open up more, share my feelings without her having to pry them from me.

"Secret for a secret?" I asked. Her little game I never played enough.

She raised an eyebrow. "Really?"

"Really."

"You first," she said.

"Whoa," I muttered, shaking my head. Was I really ready to do this?

She smiled, tilted her head and squinted at me. "You okay?"

You fool, just tell her how you feel, tell her all of it.

"For months I've been thinking about you, not just worried about you, but missing you, too. When I was at the peak, I remembered every place where we'd been, all the things we'd done together. Flying over the Flat Tops, I kept seeing you and me together, and the last few days, even though, well, still, being with you again, made me realize—"

Sometimes I needed a running start.

"I don't know if this is the right time to tell you this, but I never want to lose you again." My eyes watered. My heart raced. I took her hand. "If you'd be mine, if you'd give me another chance, I'd never turn my back. Laura, I'd do anything, if you'd just forgive me."

Her mouth opened, but I pressed my finger gently against her lips.

"I can't change the past, erase all my mistakes. But if you'll share your life with me—" I kissed her hand and closed my eyes.

She ran her hand through my hair, pulled me close, and rested her cheek against my head. Her tears fell on my face, each warm and lovely.

"Oh, baby, you know I'm yours." She kissed my head, whispered in my ear, "But I need to know you still want me, even with everything that's—I need more than a big brother."

I lifted my head, gazed into her dark eyes.

"I talked to Dr. Johnson today, about this, about us. I want you to help me feel safe again with—" She rubbed her eyes, breathed deep and slow. "I don't know how long it will take, but I don't want you out here. Maybe we could just hold each other for a while. You've got to be patient, help me."

Everything was moving faster than I expected. I figured I'd be on that couch for weeks, maybe months, and that was okay. I wanted to do the right thing. I was plenty patient, patient enough to tell her to wait longer. But would that just hurt her more? Make her think, with everything that had happened, I didn't want her anymore?

"Laura, are you sure?"

"I trust you. You've never, ever hurt me. You're the only man who's ever loved me."

I rose, took her hand, and said to Jaws, "Hold down the fort, partner."

Laura laughed through her tears.

"Hey," I said, "it's your turn—you know, secret for a secret?"

She held me, stared into my eyes. "What do you want to know?"

"What'd Kitty whisper in your ear at the beauty parlor?"

Laura winked and gave me a sly smile. "She said I had you wrapped around my little finger."

I laughed, led Laura to our bed, never looked back.

Chapter Thirty-Six

Next night, we left the trailer around nine p.m. The three of us piled into my Jeep and headed south once more, Laura and Jaws for Davis's place and me for a date with the devil. Snow fell softly and stuck to the highway. The windshield wipers swung in time to a half-worn-out cassette of The Eagles' *Greatest Hits*. Neither of us said much. Jaws kept quiet, too, lying on a piece of carpet in the back. Even he sensed my fear and apprehension. How the hell was I going to stomach spending one minute with Tucker?

A little way up Maroon Creek Road, a forkhorn mule deer jumped in front of us. I nearly hit the little buck, swerving enough to miss its ass by inches, while still staying on the road. I'd need to be that quick in Aspen.

A few miles later, we turned into Davis's driveway. Fresh tire tracks revealed he had made at least one trip into town since the storm had started. Pausing at the top of the low ridge overlooking his home, I flicked my brights a couple of times. I drove down the hill and parked alongside his Chevy. Laura and I got out and went to the back to fetch our stuff.

Davis came out of the house and walked down the steps toward us.

"Laura, Lee," he hollered, nearing us, "good to see you again."

Davis shook my hand and gave Laura a hug.

I pulled my small canvas duffel bag from behind the driver's seat of my Jeep and put it in Davis's truck. I was ready to go.

"Kid, you sure you won't have any trouble with that three-on-the-tree transmission?" asked Davis. "I've got something a little more modern in the garage if you like."

"No, sir," I said. "This'll be great." Wilbur's old Bronco, which I'd driven plenty, had the same stick shift.

Davis pulled a key from his pocket and slid into the cab, keeping the door open. "She starts real easy, just pump the gas once and choke her if the engine's cold." Following his own directions, the engine cranked over on the first try. Stepping out of the truck, he shook my hand. "Let her warm up a few minutes. You two probably want to talk, anyway."

"Doc . . . I . . . I don't know how to—"

"It's all right, Lee, someday you'll help some young rebel, too." He walked back toward the house, turned, and smiled. "Laura, come in the main door, I'll get you squared away downstairs."

Laura climbed into the Chevy and slid across the bench seat, putting my duffel bag at her feet. When I joined her in the cab, she drew near, held me.

"Everything's gonna be fine, Laura, I'm just scouting, nothing's gonna happen tonight."

"I just wish you could stay here. Why can't we just walk away from all this?"

We'd already been over this just the night before when we spent half the night holding each other, talking, trying to keep Jaws out of the bed. She knew I had to go, but it was still good to hear her beg me to stay.

"When will you be back?"

I shrugged my shoulders. "As soon as I set up a meeting with Tucker, like Parker ordered." I kissed her once more, then watched her walk back to the house, leading Jaws by his leash.

I drove slowly out the private drive to Maroon Creek Road, getting used to Davis's truck. For an old-timer, it was tight and responsive. The big V-8 had plenty of life. I had no problem with the transmission.

Traffic was bare on Highway 82. The few drivers on the road traveled slowly, like me, as snow piled on the highway. Concentrating on staying out of a ditch helped me keep Tucker out of my head.

Driving through town, I turned left at my first prospect, the Hotel Jerome, and headed down Mill Street, the route to the hospital. But this time I veered right after crossing the Roaring Fork. I climbed a short, steep hill and parked the truck in a stuffed parking lot in front of the Silver King Apartments.

I left Doc's truck there and walked the half mile into town. The route between the Silver King and town included a chunk of undeveloped ground along Mill Street and a brushy patch of river bottom. I planned to find Tucker, talk to the rattlesnake, and sneak back to the truck without being tailed. I didn't want to lead any uninvited visitors to Davis's place.

Twenty minutes later, I neared the intersection of Mill and Main. Walking around the corner, I peered into the windows of the Hotel Jerome. For off-season, the place was pretty crowded. I stepped inside to cigarette smoke and loud chatter, two reasons I hated barhopping. I paused at the doorway, pretending to look for friends. To my left, a huge mahogany bar spanned most of the wall, two bartenders taking orders from the waitresses and mixing drinks. After a few minutes, a tough-looking waitress, probably a hard-living thirty, neared.

"You got an ID? You gotta be twenty-one to be in here, buddy."

I ignored her, looked over her shoulder a few seconds.

"I don't see who I'm looking for. I'll catch you later."

She laughed, muttered, "Sure, pal, after you turn twenty-one."

Next stop was farther up Mill Street, past the Isis Movie Theater, to the walking mall. I turned left and walked along shops and bars until I hit Galena and took a right to my next stop, Jake's Abbey, a little club located below ground level. From the sidewalk,

I heard live music. I took the steps down to the entrance, waiting behind a couple of people as they paid a cover to enter. The doorman checked my ID and took my five dollars. A four-piece bluegrass band played on the little stage to the right of the bar. The place was crowded, but I managed to find a stool along the back wall.

After a couple of fast songs, a waitress found me and took my order for a club soda. About the time the gal brought me my drink, the band took a break. The stage lights dimmed and the bartender turned on the house lights, allowing me to view the other patrons. With no glimpse of Tucker or any of his lackeys, I sipped my drink and split.

I walked down the street to another subterranean tavern, Galena Street East. The joint was dark and smoky. I walked around the bar in the middle of the room to scout the entire place. Nearing the far corner, I heard loud voices joking and laughing, one of them deep and Texan. From where I stood, I couldn't see several patrons sitting at a long table. But I made out one guy facing my way, a weasel-looking bastard with a bandage on his cheek, ol' Rat Face in the flesh.

My heart skipped, my breath grew short, like spotting my quarry after a long stalk. Slowly turning away, I took a seat at an empty table, with my back against the wall. From my new vantage, I spied more of the party. Six men and three women sat together, a collection of beer bottles and highball glasses scattered about their table. Besides Rat Face, I recognized the driver, the big bearded man who had handed me Tucker's message. Two other members of the entourage I had never seen. The sixth man sat with his back to me. The women seemed like an afterthought, there for pleasure and window-dressing, but not really part of the crew. The men ignored them as they chatted amongst themselves. Sitting in the middle of the table, like Jesus at the Last Supper, was Tom Tucker, holding his unholy court.

I watched him, as if studying a dangerous beast in the zoo, but no bars, no glass, stood between us. He fascinated me. Eyes darting about, from one person to another, he seemed to measure everyone about him, like a lion deciding which antelope to devour, while he sipped his drink. After a few minutes, he handed something to one of the women at the table, a young gal, barely old enough to be in the place. She smiled, left the table, and headed for the bathroom.

Tucker wore a gray sweater over a purple turtleneck that, even two tables over, highlighted his blue eyes. I remembered he fancied himself the dandy. His sandy-blond hair reached the bottom of his collar and was casually, but thoughtfully, swept to the side. His smile, framed by a heavy and rakish mustache, seemed menacing and untrue. His skin was tanned as dark as the Old Man's elk hide belt around my waist.

A waitress broke my trance, slipping up on me from the opposite side of the room. Another toughie, she demanded my ID. When I ordered a club soda, she groaned, like she wouldn't be making any money off this pup. I halted her as she turned for the bar.

"Hold on, ma'am," I said, nodding toward Tucker, "I'd like to buy that table a bottle of champagne, a magnum of Dom Pérignon."

Her eyes widened, then a scowl crossed her face. "Let's see your money."

I opened my wallet, stuffed with twenties and fifties. "Can you give me a napkin and a pen, please? I'd like to write them a note."

With new respect in her eyes, she obliged and I penned a message for Tucker,

> *Tom,*
> *Might as well enjoy, you paid for it.*
> *Shelby*

I folded the napkin and pointed toward Tucker. "Would you please deliver the champagne and this note to that—"

"Tom?" she asked, raising her eyebrows like she didn't expect a kid like me to count himself among Tucker's pals.

"Yes, ma'am, Tom."

I sat back, took a deep breath, and waited for the sparks to fly. The waitress took the order to the bar and prepared a tray with glasses as the bartender placed the champagne in a silver bucket. When she delivered the treat to the table, everyone hooted and hollered, like it was a big deal. Everyone, but Tom. He read my note and looked down the waitress's arm pointing at me. I nodded and saluted in mock formality.

For a fleeting instant, I thought I saw a look of utter hatred cross his face. Then, like a mirage, it disappeared, masked by a toothy smile. While one of the men poured bubbly for everyone, Tucker rose and headed my way.

The sixth man at the table, the one with his back to me, turned in his chair and looked my way as Tucker neared. It was Special Agent Clyde Parker, DEA.

Chapter Thirty-Seven

I didn't have time to figure out what Parker's presence meant before Tucker reached my table. His six-foot frame hovered too close for comfort. "Well, lookee here, see what the cat drug in." He wore tight-fitting jeans and his trademark ostrich-skin boots.

The Old Man had taught me to rise when folks approached for a visit. That was the way a gentleman greeted another gentleman.

I kept my seat and kicked the chair across the table from me, sliding it into Tucker's leg.

"Sit your ass down, Tucker. Let's not make this last any longer than it has to."

I glanced over to his entourage. They were bullshitting with each other, oblivious to the duel Tucker and I were about to have. All of them except Parker, that is. He watched us closely.

"So you thought you'd just mosey into town, see your old friend, Tom."

When he sat at the table and leaned my way, I instinctively recoiled against the wall.

"What's it gonna take, Tucker, to make things right, get you off my ass?"

He sipped his drink. It looked like whiskey, neat. "I told you that already, Shelby, the night you called."

"You said you wanted the coke and the money—"

"And more, Shelby," Tucker snarled. "I said I wanted more."

"What the hell do you want?"

"I want Laura back."

Ever since Tucker and I had spoken on the phone, I'd suspected this was coming. Still, the thought repulsed me. But I needed to tell the snake what he wanted to hear and get him to a meeting. Give him back his dope and let Parker lower the boom on him. The trick was to not make it look too easy or he might smell a rat. But, then again, Tucker did have that blind spot—his ego.

I looked down and shook my head. "Are you nuts? You'd have to stick a gun to her head—"

"That could be arranged," interrupted Tucker. He smiled again, raised his hand in a reassuring gesture. "Really, though, I know we had a tiff, but give me fifteen minutes, and I'd have her eating out of the palm of my hand." He sipped his drink and winked at me.

"You really think she'd come back to you?"

"Hell, yes, sonny," Tucker laughed. "Doherty said she looks real good, too. Said she put on some weight. He says that short haircut makes her tits look even bigger."

"I gotta admit, Tucker, things have been rough, this time around—"

"Sure they have, Shelby," said Tucker, almost with sympathy. "She's used to living a lot higher on the hog, now, than that damned trailer of yours. No offense, pard."

"No offense taken. I know I live in a dump."

"Ah, hoss," said Tucker, "you'll be all right. She's just not the right gal for you."

I said nothing, but thought, *she's the only gal for me.*

"Shelby, I really want her back." Tucker glanced over his shoulder toward his table. "Not one of those fuckin' bimbos has half the soul Laura's got in her little pinky."

Soul? What the hell do you know about soul? Laura didn't have any left after you were done with her—after you beat her—gave her to your pals.

"I'm gonna treat her better this time, though." Tucker stared into emptiness. It chilled me. He really believed what he was saying. "This time I won't let her have so much blow. I'll keep her in a little place I got up Old Snowmass. Won't share her or make her work. Yeah," he said, returning his attention to me, "things'll be better this go around."

Sweet Jesus, in his own sick way, he really does miss her.

"You're really throwing a curve my way, Tucker. I'm gonna need some time to think about this, talk to Laura, make sure she's okay."

"You've had your fuckin' time, sonny. Now I wanna get this business done."

That's it, swallow the hook, you rotten bastard.

"How much time you gonna give me, Tucker?"

"One day. Then your ass will be in the Moffat County Jail," said Tucker. "It's all I can do to keep Doherty from running you in. I can't hold him off forever." Tucker grinned, figuring he had me by the balls. "I'm not even gonna come after you for the money. That's my supplier's hard luck. We'll call it the spoils of war, but I want my dope and I want Laura."

"Okay. Here it is. I got five keys of cocaine. Five thousand grams of that shit for you to sell." I glanced about the half-full club. "In a few weeks, this ski town's gonna be stuffed with toot-snortin' turkeys. You'll make a killin'."

"Sonny, tell me something I don't know."

"I'll give you that shit and Laura. But I don't want to be looking over my shoulder, worried about you and your crew—"

"You take care of your end of the bargain, and you won't have a thing to worry about."

Like hell, you'd still cut my throat for robbing you and keeping your seventy-five K. Too bad I'm not giving you the chance.

I remembered what Parker had told me about not getting too

specific, yet. And I wanted to get the hell out of there. I decided to go out with one last flourish, try to put up a little fight.

"Tucker, I'll call you in the next day or two. But I'll tell you this right now. You've got one chance to get shit straight, then I'm dumping your 'caine in the goddamned river and taking Laura a long ways from here." I slipped out of my chair and strode for the door.

I darted across the road, nearly slipping on fresh snow. Cutting through an alley, I paused to study my back trail. No one followed.

I walked to the edge of Wagner Park, a grassy oasis in the middle of town, replete with a rugby field, now under two feet of snow. Turning south, I reached Mill Street and headed downhill to the Roaring Fork. I fought the urge to run, rush to Laura. I'd never tell her what Tucker wanted. I just wanted to hold her and try to rid my mind of that monster. Would this nightmare ever end?

Nearing the river, I turned to check my trail. Someone briskly walked my way, a couple of hundred yards up Mill. Could be one of Tucker's lackeys, could be another fellow headed for the Silver King. Either way, I wasn't taking any chances. Just short of the bridge, where the road doglegged to the right and out of the stranger's view, I stepped into a patch of willows and slipped the revolver from my waistband.

A couple of minutes later, a man came around the bend in the road and slowed where my tracks in the fresh snow headed into the stream bottom. My heart skipped and my breathing drew short. I slipped deeper into the willows, my own footsteps masked by the Roaring Fork. In the brush, I no longer saw my pursuer. I moved swiftly, running forty or fifty yards up the river, then I doubled back on my trail. I kneeled and waited for my pursuer to pass.

A nearby streetlamp dimly lit the snowy river bottom. I eyed my trail a few yards away, like a wounded bear waiting to maul an unwitting hunter. First, I saw willows parting ahead, then a big man appeared in the clearing, oblivious to me. He stopped and looked about, like he realized the folly of his pursuit.

"Parker, what the hell are you doing?" I yelled over the river's dull roar. "You scared the shit out of me."

He stumbled through thick undergrowth, coming so close he nearly ran into me. "Take it easy, Bobby Lee. Looks like you did real good. Tucker's all puffed up like a damned buck bullfrog."

"I'll tell you one thing, Parker," I said, sliding the pistol back into my pants, "you're not paying me enough for this work."

Parker laughed. "He is a rotten sumbitch, but then again, you knew the score when you ripped him off, didn't you?"

"Yeah, but, I didn't know—"

"Well," said Parker, "What's he want?"

"The crazy son of a bitch wants Laura back. Can you believe that shit?"

"Of course he does, Bobby Lee. Tucker's got a damned ego bigger than Texas. He can't stand to see you with her. What else did he allow?"

"Wants the dope, said I could keep the cash, which we know is bullshit."

"Sure, he'd never forgive you for ripping him off and he damned sure isn't going to let you keep his money," said Parker. "But, it doesn't matter. He's gonna be in jail or dead."

"He said if I didn't call him tomorrow, that crooked cop of his would be arresting me. They know about what happened with the Wyoming deputies in Moffat County, too."

"Okay, Bobby Lee, you call Tucker, set up the meeting, then call me."

Parker looked pleased with himself. A big shit-eating grin on his face. "Tell Laura not to worry, we'll protect her at the meeting, won't let—"

"Wait a minute, Parker, I told Tucker what he wanted to hear, but Laura won't be there. There's no goddamned way I'm giving her to—"

"Wake up, Bobby Lee," Parker barked. "None of this shit's for real. We're just trying to get Tucker to take the bait." He softened his tone and tried to reason. "Now, you're gonna have to talk to her about helping us. She's got to be there when—"

I snapped and hit Parker in the jaw with a right hook, dropping him in the snow. "She's off the table, you son of a bitch. She's been through enough. Leave her alone!" I caught my breath as Parker struggled to his feet. "You best forget about her, or I'll dump that dope in the Colorado." Still fuming, I tried to kick Parker before he rose.

As I lifted my foot, he ducked and punched me square in the balls. Might as well have shot me with a .44 Magnum. I crashed to the snow, clutching my groin and fighting for breath.

Parker staggered to his feet and hovered over me. "Bobby Lee, how fuckin' stupid do you think I am? My boys already got your pack out of the train station, and you and Laura are delivering it to Tucker . . . or your ass is going to prison."

When I rolled over, got on my hands and knees and tried to stand, he kicked me in the ribs, knocking me into the willows.

Parker lurched through the knee-deep snow and stood over me. "Bobby Lee, it's the same deal as before, you help me pinch Tucker or your ass is mine."

"Fuck you, Parker," I gasped, "just send me to jail."

"Oh, yeah? Then who'll take care of Laura? Tucker?" Parker leaned over me and grabbed my collar, pulling my face close to his. "You call Tucker tomorrow, set up the meeting. Tell him whatever it takes to get him to come." Parker shoved me deeper into the willows and trudged through the snow back to the road.

Chapter Thirty-Eight

I don't know how long I lay in the snow, maybe an hour. When I got so goddamned cold I feared I might freeze, I summoned the will to rise and stumble back to the road. I'd caught my breath and my nuts no longer ached, but the pain in my ribs worsened.

After an excruciating tramp through the snow, I reached Mill and staggered back to the Silver King like a drunk making his way home. I climbed into Davis's Chevy, followed his instructions, and cranked the engine. Every movement requiring a twist in my torso sent a shooting pain through my chest. Parker had really screwed me up with that kick to my ribs. The hard ridge of the pistol in my side hurt so badly I had to pull the gun from my waist and lay it on the seat beside me.

I drove the back way out of town, eschewing Main Street for Bleeker. Intersecting Highway 82 a block north of the Hickory House, I motored across Castle Creek and drove to the Maroon Creek turnoff. Once I left town, I didn't see another car in the snowy night. By the time I reached Davis's place, it was nearly two a.m. But his lights were still on upstairs.

I parked the truck, packed my pistol in the duffel bag, and slowly walked toward the front door, trying to conceal the shooting pain in my chest. When I reached the bottom of the steps, Davis stepped outside.

"Mission accomplished?" he asked.

I paused and allowed a small grin. "I imagine so, Doc." I climbed the stairs. Each step felt like a knife thrust into my side.

Reaching the deck, I slipped and struggled to keep my legs underneath me.

Davis rushed to help me inside. He closed and bolted the door, then reset his security system, while I sat on a bench and removed my Sorels.

"What happened, kid? You look like shit," said Davis.

I took off my down jacket and pulled up my sweater and turtleneck. "You tell me, Doc."

He put on his reading glasses and looked at my back. "You have a bruise back there the size of a pancake." When he lightly felt it, I nearly jumped through the roof.

I chuckled, then stopped for the pain. "You should see the other guy."

"You fight Tucker?"

"No, sir. Parker."

"Parker? Shit, kid, you two are on the same team."

"That's what I thought. Now I'm beginning to wonder which one is the bigger crook." Before Davis could say anything, I nodded toward the stairway. "How's Laura?"

"She's fine, went to sleep around midnight with that beast of a dog. We had a good talk tonight." Davis pointed toward my back, "I'd offer you a stiff one, but Laura said you swore off booze—for her."

"Yes, sir, from what I've been reading, I ought to be helping her get into some kind of program," I said. "How 'bout you, Doc, never seen you tip one yet."

"Quit nine years ago, kid, and I can tell you all about the program," he said. "I had to drink my way through four marriages before I got the cure, well, actually, I'm not cured, but I am sober, today."

"No shit, Doc, You're—"

"An alcoholic, Lee, and I want to help Laura. That's one of the things guys like me do."

I said nothing.

"Laura's got something else going against her." Davis smiled softly. "She comes by the coke habit honestly, if you will, having an alcoholic father. Addiction runs in families."

"Damn," I muttered.

"You did well, though, Lee, keeping her away from Tucker. She hasn't been on the stuff very long. Couple of months is better than a couple of years."

"Think I—we—can get her straight?"

"Hell, yes, kid. She has to want it, and she does. She's already been clean for close to three weeks."

"Been tough, Doc."

"On her and you, kid."

"I want to go downstairs, Doc, see her." The hope of being with Laura was all that had gotten me home from my brawl with Parker. "I don't know how I'll ever repay your—"

"Lee, I take care of my crew," said Davis. "Let's get you to bed."

I thought it was pretty sorry, an old man helping me downstairs, but I needed all the help I could get. Still out of Laura's hearing at the base of stairway, Davis said, "We may have to take you into Aspen Valley Hospital tomorrow morning. See how you sleep."

I crept into the room and sat on one of two big couches. I heard rustling in one of the bedrooms and, an instant later, light leaked from beneath the door. Laura stepped into the room, wearing an old pair of flannel pajamas I gave her that had shrunk too much for me. From the worried look on her face, she knew I was hurt.

"Can you help me?" I unbuckled my pants. "Help me take these off?"

She rushed to hold me. Just as quick, I raised my hand. "Careful, sweetie, hold on now, I'm a little beat up."

"What happened? Who hurt you? Did he do this?"

I took a deep breath. "Just help me get my clothes off. I've been dreaming of getting in a warm bed—"

She finished pulling off my pants, while I shucked my sweater and turtleneck. I rose on wobbly legs and pointed toward the bedroom. "Please, get me in there. I just want to warm up. I don't even care if I have to sleep with Jaws."

I put my arm over her shoulder and hobbled to the bed. She pushed Jaws off the comforter and made a place for me. I crawled under the sheets and sighed deeply. I didn't remember anything ever feeling as good as that soft, warm bed. Laura turned off the light, then slipped in next to me.

"You're freezing, Slim. Maybe you should take a hot bath."

"I'll be all right. Just want to lie with you, warm up, sleep."

She had all kinds of questions. I had vowed to be more open and forthcoming, but just now, I didn't want to even think about Tucker or Parker, much less talk about them. All I knew was I wasn't getting her involved any further in this mess. I'd gladly go to prison before I'd let Parker use her as a pawn in his dangerous game.

"Laura, I promise I'll tell you about it all in the morning, but right now I just want to be with you and try to forget about everything else." I whispered three words in her ear, then closed my eyes.

Her warmth helped me bury all my fears somewhere in the back of my mind. Then I heard the tinkling of Jaws's dog tags as he stalked our cozy bed. An instant later, I was sandwiched between a hundred and twenty pounds of pretty girl and a hundred and twenty pounds of black dog. Someday, I hoped to get Jaws his own bed, inside a good, stout doghouse.

"Jaws, you ever heard three's a crowd?" I muttered under my breath. As he snored in my ear, I figured he'd argue that I was the odd man out.

Chapter Thirty-Nine

"I don't know what to do, Doc." I sat stiffly at his kitchen table, my back still sore as hell. Through the window, the Maroon Bells shimmered in the morning sun. Between a good night's sleep and a perfect new day, my morale improved. But I was in a fix, hoping Davis could help me think things through while Laura still slept downstairs.

"Lee, I don't think you have any choice," Davis said. "You've got to call Tucker, arrange that meeting." He cleaned his eyeglasses on his shirttail and sipped his coffee. "Seems to me that's all Parker can ask of you, especially since he took the dope out of your locker."

"I don't follow you, Doc."

"What I mean is, you make the offer to meet Tucker, but if he won't agree, what more can you do?"

I remembered Parker's last words before he left me in the snow. "Doc, he told me to do whatever it took to get Tucker there, even—"

"I know, kid, even promise you'd give him Laura." Doc gave me a mischievous grin. "So just keep telling Tucker what he wants to hear."

"Doc, you're not saying I should ask Laura—"

"Hell, no, Lee." Doc's smile faded. "I wouldn't let her anywhere near that sorry excuse for a man." He paused, rubbed the stubble on his chin. "But what's Tucker going to do when you show up without her? Not take back his dope?"

"No. I guess not."

"You tell Laura about Tucker asking for her?"

"Hell, no."

"Good, Lee. Keep it that way," said Davis. "How's she doing right now? She seemed pretty good last night."

"She's doing a lot better, Doc."

"Thing is, kid, right now she's white knuckling that drug habit—"

"What's that mean?"

"It means she's going to have to realize she can't do it all on her own," said Davis. "In the long run, she's going to need help. You two have been together just about every second of every day, so she really hasn't had a chance to slip yet, right?"

"I got you, Doc. When I was waiting around at the hospital, I got some info on premarital counseling, addiction therapy, stuff like that. But I have to get all this shit with Tucker and Parker behind me first."

Doc rose from his chair, coffee in hand. "Follow me to my office, no time like the present."

I gripped Davis's arm, slowed him. "I still can't believe how much you've helped us. I feel like a huge imposition."

"Nonsense, kid," said Davis, pointing to his backyard. "We haven't had this much excitement around here since Henry Kissinger got drunk off his ass and fell in that beaver pond."

I laughed and followed Davis into his office, a little nook off the living room, not much bigger than a walk-in closet. A small table with his old manual typewriter and a desk lamp sat against one wall, shelves of books against another. The room was spartan. No windows, a couple of uncomfortable wooden chairs, and a few photographs on the wall. A cork bulletin board hung over his desk where he posted photos and other information for his latest story. I suspected the little inner sanctum more accurately reflected the man's true nature than the rest of his place.

Davis motioned for me to take a seat next to his desk and slid the telephone my way. He pulled a portable cassette recorder from a shelf and stuck a small suction microphone on the handset.

"Only way I know how to listen in," said Davis. "Call Tucker, right now."

I glanced at a small clock on the desk. "Shit, Doc, it's not even nine yet—"

"That's the idea, kid, wake him up. Catch him before he's thinking straight."

Davis turned on the tape recorder and put on a set of headphones, while I fumbled through my wallet to find Tucker's number. I dialed the phone, imagining the sorry bastard dragging his ass from a warm bed to quiet that damned ringing and ease his booze-and-cocaine-laden hangover.

On the seventh or eighth ring, a woman answered the phone, her voice scratchy and weak. "Hello?" she pleaded more than asked.

"I need to talk to Tom."

"He's still sleeping, can I have him—"

"No, tell him it's Doherty," I lied. "Tell him the shit's about to hit the fan."

Davis grinned and gave me a thumbs-up.

A minute later, Tucker came on the line. "Goddamnit, this better be important."

"Oh, it is," I snickered.

"Who the fuck is this?"

"It's Shelby."

"Well, got to thinking 'bout last night, didn't yah, want to make a deal, huh?"

"I gotta admit, Tom, you know Laura a hell of a lot better than me." I remembered what Parker had said about Tucker's Texas-size ego. "She and I talked last night. She's sick of me already, wants back with you. It's killin' me, man, but what can I do?" I paused, added, "I think she's crazy, but if she wants you—"

Tucker cleared his throat and laughed. "I told you it'd be like that."

I looked at Davis, wasn't sure what to say next. He scribbled on a piece of paper, *Set up the rendezvous.*

"Listen, Tucker, I need to get on with my life. I want to get this dope to you and get Laura off my hands pronto, what do you say?"

"Anytime, pard."

Davis stuck his finger in his mouth, imitating a hooked fish.

"Tonight, then," I said, "but I'm only dealing with you, Tucker, not your damned lackeys."

"Why's that?" Tucker asked.

Davis winced, raised an eyebrow.

"Because I'm not giving just anybody half a million dollars of nose candy and the prettiest girl in town. I want to make sure you take delivery. I don't want to hear later you got ripped off and I'm still in Dutch."

Davis smiled and nodded his head in approval.

"All right, partner, but I'm not saying I won't have some friends with me," said Tucker. "And one other thing, Shelby—"

"What's that?"

"You pull a gun on any of my boys again, you better be ready to pull the trigger."

"I hear ya, Tucker."

"Let's meet around ten tonight behind Smuggler Trailer Park at the gravel yard. Know where that is?"

"Yeah." I'd been there plenty of times, passing through on my way up Smuggler Mountain to hunt and fish.

"I've got to tell you, Shelby, I don't know when I've felt so cocky," said Tucker laughing, then he hung up on me.

Davis paused the tape recorder and removed his headset. "I think he bought it, kid."

"One more call?" I asked.

"Sure," said Davis, starting his recorder.

Parker answered on the first ring. "Now, how hard was that, Bobby Lee?"

"You've got Tucker's phone tapped?" I asked.

"Yep, and your good buddy Davis, too." Parker laughed. "Did you really think I wouldn't figure out where you'd gone?"

Hearing his phone had been bugged, Davis pounded his fist into his other hand.

"Okay, what do you know about this gravel yard behind the Smuggler Mountain Trailer Park?" asked Parker.

I knew plenty. In the summer, lots of guys rode motorcycles around and over all the piles of gravel. A little stringer of pines ran to the edge of disturbed ground. A construction buddy of mine had told me earlier in the summer about a poached deer he'd lost in the patch of trees to a bunch of unleashed dogs that raised hell in the area. An empty irrigation ditch ran through the middle of the yard where cops sometimes hid to catch folks trespassing on the private property.

"Parker, there's all kinds of places for a man to hide back there," I said. "Lots of little hills, trees, an empty ditch. You could hide an army back there."

"That's what I'm planning to do, Bobby Lee."

Almost afraid to ask, I said, "Where do I come in?"

"You're the star of the show."

"What's the game plan, when do you need me?" I felt a mixture of apprehension and elation. With luck, I might be putting this nightmare behind me by the end of the day.

"I want to see you across the road from where we had our little tussle last night, way back near the trees," said Parker. "Be there at nine p.m.—sharp."

"You heard everything I told Tucker?" I asked.

"Sure did."

"I was telling him what he wanted to hear, to get him there, but there's no goddamned way I'm bringing Laura."

Parker chuckled. "How is she?"

"She's fine, she's sleeping in."

"You sure about that?"

Davis flinched and pulled off his headset. He bolted from the room. I heard him race for the stairway.

"See, Bobby Lee, after last night, I knew there was no way you'd go along with what we needed to do, so I had to take matters into my own hands."

Hearing Davis running back to the office, I put my hand over the phone.

"She's gone, kid! Looks like they did something to the dog, too." Davis slammed his fist against the wall and put his foot through a panel of drywall.

At first, I was too stunned to be angry. "You took Laura? You kidnapped her?"

"Don't worry, Bobby Lee, we didn't hurt her," said Parker. "Technically, she's under arrest, but we'll let her go just as soon as the show's over tonight."

"Where is she? Is she all right?"

"I can't tell you where she is, but I'll guarantee you, we're taking a hell of a lot better care of her than Tucker did." Parker chuckled, then added, "We didn't hurt that fuckin' dog of yours either, just gave him something in a little treat of hamburger meat to make him sleepy."

"You lousy bastard. I don't know who's worse, you or Tucker."

"Calm down, Bobby Lee, you can have her back just as soon as we get Tucker."

"Listen to me, Parker, you know the gauntlet I've gone through to get that son of a bitch."

"Yeah," said Parker, "I got to hand it to you, you don't give up—"

"That's nothing compared to how I'll hunt you down if anything happens to Laura—anything, cocksucker."

"Now listen—"

"You listen, Parker. You take care of her or I'll have your ass."

"You just meet me at nine, Bobby Lee." Parker hung up.

I slammed the desk and ran downstairs, followed by Davis. The basement door had been jimmied open and the outside security panel lay on the porch, its wiring harness severed. I glanced about and spotted Jaws, sprawled on the snow.

"Help me get him inside, Doc. It'd crush Laura if he didn't make it."

We brought the big bastard in and laid him on the couch.

Davis was nearly in tears from anger and frustration. I put my arm across his shoulder. He might have been a hell of a lot more worldly than me, but he hadn't been around the kind of people I'd been dealing with lately. Desperate, evil, cunning, ruthless— both sides of the law.

"Doc, I know this is my mess, but are you ready to get your hands dirty?"

"Parker made it my business, too, Lee, when he broke into my house and kidnapped Laura."

"All right, then let's get to work," I said. "We've got a lot to do by dark."

I felt a cold steel resolve harden up my spine. No panic, no fear, just icy determination to get the job done, to save Laura, to finish Tucker—for good.

Chapter Forty

Davis and I drove into town in one of his other vehicles, a new Jeep Wagoneer. Our first stop was the Aspen Animal Hospital. We carried Jaws into the office, my back killing me every step of the way. I sat on the floor with the unconscious brute while Davis explained the situation to the receptionist and got us into the examining room. A little while later, a young vet technician came through the double doors of the hospital, pushing a stainless steel gurney. I helped him roll Jaws into the back, where the vet waited, an old guy at least Davis's age.

As surprised as the vet was to hear about what had happened to Jaws, he was really taken aback when Davis nodded at me and said, "Think you could take a look at this kid's back, I think he might have some broken ribs."

"Why don't you just take him to Valley?"

I knew we didn't have time for that. I'd probably be sitting on my ass all day until they got to me. But getting treated by a vet?

"I'd really appreciate it," said Davis. "Make it worth your while."

I sat on an examining table, looking at posters of dog and cat anatomy. "Are you okay, looking at me?" I asked. "Have you ever—"

"Haven't had any complaints from my patients, yet," snorted the vet, before sharing a laugh with Davis.

After the vet wrapped my ribs, we left Jaws behind, with instructions to make sure the dog was okay and to hell with the expense.

Our next stop was Davis's bank. He ran inside, while I waited in his double-parked Wagoneer. His mission was to secure the cassette tape of our conversations with Tucker and Parker in his safety deposit box. He called the tape my "get-out-of-jail-free card." Having seen Parker's methods first hand, we weren't taking any more chances.

We flew back down the valley to my trailer at Woody Creek. Sure as shit, someone had broken in, rummaging all around the place, rifling through drawers, closets, and cabinets. But they didn't find the money hidden under the flooring and they didn't find my .22 rifle, hidden behind a false wall in the bedroom closet.

Looking over the mess they'd left behind, I said, "You were right, Doc, Tucker's boys would have nabbed Laura if we'd left her here." It didn't look like the DEA had lifted a finger to keep the crooks out of my place. They were more worried about revealing their presence to Tucker.

I knew Davis was sick about losing Laura at his home. I was too, but as rotten as Parker was, I knew he'd protect her at least long enough to ensure our showdown with Tucker. But I harbored no illusions that he would put her squarely in danger during the melee about to unfold at the base of Smuggler Mountain. I glanced at my watch, the hands pointed to a little past noon. We had a few more hours of daylight, then a long wait.

We drove up Woody Creek Road a few miles, muscling through a foot of fresh snow. Passing the Forest Service boundary, we pulled off the road at the edge of an open, grassy slope gently rising to a curtain of pines. I trudged up the hill and tacked a target on the trunk of a dead tree. Returning to the Wagoneer, I improvised a steady shooting rest on the hood from a blanket and sleeping bag Davis had for emergencies. I loaded the old Remington target rifle and fired at the one-inch bull's-eye, around fifty yards away. Davis called my shots, spying the target through my binoculars. After all five of my shots cut the black, I reloaded the clip and let Davis try the rifle.

His first shot landed several inches to the right, nearly off the paper. He backed away from the scope and shook his head. "Damn, that one got away from me, kid. That's some trigger— pretty light."

"Sure is, Doc," I said. "That's why you're starting off on paper."

He settled back onto the front of the rig and fired again.

"That's the style, Doc. Bull's-eye."

He lobbed three more rounds into the black, and we called it good, not even bothering to shag our target. Finding a wide spot in the road to turn around, we headed back for Aspen. Up to now, we hadn't had much of a chance to talk or plan. But on the way back to town, Davis asked, "Lee, what have you got up your sleeve? I'm ready to pitch in, but I'd like to know what I'm doing."

"Doc, I'm thinking of two jobs for you. One is, you're my guarantor and Laura's. That's where that .22 comes in."

"What have you got in mind?"

"I want to hide you in the back of my Jeep. If things go to shit, I want you covering my back with the rifle." His face knotted up. I tried to reassure him. "Doc, think of that little rifle as a scalpel, not a sledgehammer."

"What's that mean, kid?"

"If we can get close enough, you already know you can shoot the balls off a mosquito with that Remington. It might come in handy if you need to shoot out someone's headlights or whatever."

Davis brightened. "I could do that."

"Hopefully, you won't be doing any shooting, but I don't trust Parker any farther than I can throw him."

"I can't blame you there, kid," said Davis. "What's the other job?"

"Doc, that depends on what the vet tells us."

Thirty minutes later we parked in front of the vet's and hustled inside. The receptionist had good news. "Oh, Mr. Davis, your dog, aah, Jaws, is coming out of it already. Dr. Taggs pumped his stomach right after you two left. He should be able to go home tomorrow."

"Ma'am," I interrupted, "we're gonna need him today."

"Well, I don't know, we usually keep them overnight for obser-vation after this kind of procedure."

I asked, "What time is the clinic closed?"

"Five thirty."

"That'll have to do," I said, with an air of finality.

We motored back up Maroon Creek to fetch my Jeep and get our gear together. I changed into long underwear and wool. I planned on a long, cold night. I grabbed some of Laura's clothes, too. Her stocking cap, mittens, scarf, Sorels, down jacket, all the stuff Parker's boys hadn't given her time to round up in their haste to sweep her out of the place.

Rotten bastards.

I met Davis in his hallway by the front door. By now, he had warm clothes, his camera, binoculars, all the other gear we'd dis-cussed on the drive back from Woody Creek.

"Doc, we ought to take two cars into town."

We'd originally planned to take my Jeep, but I got to wonder-ing if Parker or Tucker weren't keeping an eye on us, even all the way up Maroon Bells.

"You think somebody's watching my house?" asked Doc.

"Could be," I said. "Let's meet up in town. I don't care if someone sees us together. I just don't want them to see us in the same car."

I didn't want Parker or Tucker knowing Doc would be attend-ing the festivities tonight, hidden comfortably in the back of my Jeep. Just like Wilbur had concealed me in his Bronco.

"Kid, you know where the Ute City Banque is?"

"Sure."

"Let's meet there, get something to eat, and cool our heels until we have to go back to the vet."

I met Davis at the joint on the west end of an arcade in the heart of downtown, a block from my showdown with Tucker the night before. Davis had beaten me into town, his new V-8-powered Wagoneer smoking my Willys. I found him with his back to the wall in a booth in the back corner of the old bank, converted years before into a bar. He was learning.

I didn't feel like eating or drinking. I kept seeing Laura, scared as hell, held prisoner by Parker's crew in some shitty hideout or hotel room. When our waitress came, Davis ordered a couple of cheeseburgers and two iced teas over my weak objection.

I glanced at my watch. We had a couple of hours to kill before getting Jaws.

We sat in awkward silence while waiting for our food and drinks.

"Lee, back at the house, you said something about premarital counseling?"

"Think I'm crazy?"

"I'm a good one for giving marital advice, I know, kid, but if you ask me——"

I didn't say anything, curious as hell about what he thought.

"Lee, you'd be nuts to let her get away," said Davis. "I wouldn't rush off to Vegas or anything, but I don't see anything wrong with a long engagement. Give you both something to look forward to, work for." He smiled. "That premarital counseling sounds perfect, kid."

I didn't want to jinx things. I—we—still had one hell of a dangerous night ahead of us.

"You superstitious, Lee?"

"Are you a mind reader, Doc?" I grinned and nodded. "I wore

the same socks for every cross-country meet my senior year at
Mesa, had all kinds of crazy little rituals, stretched exactly the
same way before races, shit like that."

Davis laughed. "Here's one I always had. When I was waiting
on something big, something important, like a book deal, say, I'd
go out and buy whoever the hell was my wife at the time something
nice, spend a little of that advance ahead of time. Betting on the
outcome, you might say."

"Really? I thought a guy didn't spend money he didn't have
yet, or count chickens, you know, all that stuff."

"Those are the rules, all right," said Doc. "But I always
thought a little positive thinking was part of my success."

"What are you getting at, Doc?"

"Finish your chow and I'll show you."

After tiring of shoving the food around on my plate, we left
Ute City Banque and wandered back through the arcade to a little
jewelry store tucked away in the east end of the building, The
Golden Bough.

Davis led me inside. The saleswoman, a beautiful woman
around forty with short blonde hair, greeted Davis. I suspected my
new boss had dropped a lot of money in the place. She let us
browse around without hovering over us like a damned vampire.
Custom jewelry was displayed in little glass boxes resting on plas-
ter-covered stands. I finally took Davis's meaning and focused on
the diamond rings. Fortunately, I had my own cash. No way would
I buy anything in there with Tucker's blood money.

After a bit, the saleswoman came from around the counter.
"Anything special you're looking for?"

Davis had deserted me, nosing around the other side of the
store. I was on my own.

"An engagement ring?" I said, feeling my face redden.

She smiled. "I think you're in luck."

Thirty minutes later, with a little encouragement from Davis, I parted ways with a thousand dollars, about half my net worth. I stuffed the little leather bag containing the ring in my pocket and headed for the vet, hoping Davis's superstition worked for me and Laura.

Chapter Forty-One

Davis beat me to the vet's, too. By the time I walked inside, the young tech already had Jaws on a leash in the waiting room. The beast lunged for me, pulling away from his handler. It was the first time I realized Jaws had adopted me, too, not just Laura. I knelt and examined him. His eyes were clear and alert. He looked okay.

"You shouldn't feed him for at least a day," said the receptionist.

I shuddered. Jaws could be irritable as hell when supper wasn't right on time.

Over my protests, Davis paid the bill and we left the office as darkness descended on the town.

"Now what?" asked Davis.

"I'll pick you up at the gas station across the street from Carl's Pharmacy, say ten 'til nine," I said. "Don't look at me, don't say anything, just climb in the back of the Jeep and cover yourself with the tarp when I go in to pay for my gas."

We shook hands, and I led Jaws to the back of my Jeep, wondering how to kill another three hours.

I ended up at the public library on Main. More and more nervous, I paced about, sitting here and there to browse magazines and books. Every hour, I checked on Jaws. Fifteen minutes before I needed to leave, I found a quiet spot in the back of the building, a little study table, and prayed. The Old Man and I hadn't been regular churchgoers, but I pleaded for help in the bowels of the library, begging for courage, protection, and justice. I walked to the Jeep and drove to the gas station.

I filled my half-empty tank with regular and walked into the shop to pay. Out of the corner of my eye, I saw Davis slink from Carl's, trot across the road, and slip into my rig. I paid my bill and returned to the Jeep. Adjusting the rearview mirror, I saw a squirming, canvas-covered lump in the back.

"You and Jaws got enough room back there, Doc?"

"We'll be all right," he said, his voice muffled by the heavy tarp.

"Watch that rifle," I said, "don't want to bump it, move the scope."

"I know, kid, it's jabbing me in the ribs."

We drove out of the station, caught Mill, and headed downhill to our appointed meeting site. Just short of the Roaring Fork, I turned left and drove through a graveled, undeveloped area along the river until I reached the edge of a patch of willows. The tail-lights of another car reflected from my headlights. I parked fifty yards behind the vehicle and whispered, "Okay, Doc, I'm going now, just try to keep Jaws quiet, and I'll be back as soon as I can."

"Good luck, kid," Davis whispered from under the tarp.

I grabbed Laura's extra clothes from the front seat and left the Jeep. Making my way to the van, a white Dodge without windows, I noted a clear sky and the moon rising over Smuggler Mountain. I knocked on the back and an instant later the double doors cracked open a few inches. I recognized Parker's voice whispering, "Everything clear, Bobby Lee? You by yourself?"

"Yes," I lied.

"Come in," he said, "I got somebody I think you're gonna want to see."

When I stepped inside, Laura crawled across the carpeted floor and held me, crying in my arms. At once, I was relieved to be with her and furious with Parker for subjecting her to more danger.

I leaned against the side of the van and let her cry on my chest while Parker closed the doors.

"Laura, you all right? They take care of you, they didn't hurt you, did they?" I asked, glaring at Parker in the dimly lit van.

"I'm okay, baby," she said, "just spent the day in a hotel room."

"I hate to break up this little reunion," said Parker, "but we got some stuff to talk about."

I studied the slimy son of a bitch. He wore a loose-fitting blue nylon jacket, with DEA stenciled on front and back, over a pullover bulletproof vest. He was expecting trouble.

Laura stayed in my arms, turned to look at Parker. My eyes adjusted to the weak overhead light. I glanced at Laura. Other than her red eyes, she seemed okay.

"I'm gonna cut you two loose here, in a little bit," said Parker. "But first we need to plan out this dance." He reached toward the front of the van and dragged my rucksack across the floor. "Okay, Bobby Lee, here's the cocaine—all present and accounted for, just like you promised. Good job."

If he was trying to make amends, I didn't give a shit. I was pissed as hell.

"You were right about that gravel yard, too," he said. "I got half a dozen guys hidden back there. Tucker's not gonna know what hit him."

I reached toward Parker and softly tapped his vest. "Got one of those for her?"

"Sorry, Bobby Lee," said Parker, "can't do it."

"How come?"

"Look how bulky this thing is," said Parker, "Tucker'd spot it right off, know something was up."

"Not if she wore this." With my free hand, I dug into the paper grocery sack I had stuffed Laura's clothes into and pulled out her fluffy down jacket.

Parker shook his head. "Still can't do it, can't take the chance."

"Some gentleman you turned out to be, Parker." The worst insult you could give a true Southern man.

"Let's just stop that right now, Bobby Lee."

I shook my head and breathed deeply. "What's the plan?"

Parker studied his watch. "Okay, you're gonna head up to the yard a little early, wait for Tucker. He drives a—"

"Old Mercedes."

"That's right, of course you know that, don't you, Bobby Lee." Parker laughed, went on, "When Tucker shows, along with anyone else he might bring, you two get out, take him that pack. It's important that gets in his car, got that, Bobby Lee?"

"I got it."

Parker took a deep breath. "Here's the tricky part—we want to take him down after he gets in his car—with Laura."

Laura raised her head from my chest, eyes wide, mouth open in shock. I held her against my chest, again, kissed her head, whispered softly in her ear, "Trust me." By now, nothing Parker did or planned surprised me. I'd come to expect the callous, uncaring worst from him. That's why I had my own plan. Just like with Tucker, though, I had to put up a little fight.

"Why the hell does she need to take that risk? Parker, you don't give a shit about anything but—"

"It's safer this way, for everybody," said Parker. "Can't have much of a gunfight, if Tucker's people are stuffed in his car."

"That's bullshit, and you know it, Parker. How'd you like to be in that car?"

"Listen, Bobby Lee, I got a crew of men to think about, too. You just shut the fuck up and maybe, just maybe, I'll get you off the hook up north."

I figured that was enough of a fuss. "I brought some clothes for her, we might get cold waiting."

"Go ahead and change then," he said to Laura. "Then you two can leave."

She took off her cowboy boots and jammed her feet into the Sorels. In the tight quarters, she pulled on a sweater, then her down jacket. I handed her the stocking cap and gloves.

"We're ready to go," I said.

Parker slid past us and opened the rear doors. He followed us near the Jeep. Over the roar of the river, I thought I heard Jaws growl. I walked away from my rig, motioning Parker to follow. I feigned to parley, away from Laura's hearing.

When Parker put his hand on my shoulder, it was all I could do to stand his touch. "Don't worry, Bobby Lee, it might seem a little hairy, but everything'll be okay."

The worst part was shaking his hand. "You bet, Parker, let's just get this done."

I turned on my heels and led Laura to the Jeep, the rucksack slung over my shoulder. Parker following us part way. Thank God he stopped short. I spun gravel, peeling away in reverse, before I turned around and headed for Mill. At the same instant, Jaws crawled from under the tarp, nudging Laura's shoulder with his head.

"Jaws! You're okay." She grabbed him by the neck and rubbed her face against his.

"That's not the only stowaway we've got, sweetie."

Laura looked over her shoulder past Jaws. Davis pulled his head out and breathed heavily.

"My God, it's good to breathe fresh air."

"Doc, you're here, too!"

I drove over the river, turned right at a fork in the road, and headed uphill toward Smuggler Mountain. I took a detour to the Silver King Apartments and found an empty stall in the sprawling parking lot.

"Laura, Doc and I have a little different take on what's happening tonight."

"Slim, it's bad enough I have to see that bastard again, but I don't want to get anywhere near his car—"

"You're not getting in there with him," I said. "Did you hear that, Doc? Parker wants her to leave with Tucker before they bust him."

"Unbelievable."

I turned to Laura. "Follow me outside." I jumped outside and stepped to the back. I opened both zippers at the back of the rag-top and unbuttoned all the snaps attaching the rear vinyl window to the tailgate, save for one at each end. Sticking my face through one of the gaps in the top, I said, "Doc, when we're parked, un-button these last two snaps and rest the barrel of the rifle on the tailgate."

"Got it, kid."

"And keep Jaws quiet."

I led Laura to the front of the Jeep. We were alone for the first time since we'd been reunited. Holding her close, she felt warm, soft, brave. I looked overhead at countless stars and a bright, full moon. Pulling a small leather bag from my pants, I stuffed it in the front pocket of her jeans. She gave me a look of surprise.

I leaned down until our lips almost touched. "I'll explain when we put all this behind us."

Chapter Forty-Two

We drove back to Gibson Avenue and headed left, soon reaching Smuggler Mountain Trailer Court, about the closest thing Aspen had to a ghetto. None of us spoke as I maneuvered through the tightly packed trailers, each with a host of vehicles parked outside. Careful not to swipe a vehicle or one of the loaded residents staggering in the park, we emerged at the base of Smuggler Mountain, rising from the valley floor like a dark wall. The paved road gave way to gravel, then a snow-packed two track leading to old mine tailings dating to the silver boom a century before.

The four-wheel-drive road wound through a long sloping bench, studded in sagebrush, mountain mahogany, and buckbrush. The trail led to the top of Smuggler, a popular hunting and fishing destination for locals. From the looks of the road, a lot of rigs had traveled this way since the last storm. We came to a fork and turned left, abandoning the peaceful way up the mountain for the gravel yard and our date with Tucker. Slowing, I glanced at my watch. We were early. I scanned the flat graveled plain surrounded by mounds of earth and tailings, but spotted no vehicles.

I drove to the far edge of the yard and backed into the tail end of a thin pine grove. Our hideout provided a commanding view of the gravel flat, the trailer court, and Aspen shrouded in a mantle of wood smoke. With time on our hands, I started second-guessing my plans. A lot of things would have to go right for Laura and me to walk away in one piece. Could I trust Parker to come to the rescue in time to keep us from getting shot? Why had he wanted

Laura to get in the car with Tucker? The more I thought about it, the less I wanted to risk everything on one final showdown. I let go of Laura's hand and reached for the stick shift.

"Doc," I said, "I'm thinking we ought to get the hell out of here, this doesn't feel right."

Davis sat up. "It's your call, but I don't see any other way."

"There's got to be one honest cop in town, or maybe the sheriff's office," I said, looking at Laura. "We could get her out of trouble, tell him what Parker did."

"Kid, you could probably do that, but then your name's mud with the feds."

"I don't care about that, Doc, I just don't want anything to happen to—"

"Wait a minute," said Laura. "I know what you're doing, Slim. It's no good."

"I'm just trying to protect you, get you out of this—"

"I don't want out, not if it means you have to go to jail. Let's take the chance—all or nothing, you and me."

"Damn," I muttered, but I had never loved her more.

Laura pointed ahead. "Someone's coming up the road from the trailer court."

We watched the car snake its way along the trail, then enter the far end of the yard. It headed into the middle of the flat, then its light died. I raised my binoculars and viewed Tucker's other vehicle, an immaculate Land Rover.

"That's Tucker," I said.

I started my Jeep and drove out of the trees. Passing the driver's side of the car, I counted four passengers. I drove on toward town, then parked, the rear of my rig now facing our adversaries.

"Doc," I whispered, "Tucker's car's about forty yards behind you, tops, and it's full of passengers, at least four men. Tucker's driving."

I held Laura's hand and smiled. "Trust me. Follow my lead."

She forced a weak grin. "Okay."

I pulled my rucksack from behind the back and stepped outside. Walking to the rear of the Jeep, I paused to block the view of anyone in the Land Rover. Hearing Davis unbutton the last two snaps, I slowly headed toward Tucker. Laura came along my left side, remembering not to take my hand. We couldn't look like a sad couple, about to part. We veered imperceptibly to our left, trying to provide Davis with a clear view of our adversaries.

Halfway to the Land Rover, we stopped. My eyes flicked about, wondering where Parker might have placed his men. With a full moon rising well above Smuggler now, the snowy gravel flat was well lit. You could have read a book without a flashlight. Little hills of earth and gravel, twenty- to thirty-feet high, rimmed us, less than a hundred yards away.

My heart, already at redline, skipped when Tucker opened his door and headed our way. Then, the other front door opened and another man emerged, walking next to Tucker.

The two neared, stopped a few yards from us. Tucker's sidekick was Doherty, the crooked cop, dressed in plainclothes, down jacket, jeans, and Sorels. I slipped the rucksack strap off my shoulder and skidded the pack across the snow to Tucker's feet. As scared as I was, I almost laughed. He still wore those damned ostrich-skin boots.

"There's your shit, Tucker."

He took the pack, handed it to Doherty. "Stash this in my Rover and come back."

Doherty complied and Tucker ignored me, turning his attention to Laura. "Been missing you, baby," he said, in his deep Texas best. "Everybody's been sayin' how great you look. They're right."

I glanced at Laura. She said nothing and gave Tucker no hint of encouragement, just a blank stare masking her terror.

With the dope squarely in Tucker's car, I looked for an opening to get Laura back to the Jeep.

To hell with Parker.

Doherty returned to Tucker's side. "Tom," he said, nodding my way, "can I take care of him, now?"

"In a second," said Tucker. He looked at Laura. "This might hurt, little girl, but it's got to be done."

Out of the corner of my eye, I saw her face twist into a silent question.

"See, sonny," Tucker said to me, "you got damned lucky, ripping me off like you did, last month." He chuckled. "Hell, even a blind squirrel finds an acorn, now and then."

I said nothing and tightly gripped the pistol in my coat pocket.

"Did you really think I was gonna let you rip me off—keep my money—live to tell about it?"

"I never expected a sorry bastard like you to keep his word."

Tucker laughed. "I'm gonna show you how the cow ate the cabbage, tonight, Shelby. Teach you a lesson. Your last fuckin' lesson."

Doherty pulled his own revolver from his coat pocket, had the drop on me. In the bright moonlight, the muzzle looked big, black, and deadly. "I've been wanting this ever since we met." He grinned and cocked the hammer. "Where's that smart mouth of yours now, Shelby?"

Laura screamed, "No! No! Tom. I'll do anything, but don't—"

At the same time a rifle cracked behind us, Doherty's pistol flew from his grip. When the crooked son of a bitch staggered in pain and clutched his crippled hand, Tucker lunged for Laura and seized her wrist. She screamed, dragging her heels and fighting to pull free. Two more men piled out of the Land Rover.

I felt carried outside myself, suspended from above, as time passed in slow motion. The blur of a black shadow brushed my side, then catapulted onto Tucker's back, knocking him to the ground. I grabbed Laura's hand and led her away from the other oncoming men. With guns blazing all around us, I abandoned our flight and tackled Laura into the snow, shielding her as best I could with my body. I saw Jaws maul Tucker, ripping at his face and neck, as the rotten bastard tried to protect himself with flaying hands and arms. Even over the gunfire, Jaws's guttural roar and Tucker's cries of pain echoed in the gravel yard.

Beyond the gruesome mauling, muzzle flashes, like flashbulbs, glittered from the hills overlooking us. Over Laura's screaming, I heard bullets whizzing all about us. Then, the world exploded into blinding light, followed by silent darkness.

Chapter Forty-Three

I have no recollection of the trip to Aspen Valley Hospital. I remember speaking to my parents, hugging them both for the first time in years. The Old Man came to see me, too. He asked about Wilbur and our place on the peak, told me he was so proud I'd finished college. But I never saw Laura.

It took me a long time to awaken. I fought for consciousness, like a free diver gone too deep, struggling to regain the surface. When my lids finally fluttered open, bright light seared my eyes. I came to in fits and starts, sleeping a while, then stirring. I heard distant, muffled voices, unintelligible words echoing in my fuzzy head. Gradually, I emerged from my stupor long enough to survey my surroundings.

I lay in a tall, single bed, covered with a white sheet and a thin brown blanket. Across the white room, a TV hung from the wall. When I tried to move my head, I winced in pain. I scanned to my right. An open door led to a hallway. After a bit, my blurry vision focused. I saw a nurse walking back and forth. A blue curtain partitioned the room. I clenched my teeth and twisted my neck to the right. Against the wall, next to my bed, Davis sat in a chair, book in his lap, head bowed, gently snoring. Movement in the doorway caught my eye. A man in black looked my way. *A policeman?* Then, I recognized the clerical collar of a minister. I blinked and he was gone.

I tried to speak, but no sound came from my recalcitrant lips. Fighting my stiff neck again, I gazed upon Davis, still in his own stupor. "Doc," I whispered, "Doc." But if I couldn't hear myself, how could he? I raised my arm, nearly as stiff as my neck and slapped the bed frame. "Doc," I whispered, then slapped my bed, over and over and over.

His head bobbed, his eyes, like mine before, fluttered, then opened. Turning my way, his look of surprise melted into a gentle smile. "Kid," he said softly, "welcome back."

"Laura?" I whispered.

Davis shook his head.

"Laura?" I tried, louder. Tears welled in my eyes.

"Lee," said Davis, "I can't make out what you're saying." He rose over me, took my hand, and put his ear inches from my lips.

"Laura?"

Davis grinned and nodded to my left.

I winced, willed my neck to twist. Tucked in the corner, sleeping on a short-legged cot, lay Laura, her back to me, her stocking feet sticking out of the blanket. Tears ran down my face. Now I knew why I hadn't found her before.

Davis let go of my hand and walked around the bed. He knelt down and gently patted Laura's shoulder. She jerked awake, sprung from the cot, and stepped to my side.

She held my hand and lightly kissed my cheek. I tried to speak, with no luck. She took a cup of chipped ice from my bed stand and put a few pieces in my mouth.

"They said to give you this, baby."

With a little moisture to relieve my cottonmouth, I gained a whisper of my voice. "You got some new jewelry?" I nodded at the hand she used to feed me ice.

"I sure do," she said, admiring the ring, "and you're never getting it back."

"That mean 'yes'?"

"What do you think?"

Like I said before, she could be a real smart-ass.

"A bullet grazed the side of your head," said Davis, stepping near my bed. "You have a concussion, but another inch or so, and—"

I touched the right side of my head and felt gauze above my ear. I looked under my gown and saw my chest was bandaged.

"Don't worry, kid," said Davis. "You didn't catch one in the chest. That wrapping is for your ribs. That's right, you've been running around the last couple of days with two fractured ribs."

I glanced toward the doorway, saw that minister walk by.

"Yeah, he's attending to Doherty," said Davis. "They don't think he's gonna make it, took a bullet in the lungs."

I hated to mention his name, but I had to ask. "Tucker?"

"He's here, too," said Davis. "Jaws took care of him." Davis grimaced. "Last I heard, he needed over a hundred stitches on his face and neck."

"Good God," I whispered. "How's Jaws? Where is he?"

Davis stepped close and gazed toward the open door and blue partition. "Jaws is in a little hot water," he said quietly. "He's on the lam."

Laura nodded, a sly grin crossing her face. "We got him hidden at Doc's place."

"Last night, when the dust settled, I managed to pull him off Tucker, get him back in the Jeep," said Davis. "Parker didn't care about the dog tearing up Tucker, but the local police are asking questions."

"Screw 'em," I muttered.

"My sentiments, exactly," said Davis.

"Doc, that was a hell of a shot."

"Lee, I kept waiting for the cavalry to ride over the hill. I think Parker would have let Doherty shoot you, at least he was cutting it pretty close. I just remembered what you said about that rifle being a scalpel."

"What about Parker?" I asked.

"He's around here somewhere. None of his guys got hit, not hiding behind all those gravel piles." Davis shook his head. "He's mad as hell, though, about us working our own game plan."

"What's he gonna do about it?"

Davis and Laura looked at each other and laughed.

"You know, kid, I couldn't help you with Tucker, you had to straighten out that mess. But I've got a friend of a friend in the Justice Department."

"So?"

"So, I told Parker if he doesn't want his next assignment to be busting Eskimos for smoking pot in Alaska, he better pull his head out of his ass."

"Baby," said Laura, "when you get back on your feet, we have to go up to Craig, straighten things out."

"Yeah," said Davis, "Parker's going to help you out with that, too, or he'll be living in an igloo, dining on whale blubber."

I laughed, then winced at the shooting pain in my chest.

"Doc, could you give us a couple of minutes alone?" I asked, looking at Laura.

"Sure, I'm gonna go find the doctor, tell her you're awake."

Laura sat in the chair next to the bed, still clutching my hand. "I can't believe this, Slim. We're finally free."

"I wanna get into counseling now, get on with our lives."

"Me, too," she said, her eyes watering. "I'm sorry for every-thing—"

"No one's to blame, we both made mistakes, but now we've got a second chance."

"I know I'm the luckiest girl in the world. You're not getting away from me again."

"I don't want to get away—ever."

We talked for a little while, then I slept.

I was in the hospital for three more days. I had a hell of a headache, and my ribs were sore, but soon I was walking the halls, first with a walker, then with a cane and Laura's help.

On my last morning, Parker came to my room to make amends. I was still pissed, but tried to hide my anger. He congratulated Laura and me, said things were working out like he'd hoped they would, and promised to help me up north. True to his perverse nature, he provided a final, odd gesture of goodwill. He whisked me through armed security and accompanied me to Tucker's room. I gasped when I saw the son of a bitch. He looked like a mummy, his head and neck shrouded in gauze. He peered at us through two holes in his bandage, raised a little from his pillow, then lowered his head again. Leaving the room, I couldn't help myself, and gave the miserable bastard one last parting shot.

"Hey, Tucker, how cocky do you feel now?"

The next day, Davis drove Laura and me up to Craig. While they waited in the lobby of the Moffat County Sheriff's Department, I met with the undersheriff and several officers from Wyoming. They tape-recorded our conversation, while asking me about the night I hitchhiked from Baggs to Colorado. Parker sat next to me and verified my story. Near the end of the interview, a big man in civilian garb entered the room, a brown paper sack in his hand. He sat across the table and listened to me as his eyes welled with tears. When I was through, he pulled a jean jacket from the bag and handed it to me. It was ol' Hoss, Chance Stewart, the Wyoming deputy, come to tell the board I'd saved his life on a lonely highway south of the border.

Laura and I lived together that winter in my trailer at Woody Creek. By then Jaws was no longer a wanted dog and joined us. Tucker might have called it a dump, but with Laura, I felt like I was living in a mansion. Davis found her a sponsor, and she attended DA meetings while we underwent premarital counseling, learning about our strengths and weaknesses as a couple. Mostly we worked on how to talk to each other, how to communicate. As we both healed, we grew closer every day. Like I had promised Laura, things weren't the same as before—they were better.

The next summer, we were married in a little civil ceremony at the Moffat County Courthouse. Davis gave away the bride and Wilbur was best man. Neither Laura nor I wanted to live high on the hog off Tucker's blood money. We gave twenty thousand dollars to Juan, to help him get his family to the U.S. Then, we talked Darlene Preston into hiding away thirty thousand dollars from L.Q.'s scheming eyes for her son's college education. To this day, I receive a Christmas card every year from Billy, now the principal at Moffat County High School, thanking us. A few years ago, I antelope hunted with him and his teenage son, Laverne Quincy.

Wilbur passed a few years shy of his eightieth birthday, at an assisted-living center in Grand Junction. Irascible and cantankerous to the end, we remained friends and hunting buddies. Even after he left the peak, we'd visit, talk guns and hunting, and laugh about the fall we gave the cops the slip. I miss him dearly.

Shortly after Laura and I were wed, Davis put me to work, scouring the country for information and details to support his writing in the days before the Internet and Google. Laura accompanied me on every trip, learned to type, handle a camera, and search library and courthouse records like a private eye. Davis paid well and worked my ass off. He was my mentor and the main cause for my later success as a journalist. After nearly seven years on the road, Laura and I settled down in a small town in western Colorado, where I still edit the local weekly and freelance on the side. Laura traded her detective and research skills for motherhood, giving me two wonderful daughters.

A few weeks shy of our thirtieth anniversary, we learned Tucker had died in a federal prison. With his death, Laura wanted full closure on this chapter of our life. She asked me, made me promise, to tell this story. We'd always been vague about the things we went through to be together. They were personal. People didn't need to know all the mistakes we'd made in our youths. But Laura wanted me to show others the uncommon love, acceptance, and bravery it took for us to be a couple. She wanted others who needed hope to know of her salvation.

I wanted to tell this story right, the way it really happened. To do that, I had to retrace my footsteps from thirty years ago. Some of the trails had grown cold, others were still fresh as the morning dew. I traveled from Aspen to the Front Range, up to Wyoming and across the southern half of the state to Baggs, then back down to Aspen, by way of the muddy Colorado and the crystal-clear Roaring Fork. I have to admit, the trip wasn't nearly as woolly this time, as I eschewed hitchhiking, running, Wilbur's Bronco, and L.Q.'s Champ, for the convenience of my own car. Nor did I have the law or Tucker nipping at my heels the whole way.

Still, the journey helped me remember the wildest weeks of my life. Along the winding trail, I'd close my eyes, and I'd be back, a skinny, idealistic kid, trying to save my only love and the world, all at once.

I know I didn't change the world by putting Tucker out of business. Nature abhors a vacuum, and no doubt some vermin took his place. But I did change the world for Laura and me, and I'll always remember the fall I saved her from evil and she taught me to trust my heart.